ABOVE OUR PLATFORM A COUNTDOWN STARTED FROM TEN, and Regan sprinted over to join me. Without saying a word, we grasped hands. There was a time that I'd do just about anything to get some distance from Regan Fitz, but right now, at this moment, there wasn't anyone else I'd rather be hurtling through time beside.

"At what point are you going to tell me the plan?" I asked as the numbers ticked down toward zero.

"There is no plan," Regan said as everything went black.

GLITCH

LAURA MARTIN

HARPER

An Imprint of HarperCollinsPublishers

Library of Congress Control Number: 2019955936
ISBN 978-0-06-289436-6

Typography by Ellice M. Lee
   22 23 24 25 PC/BRR 10 9 8 7 6
❖
First paperback edition, 2021

To all the heroes throughout history who have struggled to make their tomorrow better than their today. And for the kids who read this who will do the same.

CHAPTER ONE

REGAN

April 14, 1865. Gosh, I was sick of that date, and it wasn't just because that is when our sixteenth president was assassinated. Nope. I was sick of April 14, 1865, because I kept getting sent back to it for training purposes. Although training purposes was just code for, *You screwed up again, Regan; get it right this time.*

I materialized in the back row of Ford's Theatre for the fifth time this year just as the play, *Our American Cousin*, began. I always materialized into seat 10B when I did this particular practice simulation. It was supposed to contain Mrs. Margaret O'Hana, but she'd gotten sick with the measles and hadn't been able to make it to the performance that night. Her change of plans had left a convenient place for time travelers, or Glitchers, as we're called now, to slip in and out of history on the infamous night Abraham Lincoln was shot by John Wilkes Booth.

I'd see Booth momentarily, but I wasn't here to fix him. He would be allowed to murder our president without any interference from a Glitcher like myself. Interfering with him is against the law. Interfering with him was why I was here on a training mission in the first place.

I opened my eyes and looked around. Because I'd been here countless times before, I barely noticed the immaculate and stately Ford's Theatre, the theatergoers around me wearing their best dresses and suits, or the smell of a generation who handled body odors by covering them up with heavy colognes and perfumes. Even though I'd done this a lot, I still couldn't stop my eyes from automatically going up to the balcony where Mr. and Mrs. Abraham Lincoln would be taking their seats any minute. They would arrive late to the theater tonight and would be safe until the intermission, when their bodyguard would decide he'd rather go sit at a saloon and have a drink instead of protecting the president. There wasn't such a thing as the Secret Service yet. Although, in a weird ironic twist, Abraham Lincoln would sign the document that would create the Secret Service right before he left for the theater tonight. With some reluctance, I tore my eyes away from the balcony. I had less than ten minutes to find the Butterfly and complete the mission. It was time to get to work.

The last time I'd done this training mission, I'd immediately stood up and made my way to the lobby of the theater, sure that the Butterfly would be in wait there to waylay Booth. Unfortunately, I'd thought wrong.

I hated this simulation. It felt ten kinds of wrong to allow something horrendous like an assassination of arguably one of our greatest presidents, but it was all part of the job. It was why *this* particular simulation was so important to our training. We had to learn that what *we* thought about right and wrong didn't matter. At least not when it came to changing history. As a Glitcher, it was my job to make sure things stayed exactly the way the history books described without interference from a Butterfly.

The term Butterfly had thrown me for a loop when I'd first heard it. It seemed too, I don't know, fluffy to describe a time-traveling criminal the same way you describe a really pretty bug. I mean, a time-traveling criminal is usually someone attempting to manipulate history with the full intention of screwing up the future, and there was nothing fluffy about that. But I learned quickly that the term Butterfly did not come from the beautiful insects I saw landing on the flowers outside my window. Instead, it referred to the butterfly effect.

In 1963, this guy named Edward Lorenz presented a theory to the New York Academy of Sciences that "a butterfly could flap its wings and set molecules of air in motion, which would move other molecules of air, in turn moving more molecules of air—eventually capable of starting a hurricane on the other side of the planet." And everyone thought he was crazy for thinking something as small as a butterfly could start a snowball effect capable of wiping out whole cities.

He was laughed at.

He was called a fool.

And then thirty years later, they realized he was right.

So we called time-traveling criminals Butterflies, despite the fluffiness of the word, because they traveled back to the past to change something. They were the people who believed Hitler should have won World War II, that slavery should never have been abolished, or that women shouldn't have been given the right to vote. That's where Glitchers come in.

I glanced down at my watch. It was the exact same one the woman three rows up and two over was wearing. Everything from my light blue dress with the ten crinolines underneath to the way my hair was curled and pinned up to the back of my head like a poodle was historically accurate, down to the last piece of lace trim. Of course, I wasn't exactly historically accurate, since unchaperoned twelve-year-olds weren't a common sight at Ford's Theatre, but that didn't matter for a simulation. If I ever actually did this Glitch for real, I'd be an adult with years of time traveling under my belt. I swallowed hard and ignored the fact that the thought made my stomach feel like I'd swallowed a bucket of live snakes.

Shaking my head, I forced myself to focus. I looked just like anyone else at the theater. The problem was that the Butterfly, wherever he or she was, did too. There was movement in the balcony to my right, and I glanced up to see the president and his wife taking their seats with their friends Clara Harris and Major Henry Rathbone. Those friends were one of the reasons they were late; they couldn't get anyone else to come with them tonight. Had Ulysses S. Grant's wife not been mad at Mrs. Lincoln, he would have been here instead of Rathbone, and Lincoln's wouldn't have been the only assassination.

A movement to my right caught my eye; a slim man, probably thirty or so, had just stood up from his seat. I watched him leave, looking for a clue that would let me know he was the Butterfly. Because if he wasn't, and I took him down, then I would cause even more damage to the future. It was one of the biggest rules of Glitching: you could not, under any circumstances, accidentally become a Butterfly. You had to be in the past, but not interfere or interact with it in even the tiniest, most inconsequential way. I had to make sure I touched no one, talked to no one, and didn't change the course of anyone's future by my actions. I was here to take down the Butterfly. That was all.

The man in question paused to talk to someone sitting in the aisle, and I immediately dismissed him. Butterflies never knew anyone from the time period they were messing with. Then I saw her. Two rows up on my right, a woman got up and made her way quickly down the aisle toward the exit. She was the Butterfly. Don't ask me how, but I knew it instantly at a bone-deep level, but because I'd have to give a concrete reason for the identification in my debriefing, I took the extra half second to identify where she'd gone wrong. Like me, she wore an elaborate dress trimmed with lace and her hair was twisted back into a knot at the base of her neck. I bit my lip; nothing was out of place there. Then I saw it. In her ears were three tiny holes where earrings were supposed to be. No one in 1865 had multiple piercings. She was it.

I carefully got up and made my way down the aisle, never taking my eyes off her as she slipped out the exit doors. I had two options. Option One—I could follow her into the lobby and take the chance of her making a scene. Option Two—I could intercept her somewhere out of the way before she made her move to take down Booth. Option One was easier, but I really didn't want to have to redo this simulation for the sixth time, so Option Two it was.

I slipped out the side door and into one of the theater's many hallways. It felt narrow and dark with its thick velvet draperies and busy wallpaper. Suddenly there was a noise to my left, and I saw a flash of blue skirts. Turning, I walked quickly in that direction. I'd have liked to run, but running wasn't something a lady did in a gigantic dress and ridiculous shoes that pinched. I had to blend in on the off chance that someone noticed me. Rounding the corner, I hurried up the narrow stairs toward the second floor. My lungs fought to expand inside the stupidly tight dress as I looked left and right down the empty hallway. To my left I could see the curtain that hid the president from view. According to my watch, I was minutes away from John Wilkes Booth coming up the same staircase I'd just used, gun in hand. I felt my first flutter of panic in my chest. Where had she gone? Should I go back down to the theater and risk missing her or stay where I was and hope I saw Booth before she did?

As I stood there, frozen, trying to decide which was the right answer, I heard a small sound directly behind me. It was the sound of someone unwrapping something covered in plastic. Plastic, a material that wouldn't be widely used until the 1960s. I whirled and saw the curtain behind me quiver just as the sound of booted feet on the stairs came from below. John Wilkes Booth was on his way up. Without stopping to think, I threw myself behind the curtain and wrapped my arm around the startled woman's neck. She let out a muffled gargle, and I saw the long lethal-looking syringe in her hand. She stumbled sideways, throwing us out into the open, and I fought to keep my balance without losing my grip.

Her eyes went wide as she realized that her opportunity to change history was about to be taken away. Her fingernails and teeth dug into the arm I had wrapped around her neck, but it didn't matter; I had her. The thump of Booth's boots was getting louder, and I knew I had mere seconds to get this done. If he came up the stairs and saw a woman and a twelve-year-old girl brawling like a couple of ultimate fighters in big frilly dresses, it might be enough to deter him from his plan and forever change history. I reached for my belt with the arm that wasn't getting gnawed on and grabbed my Chaos Cuffs. It took a second or two of fumbling, but I got them on her wrists just as the handsome face of John Wilkes Booth made it up the stairs. A heartbeat later and we'd disappeared, leaving him free to commit one of the most heart-wrenching crimes in history.

CHAPTER TWO

REGAN

My eyes snapped open inside the narrow white simulation room, and I immediately became aware of how bone-numbingly cold I was. Large computer monitors lined the walls around me, and I could see the frozen image of the woman and me mid-struggle with Booth's surprised face staring right at us. I almost groaned out loud in exasperation, but I swallowed it at the last second. The commander's daughter wasn't allowed to whine like that.

"So I failed?" I asked. "Again?"

"That's right, cadet," said Professor Brown with a sympathetic smile as she leaned down to remove the probes on my arms and legs so I could sit up.

"By how much?" I asked, glaring at the screen.

She consulted the slim black tablet she held for a moment and then sighed. "One second."

"Tell me you're kidding," I said.

"I'm afraid not," she said. "In that second, Booth saw you disappear in front of his eyes, and it was enough for him to call off the plan. As you may recall, he'd already gotten cold feet once in his attempted kidnapping of Lincoln, so it didn't take much to spook him that night."

"Well, that stinks," I said.

"One way of putting it," said Professor Treebaun as he looked up from his tablet for the first time. "Although it seems a bit tame considering that if this was a real mission, you'd have just irrevocably ruined the unity of the United States of America."

"I know, I know," I said, really not wanting to hear yet another lecture about all the awful things that happened in the future if Lincoln survived his night at Ford's Theatre. Knowing that something that seemed so 100 percent right, like saving the president of the United States, could actually have catastrophic consequences didn't make it feel any less awful. I'd heard all that before, the last time I'd failed this simulation. But at least last time I hadn't failed by one measly second.

"So, I'm off to the recap review room?" I asked,

silently praying she'd let me off the hook. I mean, how many times could you watch the same recap?

"Correct," said Professor Treebaun, and I stifled a sigh. Five. You could apparently watch a recap for the same simulation five times.

Professor Treebaun scowled at me, as though he'd read my mind. "You will watch your recap, and you will continue watching recaps until you learn the importance of a second. We will get this simulation on your schedule for next week."

"Does my mom already know?" I asked, trying and failing to keep the slight pleading tone from my voice.

Professor Brown nodded. "She watched your simulation live from her office."

"Peachy," I said, shutting my eyes for a second so I could block out the screenshot of my failure for a moment. Professor Brown finished pulling the electrical sensors off my arms and legs, and I barely flinched as the sticky pads yanked out my arm and leg hair.

"What was that, Cadet Fitz?" asked Professor Treebaun sharply, and I snapped my eyes open.

"Nothing, sir," I said.

"That's what I thought," he said as he unplugged his tablet from the main computer and tucked it in his bag. "You know," he went on, eyebrow raised, "it would behoove you to study your history a bit more. There was a different access point to that particular stairwell that would have saved you that precious second. I thought you'd have memorized that by now."

"You and me both," I muttered.

"Enjoy your recap," he said over his shoulder as he left the room, the doors sliding shut behind him with an official-sounding metallic click.

I watched him walk out and frowned. He was right. I *should* know my history better by now. I'd been drilled on this particular event over and over again. I'd read countless reports on the Lincoln assassination. My mom had even made flash cards for me detailing things like the name of Booth's coconspirators, the ins and outs of the theater, the events leading up to the history-altering murder. Flash cards, for crying out loud. And all of it should be firmly planted in my head. But it wasn't. Sometimes I felt like my brain was one of those colanders our housekeeper, Mrs. Ellsworth, used to drain pasta, full of little holes that let all sorts of important things escape without my permission.

Now that Professor Treebaun had mentioned it, I did vaguely recall my mom mentioning the multiple access points to the staircase Booth used. But it hadn't stuck, and because of that I'd failed the simulation again, and the daughter of the first-ever female commander in chief of the Glitch Academy wasn't supposed to fail.

For probably the millionth time in my life, I wondered why everyone else got watertight brains, while mine was apparently Swiss cheese.

"Don't be too hard on yourself," said Professor Brown, her demeanor markedly more relaxed now that Treebaun was gone. "We don't just strive for perfection at the Academy. We demand it. And perfection is hard sometimes. You'll get it eventually." She unplugged her own tablet and put it in her bag before looking back up at me. "Please wait for your recap to upload, and then join your classmates in the recap review room in five."

"Yes, ma'am," I said, staring down at my slightly blue-tinged fingers, which were more than a little numb from the freezing temperature of the simulation room. Something soft fell into my lap—my uniform jacket—and I looked up at Professor Brown and smiled my thanks as I shrugged it on over goose-bump-riddled shoulders. Like all the cadet jackets, it was a soft green, closely fitted so it rested across my shoulders like a second supple skin, and I felt instantly warmer. The thin white tank I'd been wearing to allow the sensors contact with my skin was scant protection from the icy wafts of air being pumped into the room. There was something to that. The cold air. It allowed simulations to function better somehow. I racked my brain to remember why that was, failed to come up with anything, and gave up.

Which, I realized with a grimace, could very easily be my motto. Professor Brown turned and headed toward the doors, but she stopped and turned back at the last moment.

"And Regan?" she said, and I jumped at hearing my first name. No one used first names at the Academy. I'd grown up at the Academy, running the halls since I was in diapers, and even then I'd been Cadet Fitz. Always Cadet Fitz.

"Yes?" I said.

"Don't worry too much about your mom." With that she hit the button and the metal doors slid open, letting her out into the bustling hallway where all the kids who hadn't screwed up their simulation that day were gathering their books to leave for their dinners. The doors slid shut again and the noise of the hallway was choked off instantly. Simulation rooms were sound-proofed to an almost maddening degree, and now that I was alone, I could hear my own heartbeat like someone was holding a microphone to my chest. It wasn't a new sensation by any means, but that didn't make it any less unsettling.

I wanted nothing more than to skip the recap of my one-second failure and join the crowd heading home. My stomach gave an angry snarl to remind me that skipping lunch to study for this recap had been a big fat waste. I should have just eaten. It had been grilled cheese day too. I loved grilled cheese day. Feeling equal parts resentful and resigned, I waited until the screen in front of me showed the big green check mark that let me know my recap had been successfully uploaded before sliding off the table and heading over to the door. Waiting for the upload was part of the simulation training protocol, although it seemed redundant since as far as I knew, one had never failed to upload. Personally, I think they made us wait so we had a few moments to think things over and prepare ourselves for what came next.

The wall hummed as I walked toward it, and a second later the door slid open with an efficient click. The sound echoed up and down the corridor, letting me know the other cadets were being released too. I felt my cheeks burn a little in embarrassment, but I brushed it off. There would be time for that soon enough. I straightened my spine to my full five feet seven inches and strode out without a backward glance. So what if this was my third recap this week? It was all part of the process. We had to learn if we wanted to protect the future.

I followed the flow of cadets down the corridor and into the auditorium-style recap room at the end of the hall. Unlike the room I'd just left, this one was warm, and I felt the goose bumps on my arms melt back into my skin as I slid into a seat at the back. No need to be front and center for this. My classmates filed in around me, filling in the seats until the room was about a quarter full. I noted that three of the other kids in my year—Jennifer, Rory, and Mike—were here, a fact that should have probably made me feel better, but instead it just annoyed me. The more kids in the recap, the longer this whole mess was going to take. Besides, it wasn't like we were all buddies who would sit together to make this whole thing more bearable. They were nice to me in the way that most people were, like it was a requirement because of who my mom was, but they were a far cry from friends. Professor Treebaun stood at the front of the room, looking none too pleased about getting stuck with this particular duty.

Once the last cadet had taken their seat, Professor Treebaun pressed a button on his tablet and the doors to the recap room slid shut, sealing us in.

"Would anyone like to volunteer to begin this partic-ular recap session?" he asked, his sharp eyes scanning the room. I sank down deeper into my chair and made an effort to look anywhere but at him. Thankfully he called on someone else, and the room darkened as the floor-to-ceiling screen in the front of the room came to life so the entire class could watch a third-year cadet's disastrous simulation during the Texas Revolution. Poor kid screwed up within one minute of landing in the middle of the battle for the Alamo. He'd taken a misstep and fallen backward, knocking over three men who had the misfortune of standing near the wall of the Alamo. Professor Treebaun chose that moment to freeze the screen, mid-flail, and I saw the boy visibly shrink.

"Who can tell me where he went wrong?" he asked. Five hands shot up, but mine was definitely not one of them. Treebaun scanned the room and then pointed to someone I couldn't see in the front row.

"He forgot about the attack from the north outer wall of the Alamo complex," came a voice I knew all too well. It took everything in me to stifle my eye roll. I did not, however, manage to do the same to my exasperated groan, and of course old Treebaun heard it.

"Something wrong, Cadet Fitz?" he asked, his voice lashing out like lightning.

"No, sir," I said, sitting up straight in my chair.

"Good," said Treebaun. "After Cadet Frost you can go."

"Thank you, sir," I said, forcing a smile onto my face. Treebaun turned his attention back to the know-it-all in the front row, and nodded for him to continue. The boy did, going on at length about every nitty-gritty detail of the epic battle. I saw Jennifer and Mike exchange looks of exasperation and almost smiled.

I wasn't the only one who found this particular know-it-all obnoxious.

"Very good, Cadet Mason," Treebaun said, turning back to the class. "Now, who can explain the telltale flaw in the Butterfly Cadet Frost failed to apprehend?" With the press of a button, the Butterfly in question flicked onto the screen and began to slowly revolve in a circle so we could see every possible angle of his blood-splattered uniform.

There was the muffled rustle of clothing as everyone shifted nervously, and before I even realized I was doing it, my hand was in the air. Treebaun waited a moment, scanning the room to see if anyone else was going to volunteer before pointing at me.

"The blood on his jacket," I said.

"Go on," Treebaun prompted.

"It's too red," I explained. "If you look closely, you can see that his jacket is dry, not wet. He was disguised to look like he was injured in the battle, but blood dries brown, not bright red."

"Very good, Cadet Fitz," Treebaun said almost reluctantly, turning back to the screen. "This particular Butterfly was modeled after a real one caught by our commander in chief about eighteen years ago. He was one of the first members of Mayhem we ever caught." Everyone leaned in a little, including me, to get a better look at the guy. We all knew about the group that called themselves by the name Mayhem. But their leader, location, and members were a mystery. Their organization was even older than the Academy, which made sense since their very existence made us so necessary. We were charged with protecting history at all costs, while they were happy to change history for the right price. There were still the sporadic attacks by misguided vigilantes, but for the most part every active Butterfly was part of Mayhem. Which meant that over the years, the attempts to alter history had become increasingly more organized and better planned, which made Butterflies that much harder to spot. The only thing we had going for us that they didn't was that our technology and a lot of money was spent to stay one step ahead of them on that front. Unlike us, Mayhem used pieced-together equipment that often didn't allow them to time travel with the precision that we did, and, of course, they didn't have Chaos Cuffs. The thought of those cuffs made me smile, and I found my hand going instinctively to my hip, where a set had hung during my simulation. Superheroes had capes that marked them as the good guys. Glitchers? We had cuffs. The repercussion track for the Alamo kid started to play, and I stifled a yawn.

"Next up is Cadet Fitz," said Treebaun, not needing to consult his tablet for my particular simulation since he'd watched it in person. The press of a button and the screen changed from the bloody battle of the Alamo to the serene inside of Ford's Theatre.

"This was your third attempt at the Lincoln assassination, was it not?" said Treebaun.

I gritted my teeth and shook my head. He knew full well this wasn't my third attempt. "No, sir," I said, "my fifth." A ripple of stifled laughter went around the room, but I kept my spine ramrod straight, my eyes dead ahead. I could almost hear my mom's voice in my head coaching me. *Confidence is a skill, Regan. The more you practice it, the better you get. Learn to maintain an air of total control despite the circumstances swirling around you.*

"Right," said Treebaun. "Let's begin."

The room darkened again and the screen shimmered, zooming in on an image of me sitting in my blue dress. The recap began.

Recaps shouldn't turn my stomach anymore, but they still did. Watching myself on that screen was like having a million ants crawl underneath my skin, and not just any ants, but the fire ant variety that liked to bite. And the feeling was that much worse now that I knew Elliot Mason was sitting in the front row. I rolled my neck from side to side in an attempt to dispel the feeling as I watched myself spot the

Butterfly and exit my seat at the theater.

Did I really wrinkle my face like that when I was thinking? It made my already turned-up nose look even more piglike. Charming. And man, did the back of my hair look stupid in those tight bouncy ringlets. I ran my palm over my smooth blond strands and caught myself wrinkling my nose in the exact way I'd just found obnoxious. I rubbed it with the back of my hand, grateful that for simulations at least I didn't have to actually curl my hair or wear the dress. If I ever got to do an actual mission, I'd have to do all that. The prep would be real, and the bite marks the Butterfly on-screen was so nicely carving into my arm wouldn't magically disappear when the simulation ended. Treebaun paused the screen on the image of a wide-eyed John Wilkes Booth and turned back to the class.

"Cadet Fitz missed this particular simulation by one second. Who here knows how she could have saved herself that second?"

Just like I knew it would, a slim brown hand in the front row shot into the air.

"Cadet Mason again," said Treebaun.

"Had she used the alternate staircase, she would have arrived in plenty of time to apprehend her Butterfly," said Cadet Mason, and I could just picture the smug look on his stupid face as he said it. Treebaun

22

changed the screen to a diagram of Ford's Theatre and did a quick overview of all the ways the top balcony could have been accessed before turning on my repercussion track.

The repercussion track was different every time, depending on how badly you'd screwed up, and really, as my mom liked to point out, it was just a bunch of guesswork. Its purpose was to show the Glitcher what their actions could cause in the future.

Without Lincoln's death, things got surprisingly nasty. My one-second mistake would cause the North and South to never fully reconcile in the aftermath of the Civil War. Eventually, a second civil war would take place, this one twice as devastating and deadly as the first, making what should have been the United States of America so divided and weak that it was easily conquered. All because of one teeny-tiny, should-be-insignificant second. I watched this alternative history spiral out in flashes and blips and bit my lip. Treebaun was right—I did have to be perfect. Which was a problem, because while I was a lot of things, I was a far cry from perfect. I sighed. It would have been nice if, for once, I'd knocked this simulation out of the park, especially with Elliot Mason sitting front and center.

The screen changed to the next student, and I relaxed a little in my seat. If Elliot was in here, then he'd screwed up too, and I was going to enjoy watching him squirm. Treebaun progressed quickly through each student's recap and repercussion track, and I watched a botched Kennedy assassination simulation, a Watergate mess, and a rather iffy situation involving Ben Franklin, but none of them were Elliot's. Finally it was over, the lights went on for good, and Treebaun turned to us, his lined face serious as he took the time to look each of us in the eye.

"You will not make the same mistake again, will you, cadets?" he asked.

"I will not," I responded in unison with the rest of the room. There was no other correct answer. Everyone stood up, but I stayed in my seat a heartbeat longer. He'd forgotten to show Elliot's simulation. How had he forgotten? Treebaun never forgot anything. The rest of the kids filed out the doors as I sat there fuming. But then I saw Elliot get up, and I grabbed my stuff and shouldered my way through the crowd and out. No way I was going to allow him to gloat face-to-face. A few people grumbled, but I made it through the door and headed down the hallway toward home.

Rounding a corner, I almost ran headfirst into two cadets. I mumbled an apology and was about to keep going when I caught a glimpse of their expressions and stopped. Both of their young faces were drained of color, their hands visibly shaking as they fumbled to zip up their jackets. I recognized them as being a few years below me, but I couldn't remember their names. It was obvious that their recaps and repercussions had been bad ones, I thought, trying to place each of them in the simulations I'd just watched. The boy I recognized from a pretty bloody World War I battle, and I thought the girl was the one who'd gotten herself killed during the Kennedy assassination. I could have been wrong, though. I could sympathize. Watching myself die on-screen, even if it was just a simulation, always made my insides go cold and hard, like I'd swallowed an iceberg. These kids looked like they'd swallowed the one that had taken down the *Titanic*, and I couldn't help but feel a tug of sadness for them. They'd never asked for this life. None of us had, and it wasn't the first time I wondered what it would be like to have a life other than this one. To have the freedom to choose my own path based on my strengths instead of being crammed down one that seemed to do nothing but highlight my weaknesses. I shook my head, pushing the thought away. I was a Glitcher. I was the daughter of the commander in chief. I didn't get an option of another life, and I'd decided a long time ago that I wasn't going to let that sour the one I did get. This was the hand of cards I'd been dealt, and I was going to play it for all I was worth, even if that meant watching the same recap of Lincoln's assassination until I died of embarrassment.

Long gone were the days when someone could be born with the time-traveling gene and go unaccounted for. Everyone saw the mess that made, and it had taken years to get history straightened back out. Some things had been too far gone to correct and history had just had to bear the scars. Germany was still upset about the whole *Hindenburg* mess, but as our professors were quick to point out, the world needed a tangible reminder of what happened when time travelers pranced through history like a bunch of unchaperoned kindergartners on a field trip. Thankfully, right around the time that Mayhem started recruiting, the government stepped in and started regulating things.

Now everyone was checked for the gene at birth. They poked your heel, smeared some blood on a slide, and checked to see if you were one in a half million. If you were born with the teeny-tiny DNA glitch that allowed you to slide in and out of time like a knife through butter, you were handed over to your country's branch of the Academy. We were part of the United States branch, but there were Academy branches just like ours hidden all over the world. One of the most important and influential treaties of all time had made it possible for each country's Academy to regulate its own Glitchers, with the understanding that a Glitcher was only allowed to protect their own country's history. Of course, things always got a bit hairy when multiple countries were involved in a historical event. For example, the assassination of Franz Ferdinand that kicked off World War I had taken three weeks of negotiations and a lifetime of headaches, according to my mother. So sending your child off to the Academy was an honor above all others, but that meant that parents were allowed to see their kids only twice a year during the special visitation times the Academy carefully orchestrated with enough security to sink a ship.

One of the few exceptions to that rule, of course, was me. I'd been born on Academy property, the daughter of the Academy's commander in chief. My dad had been a Glitcher too, but he'd died on a mission before I was born. Mom didn't like to talk about him, so we didn't. I'd asked her once what would have happened to me if I hadn't tested positive for the active Glitching gene, and she'd been purposefully vague. Leading me to believe that a little blond-haired baby girl would have mysteriously ended up on the doorstep of an orphanage somewhere. While that may seem cruel and heartless to most, I knew it was just protocol. You couldn't live or work at the Academy unless you had the Glitch gene. Period.

My heart gave a painful tug as I looked at the two little faces in front of me. I could practically see the tears pressing against the backs of the girl's eyeballs, and before I could think better of it, I found myself putting a companionable arm around her shoulders and squeezing. She jumped about a foot at my contact, her curly brown hair whipping across her face as she turned terrified green eyes up to meet mine. The boy beside her was scowling, caught up in the memories of his own recap, no doubt, but when he saw me his expression changed to one of worried wariness. A moment later his hand snapped to his forehead in a salute. I ignored it and gave the girl a smile that was meant to be encouraging but now felt stiff.

"It gets easier," I said. "Every time. It gets easier."

She nodded but didn't look at me, and I could tell from the rigidity of the muscles beneath my hand that I hadn't convinced her in the slightest. How old was she? Eight? Nine, tops? Third-year cadets seemed like such babies now, even though I was only a few years older than them. This would be their first year doing full simulations, and I knew that was a hard transition. The girl's bony shoulders felt as fragile as a bird's wing under my hand, and I released it and stepped back.

"It really does get better," I assured them both. "Promise."

"Stop that," quipped a male voice behind me. "Don't you know that you don't salute the commander's daughter?" I turned to see Elliot Mason. He was staring at the two kids, a smirk twisting his mouth. "She's not anyone important. She just thinks she is."

"Lovely to see you too, Elliot," I said, smiling too brightly as I turned to the wide-eyed cadets. "Forgive him," I said. "Elliot has the personality of a constipated toad, and he struggles with remembering his manners."

Elliot's dark brown eyes narrowed into angry slits. "You aren't funny, cadet," he sneered, and I saw him stand up straighter in an attempt to offset the three additional inches of height I'd had on him since we were both eight. I fought the instinct to roll my eyes. It wasn't my fault that I'd inherited my mom's height, and just to press the fact, I straightened my spine so I could look down at him. It was then that I noticed that our audience had disappeared. The kids I'd been talking to had melted into the crowd, and it was just Elliot and me. Which, I reminded myself, was a situation my mother had given me strict instructions to avoid. *The best way to prevent a conflict with Cadet Mason is to keep your distance*, she'd said, like it was easy to do in a class as small as ours. We were two of ten students in our fifth cadet year, and avoiding him was next to impossible.

"You didn't need to be such a jerk," I said, shouldering past him as my stomach rumbled, reminding me of my priorities.

"Couldn't help myself," he said, hurrying to keep up with me. I walked faster, but Elliot just adjusted his stride and kept pace.

"Where was your recap, by the way?" I said, whirling to face him so quickly he almost ran into me.

Elliot shrugged. "I didn't have one. I like to sit in on the recap sessions. I find them helpful."

"You're kidding," I said. "You go through that voluntarily?" He nodded.

I shook my head. "You really are a freak, Mason."

"A freak that's at the top of our class," he shot back. "Last I checked, Fitz, you weren't even in the top fifty percent. That must sting a little." It did sting, but it was also an inarguable fact. If my brain was a colander, Elliot's was a steel trap.

"Doesn't change the freak status," I muttered as I hurried down the hall, but Elliot just sped up to keep pace with me.

"What are you doing?" I asked. "Don't you have somewhere better to be?"

"Not particularly," he said. "I was just wondering if you're competing in the sim test tomorrow."

"No," I said.

"You know," he went on as though I hadn't said anything, "the test where they pit us against one another?
The test you have to win ten times before you are eligi-
ble to move up to the next level of the Academy? That
sim test? But wait," he said, pausing with an overly
dramatic hand to his chin, "you haven't even won once?
Have you?"

"I said no," I snapped back, walking so fast he
practically had to jog to keep up. It was hard to win
something you'd never attempted, but I wasn't going to
tell him that. If I couldn't pass the Lincoln simulation,
I didn't have a shot of winning a sim test. I turned left
down the corridor, my access badge lighting up on
my chest as the large metal door slid open to let us
through.

"I've been prepping for the test for weeks," Elliot
went on. "I've already won nine times, which I'm sure
you know, but I heard they really make it tough for
your tenth try. They don't like kids leveling up too
young." He paused and looked at me expectantly. I
knew Elliot well enough to know that this wasn't going
to end until he made whatever point it was he was trying to make, so I stopped and turned to face him again,
arms crossed tight over my chest.

"What's your point?" I said.

He smiled. "No point. Just thought that you should

know that I'm about to be the youngest cadet to level up. Your mom currently holds that record, right?"

I didn't say anything because the question had been 100 percent rhetorical. He knew, just like the entire Academy knew, that my mom held almost every record worth holding. What was he trying to do? Bait me? I glanced up and down the corridor, but we were alone, everyone else having already abandoned the simulation wing for the mess hall and their dinners.

"Bet she'd have loved it if you'd been the one to beat it," Elliot said with a fake disappointment that set my teeth on edge. "Anyways," he went on as though he wasn't the biggest creep on the planet, "I just wanted you to know so you wouldn't miss me."

"No one has ever missed you," I shot back, and he winced. That wince brought me up short. Elliot never winced; he never showed any sort of emotion besides cocky self-assuredness peppered with the occasional temper spike. Whatever I'd said had struck a nerve, and I studied his face. And then it hit me.

Just like every other Academy kid, Elliot's family had given him up for training. But unlike every other kid, Elliot had never had anyone come on a family visitation day because his parents had both died shortly after he was born. While everyone else spent time on the lawn catching up with family, he was always off by himself, usually in the library. A fact I'd found out the hard way when I'd run into him a few years back and asked where his family was. The simple question had set him off, and we'd both ended up with our first detentions. It wasn't until after my mom chewed me out for the detention that I found out why Elliot hadn't been with his family. I'd felt like a complete jerk, especially since I knew what it was to walk in those particularly painful shoes. I'd never apologized, though. Maybe it was because I wasn't necessarily supposed to know about Elliot's parents, or maybe it was because I'd just been too embarrassed to do it. Either way, I'd made sure to steer clear of the library on visitation days from then on out because, of course, I was never part of family visitation days either. I couldn't believe that I was back in the same awful position, acting the jerk by running my mouth off to Elliot Mason. Part of me wanted to blame him, like he'd dragged me down to his level somehow, but really there was no excuse. I was just as big of a grade-A jerk as he was. Maybe even worse, I realized.

"Sorry," I said. "That was out of line." Elliot and I had disliked each other practically since we were babies in Academy day care. I had a very clear memory of three-year-old Elliot shoving Play-Doh up his nose, a memory I made a habit to remind him of every time the opportunity presented itself. Which, as it turned out, happened quite a lot. In my defense, he tossed around the story of that unfortunate field trip where I wet my pants like it was confetti, so he had it coming. I wasn't sure why we didn't get along, but I had a feeling that it was because my mom was the commander in chief, and he was just another Academy kid. Or maybe he really did have the personality of a constipated toad. The jury was still out.

Elliot forced a grin, showing off two rows of perfect white teeth. "It's fine. The only reason someone would miss you would be if your mom required it, Fitz."

I swallowed down what I wanted to say and raised an eyebrow at him, curious despite myself. "So you think you're ready to move up to level six?" I asked. The very idea made my chest tight. At that level, you actually time traveled. Not to anything major, of course, but you were put on a Glitch platform and sent to a deserted field somewhere in the past to get used to the whole experience.

The rare gene that allowed a select few to Glitch couldn't be activated at will. Thank goodness. It lay dormant, hidden inside the very DNA of a Glitcher until it was triggered by a Glitch platform in ways I still didn't completely understand. I wasn't sure how I'd handle that step when it came, but I'd have to find a way. *If* it ever came, I thought ruefully, and I hoped that thought hadn't shown on my face. The last thing I needed was to give Elliot Mason ammunition, thank you very much.

The Glitch gene was so rare that I wasn't in danger of getting kicked out of the Academy, especially with my mom being who she was, but that didn't mean I'd get to be a Glitcher. Only about 20 percent of the Academy students made it that far. The mental strain broke some, and others opted out of the program due to the overwhelming stress and pressure of it all and chose to work on campus in some other role. They weren't considered failures, just reassignments. You could label it however you wanted to, but if the daughter of the first ever female commander in chief didn't make it through, I would be a big fat failure.

"Hey," Elliot said suddenly, the mocking tone gone from his voice. "What's this?" Turning, I saw him bend down and scoop up a small white envelope off the ground. Deciding to capitalize on his distraction, I hurried down the hall, relieved not to feel his leering presence at my side anymore.

"Hey, Fitz!" Elliot called. "It has your name on it!"

I ignored him and kept walking. This was just one of Elliot's tricks. He'd get me to walk back there, and then he'd say something stupid, and I'd lose whatever cool I was managing to maintain.

"Hey!" Elliot called again. "I'm serious. It has your name on it!" I heard him jogging to catch up to me, and I quickened my pace. I was almost to the door that would take me out of the simulation building and into the sunshine. Tomorrow he'd ace that test, like he aced every test, and he'd move across campus to start the next phase of the Academy. With any luck, I wouldn't see his sneering face again until I moved up myself. I was about to put my hand on the wall sensor that would open the door and let me out, but something stopped me.

Someday, I would look back at this moment and wonder what it was that kept me from walking away from Elliot Mason forever. But whatever it was, I stopped, and I turned, arms crossed, to face him. Seeing me turn, Elliot slowed down and walked the last few feet to catch up to me. Without a word, he handed me the envelope. The envelope's paper felt unusually thick, much better quality than the thin stuff our assignments were usually printed on. I flipped it over and felt my stomach flop sickeningly. He was right. My name was scrawled across the front, but that wasn't what made me feel ill. It's that the name was written in *my* handwriting. I'd recognize it anywhere, the way the loop of my *g* was always just a tad too large. But I knew I'd never held this envelope before.

"Open it," Elliot prompted me impatiently.

I shook my head as I turned the envelope back over in my hands. My brain felt muddled as I tried to remember a time that I'd written my name on this, but I kept coming up short. It felt like trying to remember a dream after waking up, like the memory was there, but just out of reach.

"Come on," Elliot said, "open it. I want to see who wrote you a letter. Do you have a secret admirer no one knows about?"

"Don't be dumb," I said as I rubbed the paper between my fingers, noting a texture and weight to it that was completely foreign. Suddenly it clicked like a bolt in a lock.

This was a Cocoon, the equivalent of a time-traveling bomb. It was something dropped by a Butterfly to change the future in some way, usually by revealing something that was about to happen so it could be changed. I felt my blood go icy in my veins, and I turned the letter back over, looking again at *my* name in *my* handwriting. If this *was* a Cocoon, and I knew that it was, that meant that I was the Butterfly. My mind immediately recoiled from the idea. Me? A Butterfly? It was so absurd a thought that my brain refused to accept it. Never, not in my wildest of wild dreams, had that possibility ever occurred to me. I'd been raised to hate Butterflies with every fiber of my being, but the evidence in my hand was almost undeniable. There was my name, in my own handwriting, on a piece of strange paper I'd never felt before in my life. Which meant that in the future I was going to write this letter and drop it here, in this exact moment, so that I could change the future in some way. If that didn't make me a Butterfly, I didn't know what did. Snapping my head up, I looked left and right, but the corridor was empty except for a very impatient Elliot Mason and me, and despite the panic that had frozen me to the spot, I couldn't help but wonder why in the world my future self would choose a moment that included Elliot Mason. Apparently, future me was an idiot.

Looking back down at the letter, I felt fear creep up my spine like a spider up a web. If this was found out, I'd be imprisoned for life and my mom would lose her job. It wouldn't matter that I'd done the crime in some unknown future or that current me had no flying clue what was going on. The condemning evidence was sitting in my hand. But despite all that, all I could manage to do was stand there, reeling at what this meant.

"Why do you look like you just saw a ghost?" Elliot asked, peering at me. "What's in that thing?" I'd just put together that I needed to hide the letter, and fast, when his hand shot out to grab it. I jerked back reflexively, but it was too late.

My blood fizzled angrily in my veins. "What do you think you're doing!" I yelled, trying in vain to snatch back the envelope. With a smirk he stuck an arm out to stop me while simultaneously dangling it just out of my reach. I glared at it for a moment, and then lunged forward, slamming my shoulder hard into Elliot's chin as I made a mad grab for the envelope. My hand closed around his, and I started prying his fingers loose without worrying overly much about how far back I yanked them in the process. Elliot cried out and twisted so we stumbled sideways. A second later a sharp whistle ripped through the air, and we both froze.

"Cadets!" boomed a voice that made that one word into a command. We jumped apart like we'd been electrocuted, and I felt a stab of fear as I saw my envelope still grasped tightly in Elliot's sweaty hand.

The sound of heavy boots resounded down the corridor, and I didn't need to glance to my left to know that it was an officer. I stepped my foot to the left and brought my heel down on the toes of Elliot's boot and pressed. His eyes darted angrily over to mine and I frantically flicked my eyes down to where the letter was clutched in his hand and then back to him, trying desperately to communicate that he needed to hide it. Now! He narrowed his eyes at me, and for a gut-wrenching heartbeat, I was sure that he was going to do the exact opposite just to spite me. But then he shocked me and balled his hand into a fist, successfully hiding the envelope.

"Cadets?" asked the sharp male voice.

"Professor, sir!" Elliot and I barked in unison. I cheated my eyes to the left to see that it was Professor Green. Well, I sighed inwardly, it could have been worse; it could have been Treebaun again. Green was one of the oldest professors on campus, with gray hair that bushed out above his ears like the cheeks of a chipmunk. He'd taught my mother back when she was a cadet, but he'd never once compared me to her. Which wasn't something I could say about any other professor on campus. He studied us now out of faded blue eyes in a way that let us know we weren't the first unruly cadets he'd ever dealt with, and we most certainly wouldn't be his last.

"The last recap session ended ten minutes ago," Green said. "What are you both still doing in the building?"

"I was just saying my goodbyes, sir," Elliot barked. "I am testing for the upper Academy tomorrow, and not to brag, sir, but I'm pretty confident of my advancement."

Professor Green raised a skeptical eyebrow as he looked from Elliot to me and back again, probably thinking of the multiple discipline reports that had found their way onto his desk over the years with the names Elliot Mason and Regan Fitz written across the top.

"Is that so?" Green said. "That certainly didn't look like a goodbye, at least not one that I'd ever want to take part in."

At any other time, I would have laughed at the way Green made Elliot squirm. You can't butter this one up, you great big brown-noser, I thought as Green looked at Elliot like he was something interesting he'd found on the bottom of his shoe.

"I think you'd better come with me, Cadet Mason," Green finally said. "There are a few boxes of old World War Two uniforms in my classroom that need to be put into storage, and you look like just the man for the job. But before you do that, I would like to see you extend a proper goodbye to Cadet Fitz. It will do you no good to move up in the Academy if you retain the manners of a first year." Elliot's face twitched, but he nodded and turned to me, his hand extended for the customary handshake exchanged between cadets. I stared at that hand for a half second before acting on instinct and harebrained desperation. Taking a step forward, I threw my arms around him in a tight hug. He froze, because that's what you do when the universe turns upside down.

"I need that letter back," I hissed in his ear, just loud enough for him to hear me.

"What's in it for me?" he whispered back, his arms wrapping around me in what was probably the most awkward and weird hug of my life as he kept up the bizarre charade.

"Whatever you want," I said in desperation, although I had no clue what I could possibly do for Elliot Mason that he'd care about.

"Maybe," he said, raising an eyebrow as he took a step back and out of my arms. "Goodbye, Cadet Fitz," he said, the epitome of good manners.

"Much better," Green said. "Now move along to my classroom. I will meet you there momentarily." Elliot nodded and pivoted sharply on the spot. I watched him go, wishing I could bore holes into his back with my glare alone.

Green turned to me, a look of concern on his face. "Cadet Fitz?" he asked. "Anything you want to tell me?"

I shook my head, making an effort to smile, but it felt too stretched and tight on my face.

Green raised one of his thick gray eyebrows that always reminded me of a fat furry caterpillar. "Are you sure, Cadet Fitz?" he asked.

"Positive, sir," I said. "It's just that Cadet Mason makes me want to scrub my skin with sandpaper, sir."

Green snorted out a laugh. "That was an enthusiastic goodbye for someone who makes you feel that way."

My mouth went dry as I realized my mistake. "I'm just really excited that he's moving on tomorrow," I said, which was 100 percent the truth. "That's all."

Green chuckled. "Cadet Mason is incredibly focused and goal oriented, and people that driven have a tendency to grate on others." When I didn't say anything, he sighed. "You know," he said. "I've taught you both for years now, and if each of you would relax a little, you might just become friends."

"Friends?" I said, barely hiding the disgust in my voice.

Green nodded. "Friends. The life you are training for is one of extreme stress and strain. Friends can help with that." Green considered me again for a long moment before nodding his head as though he'd just figured something out. "I assume you aren't participating in the sim test tomorrow?" he asked.

"Correct, sir," I said.

"May I ask why you never participate in sim tests?" he said, and I felt my insides shrivel a bit.

"I don't want to fail," I said, deciding that honesty was the best policy when it came to Professor Green.

He'd been around so long he could sniff out a lame cadet excuse from a mile away.

"And why do you believe you'd fail?" he asked.

"Experience," I said with a shrug. "I failed my simulation again today. I'm pretty terrible under pressure."

Green sniffed. "Well, it seems to me that if you're bad at something, you should take every opportunity to practice it. Don't you agree, cadet?" With that he turned and disappeared back through the door Elliot had just gone through.

I muttered something that I hoped sounded like a thank-you and exited the building. The sun was already as good as set, the last wisps of day sliding across the grassy courtyard we affectionately called the Mall to be replaced by the lengthening shadows of twilight. I let out a breath, releasing some of the tension of the last few minutes with it. My shoulders relaxed, and I stood for a second on the wide concrete steps, letting the panoramic view of the campus calm my buzzing nerves. My brain silently named each of the large stone buildings that surrounded the Mall—the Roosevelt Building, the Revere Building, and the Edison Building with its impressive clock tower. They were as familiar to me as my own reflection, and the normalcy of the sight went a long way toward calming me down. It really was beautiful. The air had a heaviness to it, making the smell of fresh-mown grass almost over-powering, and a quick glance at the sky showed an approaching storm. Good. I liked storms. They were wild and unpredictable, and they played by their own rules. Something I both envied and admired.

Set apart from "normal" citizens for our own protection and theirs, our gated, walled, and closely guarded campus complex sprawled across an entire island in the middle of the ocean. I had no idea which ocean, because where exactly we were situated on the globe was a secret I wasn't allowed in on. Although I had some educated guesses.

Government funding for the Glitch Initiative continued to pour in daily, and the grounds showed it. Elegant fountains dotted the property, looped and connected by polished concrete walkways edged with well-manicured landscaping that gave a historic university feel to an otherwise state-of-the-art facility. Behind the classic building facades of brick and stone was some of the most intricate technology known to man, all developed to help facilitate the continuation of the Glitch Initiative. Everyone had seen what the future looked like if time travelers were allowed to muck about in history unregulated and unchecked.

Well, I amended, they hadn't exactly *seen* it, since enough of the original time travelers had had the conscience and forethought to realize what was happening and fix things before everything went too haywire. According to the legend, the founder of the Academy had taken a complete set of World History books back in time and hidden them in some remote mountain cave. So when things went off the rails, so to speak, all he'd have to do was go back to those history books tucked safely in the past, and check to see if the current history matched. If it didn't, a mission was dispatched to fix it and stop the Butterfly from doing their damage. Thankfully, we now had more high-tech ways of keeping the proper timeline documented so that a Butterfly couldn't change things without our knowledge. Mom had tried to explain how that worked once, but it had given me a splitting headache, so she'd stopped. What mattered was that the general public didn't have a problem pouring millions of dollars into training and overseeing Glitchers as long as it kept the future intact. Well, no one was complaining outside the Academy at least. Inside, I knew I couldn't be the only one who sometimes felt like the lush green lawns and immaculate buildings were just well-disguised cages. But, as I'd been reminded on multiple occasions by my mom, the security of the future was more important than satisfying a twelve-year-old girl's wanderlust.

The large clock tower to my left started chiming,

and I hurried down the path. I'd gone only a few steps when I noticed something gray shoved into one of the well-manicured hedges, and despite my preoccupation I paused to grab it. It turned out to be two drab gray shirts, each sporting a weird number on the pocket. They looked like Glitch costumes, although I had no idea what historical event they might belong to, which wasn't all that surprising for me. Still, I didn't want whatever cadets had lost these to get in trouble, so I shoved them under my arm and picked up my pace. I could drop them by the Academy laundry on my way home, but I would have to hustle. The campus crowd was already thinning out, and I didn't want another teacher delaying my dinner any further with questions about why I'd lingered after the last recap. Although it already felt miles away, the confrontation with Elliot and the letter were taking up all my available brain space. Man, what I wouldn't give to recap that. To sit back and watch the scene play out in the detail that only a recap could provide. But, of course, that was impossible. What mattered now was figuring out how to get that letter back from Elliot, preferably before he realized what he had and turned me in.

CHAPTER THREE

ELLIOT

Regan Fitz was a stuck-up brat. She always had been, and she always would be. Of course, if I'd grown up the commander's daughter, I might be a stuck-up brat too. I scowled out of Green's classroom window as I watched her turn right toward her impressive brick house on the hill. I'd always wanted to see inside that house, but of course I'd never gotten an invite. Whatever, someday I'd be the one who lived there, and Regan "Too Dumb for Her Own Good" Fitz would be a nobody. I put my hand in my pocket and felt the weird texture of the envelope she'd almost taken me out trying to get back, and I wondered again why I'd bothered to hide it from Green. It had been a perfect opportunity to really stick it to Fitz right before leveling up. But I was too nosy, and I'd have given just about anything to find out what made all the blood drain out of her face like that. As I watched her disappear around the corner, I felt an old familiar jealousy wrap itself around my chest, and I momentarily regretted not throwing her under the bus when I had a chance. I tightened my grip around the letter, crumpling it mercilessly in my hand before realizing what I was doing and releasing it.

"Cadet Mason," came a voice behind me, and I jumped guiltily and immediately pulled my hand out of my pocket. I turned to see Professor Green staring past me and out the window over my shoulder. "You aren't a fan of Cadet Fitz," he said. It was a statement, not a question. I shifted uncomfortably, not quite sure what to do with that. Green was my least-favorite professor. He was direct to a fault and made me feel like my skin was two sizes too small. When he looked at me it was as though my skull was the same clear glass as the window, allowing him to see all my thoughts swirling around inside my head. Every other professor was happy with their yes, sirs and no, ma'ams, but Green had never been impressed with me. Not when I aced every test he gave or finished at the top of every simulation.

"I'm not sure how I should answer that, sir," I finally

said when the silence had begun to stretch uncomfortably.

"You don't have to," Green said. "The boxes that need to be moved to the third floor are over here." I turned and followed him to the corner storage closet. He threw open the door and flicked on the lights to reveal stacks of dust-covered boxes.

"That's a lot of boxes," I said.

"Then you'd better get a move on," he said, turning to sit down at his desk. I stared at that stack and felt a new fury bubble in my veins. Why was I here and not Fitz? She'd been just as guilty as me for causing a disturbance in the hall. Probably even more so. I picked up the first box and turned to see Green still studying me, and I quickly rearranged my face into one of passive obedience.

"She isn't here because she doesn't need to build character," he said, and I paused on my way out the door. What was this guy? A mind reader?

"And I do, sir?" I said.

"She has her weaknesses, and you have yours, whether you're willing to admit it or not. Moral fiber is something that can't be taught, but hard work helps some. Being the best isn't always the best thing for one's character. It will do you no good to be the best Glitcher at the Academy if your insides don't match your outside."

I had no idea what that meant, but I mumbled something I hoped sounded like an agreement and headed out the door.

An hour later I'd hauled the last box out of Green's room and up the three flights of stairs since the elevator was conveniently getting repairs. Part of me was sure Green had known that when he made me do the job, but maybe that was giving him too much credit. Shaking my head to rid myself of the storm cloud that seemed to have settled around my shoulders ever since my run-in with Little Miss Fitz, I hurried toward the student dorms. It was late, and if I didn't hustle, the mess hall would be closed, and I'd be out of luck. With that in mind, I broke into a jog that ate up the quarter mile between the simulation building and my dorm in a matter of minutes.

My mind went back to the successful simulation I'd done that afternoon. It was over the Battles of Lexington and Concord, and I'd gone in disguised as a British soldier. I wondered if it would ever get old seeing Paul Revere in the flesh. Probably not. Early American History was my favorite, and this simulation was one of the more advanced of the program since potential Butterflies were scattered over a large area. Which is probably why it was my favorite; there was nothing I loved more than a challenge. I smiled, thinking about how I'd caught my Butterfly in plenty of time, cuffed him, and made it out before major damage was done. It had been textbook. I hadn't stayed back to watch the Recap to rub Regan's failure in her face. That was just an added bonus. It really was the extra practice that I craved. If you wanted to be the best, you had to live and breathe this life, and if I could learn from my classmates' mistakes and avoid making my own, all the better.

I reached the mess hall two minutes before it closed and earned myself a dirty look from Mrs. Smith, who was just walking over to the big metal double doors to lock them up for the night.

"Sorry," I apologized as I flashed her one of my most winning smiles. "I got tied up. I'll just grab something and bring it back to my room."

"There isn't much left," she grumbled as she locked the door behind me lest anyone else sneak in and make her night longer.

"That's okay," I called, trotting over to where the large silver trays of food sat under warming lights. She was right. It was spaghetti night, which was always a favorite of mine, but the remaining sauce had dried out and burned onto the corner of the pan, which was fine because there were only a few stray noodles left anyway. There wasn't even one lousy piece of garlic bread left. It looked like another cereal dinner. With a sigh,

I grabbed a bowl and quickly filled it with the crumbly remains of some sort of bran cereal and grabbed a milk carton from the counter, ignoring the fact that it had lost its chill hours ago.

Turning toward the door again, I almost ran full force into Mrs. Smith, who stood with her arms crossed, watching me in disapproval. I barely managed to steady the bowl of cereal before it dumped all over my front. She studied me for another second, and I wondered if I was going to get chewed out for something when she sighed and held up a finger.

"Stay," she said before turning and disappearing back into the stainless-steel labyrinth of the kitchen. I stayed. You didn't mess with Mrs. Smith. She was scary. When I was a first year, I'd seen her make a cocky fifth year mop the entire mess hall because he had the audacity to start a food fight. She'd stood over him the entire time, her eyes narrowed and mouth pursed into a thin line, and the kid had practically shrunk five inches by the time it was all over. If she said to stay, I'd stay.

A moment later, she was back, a small foil packet in her hands. Without comment she confiscated my sad bowl of bran crumbs and handed it to me. It felt warm, hot even, and I looked up at her in surprise.

"A growing boy can't grow on this," she said, holding up the offending bowl like it was full of bugs and not cereal. "Now get back to your dorm. If you get caught in the halls after lights-out, I'm not vouching for you." I stared at her another second in surprise, my fingers burning a little on the hot packet, before mumbling a thank-you and bolting for the door.

I made it back to my room in record time. Shutting the door behind me, I set the foil packet down on my desk before shucking off my Academy jacket and hanging it carefully in my closet. If everything went right, I'd be getting a new one tomorrow, red instead of green, but that didn't mean I wasn't going to keep my cadet jacket nice. I could still remember the day I'd been given it. Just like every other Academy kid, someone who had been entrusted to the Academy by my parents from birth, I'd grown up not owning much. I didn't lack for anything—food, shelter, the basics—but nothing was ever really mine either. Every toy had to be shared; every outfit was given to me and then taken back once I'd outgrown it.

The jacket was the first thing I'd been given that was mine indefinitely, with my name embroidered in gold inside the collar. The first time I'd worn it I'd felt ten feet tall, like somehow making it this far made up for never having a real family. Unlike the rest of the kids on campus, I didn't even have a picture of my parents, let alone a twice-yearly visit. All I knew about them was that they'd died shortly after turning me over to the Glitch program. Sometimes I'd catch myself staring at my hands and wondering if I'd inherited my long fingers with their thick knuckles from my dad, or I'd catch a glimpse of my nose in the mirror and wonder if I'd inherited its distinctive arch from my mother. I might learn everything there was to know about America's history, but my own history was destined to stay a mystery forever. Whatever; it wouldn't matter that I was one of the only kids without parents on parents' day if I was the best. I shook my head, clearing the thoughts of my imaginary family away as I shut my closet door. Tomorrow, I'd get a new jacket with my name on it.

My stomach grumbled at me, and I turned to the foil packet. Inside I found a large portion of the lasagna that had been at dinner yesterday, reheated so the cheese stuck in gooey puddles to the foil. God bless Mrs. Smith. I popped a bite into my mouth with my fingers, having forgotten to grab a fork at the mess hall, before retrieving the letter from my pocket. Time to see what Fitz wanted me to hide from Professor Green. I wondered momentarily what I should make her do to get it back. Something humiliating, although, if I was lucky, the letter would contain something embarrassing. Something that would put her in her place, take her down a notch. I flipped over the letter to see her name again and felt something twist sickeningly in my stomach. I took another bite of lasagna even though I knew it wasn't hunger, and for the first time I wished I hadn't decided to mess with her. Something about this letter sent prickles up my arm and made me feel uneasy, but my curiosity got the better of me, and I unfolded it and read.

I don't have much time, so I'm going to get right to the point. This letter is exactly what you think it is, but it's going to be fine. I promise. You and Elliot Mason are going to have to get over yourselves. But even as I write this, I know you won't. At least not right away. So here's the deal. Whatever happens, Elliot can't level up tomorrow. So many things hinge on that, but I don't want to freak you out with any more information than I have to. Besides, if I tell you too much, things won't unfold the way they need to, and I hate to break it to you, but there is no going back now. A lot of lives are at stake here, so don't blow this one like you just blew your Lincoln simulation for the fifth time.

Oh. And you need to know this:
Behind the curtain.
Belowdecks.

When the window breaks, grab me.
Trust the door will open when it needs to.
The prototypes are a bust.
Grab the key card when you have a chance.
Don't forget about the one in his pocket.
That's all. Good luck. Don't screw this up.

I blinked and then reread the message. There were only two things that were really clear about all this, and both of them made me feel like Mrs. Smith's lasagna was going to come right back up again. The first was the most obvious—this was a Cocoon. It was illegal, and my name was on it. Not Regan's. Although, I frowned, it was obvious that a future version of herself had been the one to write it, but that wouldn't hold up in Glitch court. Especially since she was the commander's daughter. My name, however, was indisputable, and I felt a surge of anger. There was no way any future version of myself was chummy with Regan Fitz. Even if I was, what kind of person would put condemning evidence like this down on paper? The whole purpose of it seemed to be to mess up my sim test tomorrow, something that I was not going to let happen under any circumstances. I'd worked too hard.

I sat back and stared at the dull tan wall of the dorm room I'd called home ever since I could remember. If I got caught with a Cocoon, then all that extra training, the extra simulations, the hours and hours in the library researching, would be for what? Jail time? There were no second chances for a time-traveling criminal. The world had learned the hard way that ruthless justice was the only way to ensure that the past remained untampered with.

I reread the letter. My first instinct was to march right back out the door and find Fitz. My second instinct was to make the letter disappear. If there was no evidence, there was no crime. I could just pretend that I'd never seen my name written on a Cocoon, and I could stay on track to become the best Glitcher the Academy had ever seen. All of this went away if the letter went away. But the problem was that Fitz knew about the letter, if her overreaction to me taking it was any indication, which meant that my fate was in her entitled little hands.

CHAPTER FOUR

REGAN

The house smelled like cheese and marinara sauce, and I had a piece of garlic bread in my mouth before I even registered that I'd reached for it. My stomach let out a little contented gurgle, and I reached for a second piece. I never had a chance. A familiar hand, slim and white with a small silver ring, darted out and smacked mine.

"Enough of that," said Mrs. Ellsworth. I frowned at her, rubbing my stinging fingers as I shoved the piece of bread I'd been holding into my mouth before she commandeered it. In this kitchen, she was queen, and I was nothing.

"Sorry," I muttered.

"Where have you been?" she chided me, tucking a stray wisp of white hair up into her bun. "You're late, and your mother has been waiting. Now wash up and hustle into the dining room. Chop chop." The sound of clinking glassware echoed faintly from behind the thick mahogany door, and I raised a questioning eyebrow at her.

"Officer Salzburg is here to discuss security," she said, turning back to the large cast-iron pot on the stove. "Be on your best behavior."

Being on my best behavior at all times was just one of the problems with being the commander's kid, and today of all days I did not want to play the polite and well-behaved daughter. Mrs. Ellsworth turned away from the pot she was stirring and saw me still standing right where she'd left me, and her eyebrows disappeared into the low swoop of white curls that lay across her forehead. The message was clear—move it, girl. With a barely stifled sigh, I ducked into the small hall bathroom just off the kitchen and did a quick check of myself in the mirror. The same face I'd watched flub up Abraham Lincoln's assassination just hours before stared back at me, although I looked a little paler now. My mom called my name from the dining room, and I grabbed both of my cheeks in my fingers and gave them a rough twist to pink them up a bit. It hurt, but at least I didn't look like I'd seen a ghost, or, I amended with a grimace, a Cocoon written in my own handwriting. Still feeling unnerved and slightly nauseous despite the garlic bread in my stomach, I ran my hand over my hair, smoothing it down, before taking a deep breath and walking out and into the dining room.

Our house, unlike most of the buildings at the Academy, was actually old, not just fabricated to look that way. It was built in a time when houses had things like butler's pantries and wall-to-wall mahogany wood paneling. Our dining room in particular had an elegant old-world feel to it that you just couldn't re-create today with all the strict regulations on natural resources. My mom was sitting at the end of our long dining room table in full dress uniform eating a salad with a man, also in full dress. He smiled broadly when I came in, and stood up.

"Officer Salzburg," I said, extending a hand that he shook like a limp fish. "It's wonderful to see you."

He sat back down to his plate of Mrs. Ellsworth's famous rigatoni and picked up his fork. "Sorry to interrupt your family dinner," he said with a smile that spread just a bit too wide on his face. I glanced over at my mom and saw that her face had a stiffness to it that made it clear that Salzburg, per usual, was getting on her nerves. All the officers tended to sit up a little straighter when they had dinner with my mom, but Salzburg was one of those people who laughed too loud, talked too much, and generally tried too hard to impress her. It set her teeth on edge.

"It's no problem," I said, hoping that didn't sound like the out-and-out lie it was.

"I had something exciting to show your mom, and I just couldn't wait." He held up a small black camera that was sitting on the table before plunking it back down to take another bite of his pasta.

"More security cameras?" I asked, glancing over at my mom. "Don't you think that's a little obsessive?" We live on an island, in the middle of who knows where, behind a three-foot-thick wall with security officers swarming the place like ants. How could we possibly need *more* security?

"Regan," my mom said, her voice tight. "That isn't your place. Is it?"

I felt like a tire with the air let out, and I nodded and looked down at my own plate. She was right. Security was none of my business.

"No, no," Salzburg said around his mouthful of pasta. "It's a valid question. These, my dear, are no ordinary cameras. These," he said, patting the camera by his side like it was a dog, "these detect Butterflies."

I swallowed the bite of pasta in my mouth too

quickly and choked. My mom thumped me on the back as I leaned forward to cough up a lung into my napkin. Sitting back, I took a sip of water, my eyes still streaming as my mom shot me a disapproving look.

"I didn't think we had that kind of technology," I said.

"These are a prototype," Salzburg said. "Technology stolen right out from under the noses of the Mayhem themselves."

"Really?" I said, picking up the camera with a newfound reverence.

"Really," Salzburg said. "We managed to bring in one of their agents alive, and this little gem was hidden in his pocket. They were using it to detect our agents. Well, the joke's on them, because we managed to replicate it and are planning on using these cameras to detect Mayhem members. They can threaten this Academy all they want, but the second they breach security we'll know it."

Mom cleared her throat, and Salzburg snapped his mouth shut with an audible click.

"I apologize, Commander," he said. "Did I speak too freely?" I flicked my eyes between my mom's disapproving face and Salzburg's, which was looking a lot paler than it had a moment ago.

"The Mayhem knows our location?" I said as the

hairs along my neck stood up. "Is that why you've been so busy with security recently?"

"There's nothing to worry about," Mom said. "Isn't that right, Officer Salzburg?"

"Quite right," Salzburg said a little too quickly as he took the camera back out of my hand. I fought the urge to roll my eyes. I was twelve, not two. I decided to let this one slide, for now, and made a show of shrugging and digging back into my meal. If I really wanted to find some answers, I could always poke around in my mom's office later, and besides, the last thing I really wanted to talk about after the mess with Elliot and the letter was Butterflies.

"Anyway, we will install the first batch in strategic locations on campus just to see how they do, and then, if all goes well, we can start using them in the field."

"I can't imagine carrying something like that on a Glitch," I said, eyeing the camera. "It doesn't exactly blend in."

"But only imagine if we could use them with our Glitchers to detect a Butterfly," Salzburg said. "The margin of error would almost disappear if we didn't have to rely so much on a Glitcher's intuition. Which I hear you have a particular knack for, Cadet Fitz." Salzburg cheated his eyes over toward Mom, whose face remained as impassive as stone. If he thought he was going to worm his way back into her good graces by complimenting her kid, he had another think coming. My mom was very careful to keep her work life and her home life separate, and any officer who thought praising me was a good tactical move was off base. Salzburg got the picture and directed his eyes back to me.

"Did you have a simulation today?" he asked, his desperation to change the subject almost pathetic.

"I did have a sim today," I said.

"Well," he prompted, "how did it go?"

My mom flicked her eyes to me, and I saw the tiny hint of a warning there. She knew that I'd had to do a recap session, and she didn't want me advertising my less than stellar track record in front of our guest. I felt my heart sink a little; the craziness of finding the Cocoon had kind of overshadowed the Lincoln assassination failure. Mom had helped me study for it for the entire week with her infamous flash cards, but none of that mattered.

"Great," I lied. "The Butterfly had an ear piercing that wasn't on era."

"Very good," said Officer Salzburg. "That's not an easy spot. No wonder Professor Gordon raves about you. Says you're uncanny."

My face flushed, but for once it wasn't from embarrassment. Because I *was* the best student in Professor

Gordon's class, trumping even Elliot, which brought me huge amounts of satisfaction.

"I don't know about uncanny," I said, "but I do love the class."

Salzburg sighed and smiled. "I remember that simulation like it was yesterday. Helped develop it myself after being part of the mission to fix Lincoln's assassination. At one point there were ten different Butterflies in Ford's Theatre that night. Ten! Half of them were trying to save Lincoln while the other half were trying to ensure that Booth didn't break his leg when he jumped off the balcony onto the stage! Crazy." He glanced at my mom and smiled. "You were there too, Commander, were you not?"

My mom nodded. "I was. One of the most complex missions to date."

"There was even a Butterfly hiding under the stage," Officer Salzburg said conspiratorially, leaning forward as though he was telling me a secret I didn't already know. "Planning to capture Booth when he did his walk-through of all the hidden exits of the theater earlier that day. Tricky one, that; took us multiple jumps to figure out." I nodded, doing my best to look appropriately impressed. Like all the officers at the Academy, Officer Salzburg had the Glitch gene and had gained a reputation for himself fixing and putting the future back together like it was Humpty Dumpty and he was all the king's men. But like most of the officers and professors, he was no longer able to time travel.

Some of the early technology that was used to help Glitchers time travel to specific moments in the past was unnecessarily hard on the human body. It was a similar problem to what astronauts faced when they traveled in space; the journey wreaked havoc on the fragile internal balance of bones, muscles, and nerves. As a result, he had the same longing in his eyes that so many of my professors had when we talked about our training. Some of them missed it so much they ruined their own health to do just one more jump. It was one of the reasons that the deactivation injection was now required as soon as you were done with your Glitching career. The students who didn't make it through the Academy for one reason or another received the same thing, and I'd always wondered what that would be like. Would it feel freeing, or like you'd let everyone down? Regardless, it was common knowledge that you could find many of the Academy staff in the simulation rooms after hours, reliving their glory days over and over again. Mom was in the same boat, although she was too busy with me and being the commander of the entire Academy to mess around with recreational simulations.

I glanced at her now, seeing a similar look in her eyes as she watched Officer Salzburg relive some of their most famous jumps together. For a while there, certain pivotal historical events had been almost over-run with Glitchers and Butterflies, to the point where it was hard to tell who was actually a part of history and who was trespassing. The very idea made my brain hurt. It was hard enough to spot one Butterfly, let alone worry about the other ten at the event that weren't your business. Thankfully the Academy had developed some technology to help Glitchers stay focused on their target. It was something I was sure Elliot would start learning about after he broke my mom's record and became the youngest cadet to level up. I studied my mother as Salzburg rambled on. She'd been the best Glitcher to ever grace the steps of the Academy, a fact that had quickly catapulted her up the ranks until she was named the first female commander in chief. But, just like Officer Salzburg, she'd reached her Glitching limit and been deactivated. Any more time traveling and her health would have started declining until she looked like one of the fragile Glitchers who lived in the nursing home on the edge of the Academy.

The conversation turned away from my simulation then, and back to the intricacies of running a place like the Academy. Apparently, an entire section of the campus had lost power today, something Salzburg was quick to point out wouldn't matter with the new prototypes since they were battery operated. I shot the piece of machinery in question a look out of the corner of my eye as I ate my third piece of garlic bread. If it really could detect a Butterfly, could it also tell that I'd held a Cocoon in my hand earlier that day? A Cocoon that Elliot Mason, of all people, now had in his possession. Why hadn't I held on to it tighter? How had I let Elliot get the drop on me like that? Was he reading it now? If it was a Cocoon, and I was pretty positive it was, he might already be taking it straight to a security officer, and I was done for.

Officer Salzburg set his fork down with a loud clank, and I jumped guiltily. Dinner was over, and I was excused to go to my room for the night. Usually I'd have to help Mrs. Ellsworth do the dishes, but she must have seen something in my face because she waved me away after I carried the first stack to the sink. I almost let out an audible sigh of relief as I retreated up the back staircase and into my room. I immediately sat down in front of my laptop so I could message Elliot, but before I could even touch a key it sprang to life, a message from Elliot popping up on the screen as though I'd willed it there by sheer desperation. I inhaled like I'd just been punched in the gut as my heart slammed to a startled stop in my chest. He was messaging me. That couldn't be a good sign.

My hands were trembling as I reached out to open the message. I hesitated, though, my finger hovering above the button. There were no cameras here, but I still felt exposed. I quickly tucked the laptop under my arm, grabbed my bathrobe, and went into the hall bathroom, locking the door firmly behind me. Turning on the shower, I sat down on the cool tile floor and opened the message as the bathroom filled with steam.

I know what this is. We need to talk.

I'm not sure how long I stared at that message, but I felt like I aged ten years in a matter of seconds. It was that last bit, the wanting to talk part, that threw me completely off. If he knew what that letter was, then why in the world wasn't he marching it straight to a security officer like the good little rule follower that he was? Why talk to me about it?

"Regan?!" came a voice from outside, and I jumped, my heart slamming into my throat. It was Mrs. Ellsworth.

"Yes?" I said. My voice sounded wobbly even to my own ears.

"Are you almost done?" she asked. "Officer Salzburg left and your mother wanted to speak to you before you went to bed."

"Yes!" I called back. "I'll be right out." Her footsteps retreated down the hall, and I typed in a reply to Elliot's message.

Okay. Meet me by the fountain before first period.

That done, I shucked off my clothes and threw myself into the shower. We'd apparently run out of hot water while I sat on the floor staring at that message, and I inhaled hard as icy water jolted me out of my preoccupied fog. I scrubbed quickly with the soap, making sure my hair was wet all the way through before jumping back out and wrapping myself in a towel.

A reply was already flashing on my laptop, and I dripped water all over the keyboard in my hurry to read it.

Not tomorrow. Now.

Now? I repeated. What did he mean now? It was late, way past the curfew that determined when students were allowed to be out and about on campus grounds. I was about to type back a snarky reply, but I stopped myself. It was not the time to make him mad, not when he was potentially holding the only piece of evidence needed to ruin my entire future. I bit my lip. I was just going to have to find a way.

Give me thirty minutes. Meet me at the fountain.

I was about to close my laptop so I could go get some clothes on and see what my mom wanted when a message pinged back.

What fountain? There are a million of the dumb
things on this campus.

His annoyance seemed to drip from every word,
and I had to stifle a smile. Readjusting my towel, I
typed back.

You're right. But I only shoved you into one of them.
See you there. Bring it with you.

I stared at my reply for a second before hitting send.
I didn't dare put down in writing *what* I wanted him to
bring with him. I glanced at the time on my laptop and
grimaced. If I was going to make it to the fountain in
half an hour and talk to my mom, I was going to have
to hustle. Tucking my dirty clothes and laptop under
my arm, I made my way back to my room to throw
on my pajamas. A minute later, I flew back down the
stairs, my still-dripping hair making the back of my
T-shirt wet. I rounded the bottom of the stairs at full
speed and almost ran headlong into my mom. She
caught my shoulders before I could fall backward onto
my butt and smiled.

"Easy there," she said. "I was just coming up to find
you. I wanted to hear about your simulation."

I pushed my wet hair out of my face as I looked
up at her. She knew all about my simulation. She'd
watched it live, according to Professor Treebaun, but I
appreciated that she was pretending she hadn't. "One
second," I said. "I missed it by one second. One!"

She sighed. "Come on. Let's hear it." She turned and led us into her office, where I plopped down on my favorite leather chair.

"What happened?" she asked, taking a seat behind her desk and pulling off the black no-nonsense heels that she always wore when someone important came for dinner. They gave her an extra four inches, not that she really needed them at just under six feet tall, but she liked to wear them anyway. Someone had asked me once what it was like to have your mom be the commander, and I hadn't really known how to answer them. In some ways it was pretty cool, but in others it really stunk. For one thing, I always felt like I had two moms: the public one who everyone else saw and the private one who took off her heels and replaced them with fuzzy green slippers that were almost worn through at the toe. And I really preferred the fuzzy green slippers version, even if her unrelenting expectations for me often made me feel like I had an elephant sitting on my chest.

"The usual," I said. "I had no problem spotting the Butterfly, but I couldn't seal the deal in time. I forgot about the alternate theater entrance, and I was late getting the jump on the Butterfly because of it." I pressed my lips together and waited. You didn't interrupt my mom when her brow was furrowed like that, and to be honest, I was grateful for the quiet. Mrs. Ellsworth had lit a fire in the office's small fireplace, and I pulled my knees up to my chest and reached down to dig one of the blankets out of the basket Mom kept there for this very purpose. Cuddled into the chair, waiting for my mom to pass down whatever verdict or opinion she was working on, the Cocoon and all that it threatened suddenly felt like a distant event that had happened to someone else. Maybe I could just stay here in this chair and life would go on as though Elliot wasn't holding a ticking time bomb. But the problem with time bombs, I thought gloomily, was that eventually they exploded whether you ignored them or not. Reality fell heavily on my shoulders, and the warm safety of the chair and the blanket and the fire vanished as though someone had thrown me back in that icy shower. I glanced at the clock. I had to wrap this up.

"You know my favorite Edison quote, right?" she finally said.

I rolled my eyes, because I knew exactly what quote she was talking about. "It's the one about failing ten thousand times when he tried to invent the light bulb, right? Is that how long you think it's going to take me to pass the Lincoln assassination?"

Mom laughed, a rare thing for her, and shook her head. "No, the one you're thinking of is his most famous, of course. I believe that one went, I have not failed. I've just found ten thousand ways that won't work, and I must say I like that one. But Thomas Edison had another one that I like even more." When I just raised an eyebrow, she went on. "It's one that I used to have on the wall of my dorm room when I was a cadet. I found it during a study session over Edison, and it always resonated with me." She cleared her throat and waited until I looked up and made eye contact before continuing, a trick she'd been doing for as long as I could remember. "Many of life's failures are experienced by people who do not realize how close they were to success when they gave up," she quoted.

"That's very nice, Mom," I said, "but what are you trying to get at here?"

"I think you should participate in the simulation test tomorrow," she said. "I think you need to mix things up a bit. It would be a good challenge for you."

My thoughts flashed immediately to Elliot and his smug confidence that he was going to win that test and level up. He'd talked about it like it was a sure thing. I shook my head.

"I don't want to," I said, bracing myself for a fight so familiar I could have it in my sleep.

"You are the only fifth-year cadet who hasn't participated in one yet," she said. "Win or lose, the practice would be good for you."

"No," I said again. "I won't be humiliated in front of a bunch of judges and whatever audience shows up to watch. It's bad enough that everyone just *thinks* I'm dumb. I don't need to prove them all right." I stood up and stomped out of the room and up the stairs.

"Regan!" my mom called after me, but I didn't turn around. I had bigger things to worry about than the stupid simulation test tomorrow. I had to go face Elliot Mason.

CHAPTER FIVE

ELLIOT

Sneaking out of the dorm was easy, and I thanked whatever luck had landed me a room on the first floor. All I had to do was open my window and slip out into the cool of the night. A night that felt too large and too dark. I found myself hesitating outside my own window, suddenly wanting nothing more than to crawl back into my tiny room and pretend none of this was happening. It made no sense. This had been my idea, after all. My impatience to talk to Regan face-to-face had me standing outside my dorm room after curfew, something that I'd never done before. It was against the rules, and I liked rules too much to break them all willy-nilly. I felt like I was wearing someone else's skin, and it was a few sizes too small and made completely out of itchy wool. This wasn't me. I didn't carry incriminating evidence around under the insole of my right shoe. Evidence that could end my career and Regan's in a heartbeat.

Thinking about that letter gave me goose bumps, and I shivered even though I was perfectly warm inside my green cadet sweatshirt. Finally, willing myself into action, I jogged silently down the path that led around the outer edge of the Academy next to the wall. Standing about thirty feet high and built of solid stone like something from medieval times, it wrapped around the entire campus. When it had originally been erected, some people had even compared it to the Great Wall of China, although that was pushing it a bit. Still, it was impressive, and it had a bike path built right next to it that Academy residents used regularly for exercise. Tonight, I was the only one on it. Even so, I made sure to keep to the shadows, my head on a constant swivel for a roaming security guard. When I'd demanded that Regan meet me tonight, I hadn't really thought through it all. I'd been so focused on getting answers that I'd thrown all caution out the window, and I never threw caution out the window. Being out at night made me feel exposed and vulnerable in a way I'd never experienced before, and I didn't like it. Not one bit.

The stupid fountain Regan had mentioned sat on the opposite side of campus from my dorm, and I picked up the pace. As I rounded the last corner, the fountain in question came into view. It was larger than most, standing just over fifteen feet high and carved from marble to mimic the famous Trevi Fountain in Italy. If we couldn't ever see the real world, they would re-create it in miniature for us here. I slowed my pace, breathing harder than I probably should be for such a short jog, and I made a mental note to up my cardio training sessions. Regan was nowhere to be seen. Either I'd beaten her, or she wasn't going to show.

I scowled as I remembered Regan shoving me into the icy water of this particular fountain. It had been December a few years ago, nearly Christmastime, and the fountain was decorated with large swoops of multi-colored lights that twinkled on and off. It had been a particularly good day. I'd gotten Martin Luther King's "I Have a Dream" speech as the simulation for my final and spotted the Butterfly trying to prevent King from making it to the Lincoln Memorial.

My good mood that day had come crashing down around my ears when Regan had cut me off on the path. And it wasn't even so much that she'd cut me off; it was that she didn't even notice that she'd cut me off. Like always, she was caught up in her own little world, and don't ask me why, but it was too much that day. So I'd reached a foot out and caught hers. I'd only meant to trip her a little, to bring her back to reality so she'd apologize for cutting me off. But it worked too well. She'd gone sprawling face-first into the dirty, slushy snow. She'd looked so shocked as she picked herself up, her cadet jacket all muck covered and soaked, that I'd had to laugh. Which was when she'd reached out and given me a quick stiff-armed shove that had tipped me sideways and right into the frigid half-drained fountain.

I'd come up sputtering in time to see Regan's shocked face. Just like mine, her plan had worked out better than she'd expected it to. Before I could climb out of the fountain to retaliate, she'd turned tail and sprinted toward home. I'd almost turned her in for it, but knowing my luck a camera would have caught me tripping her, and I'd have gotten in trouble too. Thinking about a camera made the hairs on the back of my neck prickle, and I glanced around nervously at the surrounding trees, glad I hadn't decided to pull that thing out of my shoe to read for the twentieth time. If I got caught now, all I'd get was a scolding for being out past curfew. Not wanting to take any chances, though, I stepped a little farther into the shadows of the trees. Taking a deep breath, I turned my attention to the fountain, the soft rush of its spouts doing nothing to ease the knot in my stomach. How much about this did Regan know? Was she playing dumb earlier when she pretended like she'd never seen the thing before? Was it all a setup? What if she decided to turn the tables and show up with security officers? The sound of a twig snapping made me jump and I spun to face Regan as she jogged out of the darkness.

CHAPTER SIX

REGAN

Elliot was leaning against a tree near the edge of the fountain, staring into it like it held all the answers of the universe, but when he looked at me, his expression made me stop cold in my tracks. Gone was his normal contemptuous and haughty look, and in its place was fury. Why in the world was he mad? If anything, I was the one who should be mad. He'd stolen *my* letter, after all. He was the reason I'd had to climb out my window and down the side of the house like a very uncoordinated monkey. At this very moment my mom could be knocking on my bedroom door, and I'd be beyond busted.

"What's your problem?" I asked, taking an involuntary step back.

"You," he said, his voice hard.

"Well, what else is new?" I asked, deciding that keeping things light was probably in my best interest. Elliot seemed to be on edge, and the last thing I needed was to push him over it. The thought had me stifling a smile as I glanced behind him, reliving the lovely moment when I'd shoved his smug face directly into that fountain. The next second I caught sight of Elliot again, and all thoughts of smiling disappeared.

"So, I'm guessing you read the letter?" I asked.

Elliot jumped at the word *letter* like it had electrocuted him somehow, glancing left and right as though to make sure we were alone. "Yes," he finally hissed, the word barely loud enough for me to hear.

"So?" I said. "What did it say?"

"It said my name," he said, coming over to lean against one of the large oak trees that bordered the fountain. "That's enough, isn't it? If it didn't have that, you'd be in jail already. But you wrote the one thing that was sure to condemn me on that, that . . ." He faltered, his face twisting in a grimace as he searched for words. "Well, you know what."

"Actually, I don't know anything," I said. When he just looked at me like if he stared hard enough my head would catch on fire, I threw up my hands defensively. "I swear," I said. "I have a solid guess what that is, although trust me, I'm really hoping I'm wrong. But judging from the stink eye you're giving me, I'm guessing I'm out of luck."

Elliot snorted. "Luck. Like you've ever needed luck. You put my name on here just to spite me, don't lie."

"I didn't," I said defensively. "Well, I haven't yet. I can't really control what my future self does, now can I?"

Elliot visibly twitched at the word *future*, glancing around nervously before turning to stare daggers at me again.

"Watch your mouth," he said. "This place is probably monitored from ten different angles."

I shook my head. "It's not," I said. "This entire section lost power today. It won't be fixed until next week sometime. No one is watching us."

He raised an eyebrow at me. "That's sure convenient."

"Perk of being the commander's kid." I shrugged. "I find out about exciting stuff like electrical shortages. Besides, if it hadn't been out, I could have ensured those security monitors were accidentally turned off." I put the word *accidentally* in air quotes, but Elliot didn't seem the least bit impressed. If anything, I'd somehow just made him angrier.

"One of the many perks of being you," Elliot muttered, picking at the bark of the tree he was leaning against.

"If you have something to say, you need to speak a little clearer," I snapped.

He stopped picking at the tree and crossed his arms over his chest. "How can I trust you?"

"Do you have a choice?" I said. "Whatever this letter is—and I think you and I both know—we are going to have to deal with it together." That was a complete bluff, but Elliot was too twitchy to notice. I had no idea if we were in this together, but I needed him to believe that if I went down, he went down too. It was pure self-preservation.

"Let's get this over with," he said. I nodded, although I was equal parts terrified and intrigued to see the piece of paper that had kept Elliot from turning me in to the authorities. He reached down and pulled it from inside his shoe and smoothed it out in his hand. Together we walked over to the fountain's edge, where a large spotlight illuminated the slightly tacky sculptures. Elliot spread the letter out and looked at me expectantly. Taking a deep breath, I carefully leaned in to read the piece of paper that would forever change the course of my life.

I read it, and then I immediately went back to the top to read it again despite the fact that Elliot was staring daggers at the side of my head as though that would help me process it all faster. I ignored him as I let the words sink in. Lives were at stake. Elliot couldn't level up tomorrow, and we were apparently going to have to work together. My future self must be delusional, I thought, shaking my head. Even though I'd grown up in a world where time traveling was completely normal, I still couldn't quite wrap my head around this. Maybe it was because *my* future self had written it, or maybe it was because my future self clearly wanted to change something about the future. The thing that I'd been training *not* to do for my entire life. But there it was, all laid out in my own handwriting.

"You just *had* to put my name in it," Elliot said practically in my ear, and I jumped.

"Don't forget, it was my name written on the envelope," I said, sitting back. "I'm just as sunk as you are if this thing gets found out."

"Oh yeah," Elliot said. "I kind of forgot about that." Then he shook his head and narrowed his eyes. "You could end my entire career with this letter. You do realize that, right? Everything I've worked for."

"Your career?" I repeated in surprise. "Your career? Are you serious right now? There is obviously so much more at stake than *your* career." When Elliot just stared back at me, I threw my hands up in exasperation. Leave it to Elliot Mason to make this all about him. "This is obviously important, or didn't you catch the part where I said that lives depend on us?"

"My future career *is* my life," he said.

I groaned in exasperation. He was *not* getting this. "If this gets found out," I said, talking slowly and clearly like he was still three-year-old Elliot who didn't understand that sticking Play-Doh up his nose was a bad idea, "my mom will lose everything, and I mean everything. You and I will be put on trial and convicted. It will be the end of our freedom."

"My freedom," he said. "They won't put the commander's daughter on trial."

I snorted, the noise too loud in the quiet night. "You can't seriously believe that," I said.

"I'll believe that when I see it," he said.

"Well, let's hope you never believe it, then," I said, "because I'd rather not go on trial if it's all the same to you. So chill for a second, will you? I need to think." I put my head in my hands and squeezed my eyes shut.

"Think about what?" he asked. "About what the inside of the Academy jail looks like? Because we know that one already. Remember our field trip three years ago?"

"I do," I snapped back. "You thought it would be funny to shove me into one of the empty cells and lock the door."

"I didn't *think* that was funny," he said. "That *was* funny, and even though I wasn't the one locked inside that cell crying my eyes out for the five whole minutes it took the guard to get it unlocked, I know I don't want to spend the rest of my life in there."

I looked back at him, eyebrow raised. "You don't do *chill* very well, do you, Mason?"

Elliot bristled at me. "Some of us don't have that luxury, Fitz. And, for the record, you're right. I have exactly zero chill. Not when it comes to this," he said, pointing at the letter.

"I half expected you to march in here with security officers," I admitted. "I might have if the situation was reversed."

"Don't think I didn't think about it," he said.

"Well," I said. "Thanks, I guess."

"You're welcome," he said. "I guess."

We stood there for a second, not saying anything as the noises of the night pressed in around us. I'd thought that seeing the letter would make things perfectly clear for me. That I'd know what to do once I had the full picture and could talk to Elliot. But in reality, nothing had changed.

"Don't you think that it's pretty convenient that it says I'm not supposed to level up tomorrow?" Elliot said, tapping the letter. "How do I know this isn't just future Regan messing with me?"

"Yeah," I said. "You're right. I'm sure future me

risked life, limb, and prison to mess with you so you wouldn't take a stupid simulation test."

Elliot stared at me a second and then sagged. "Okay, so maybe that's a bit extreme. But you have to agree that this letter is ridiculously vague. I mean, if we are going to risk everything, shouldn't we know what we are risking it for?"

I shrugged. "You're right," I said. "This letter is missing so much key information it isn't even funny. I have no idea what my future self was thinking writing it. If it was possible to give her a swift kick in the shins, I would. Trust me."

"Can I volunteer for that job?" he asked, and for the first time his voice didn't have that angry edge to it. "And you didn't just write it. You managed to deliver it to the past. To us. Which means that in the future, you're already a criminal."

"In a weird way, that actually makes me feel better," I said. "Like, the future version of myself isn't asking me to do something she hasn't already done?"

"Weird is like the biggest understatement of all time," he said, shoving his hands into his hair. We sat there another moment, both of us wrestling with the baffling implications of receiving a Cocoon. And not just a Cocoon, but one that made it clear that Elliot and I were supposed to prevent something bad from happening. I thought of all the people in my life that I cared about. Mom, of course, and then Mrs. Ellsworth, who had taken care of me just as much if not more than my own mother for the better part of my life. Professor Brown and Professor Green, along with a handful of other people on the faculty who had taken a special interest in me, and then the list kind of sputtered to a stop. Friends weren't very easy to make at the Academy, where the structure of the curriculum pitted us against one another practically from kindergarten. I'd had an exceptionally hard time of it. Between all the extra tutoring and study sessions I'd been receiving since practically day one, and the fact that I was the commander in chief's daughter, well, there wasn't a whole lot of time for that. I didn't live in the dorms with everyone else, and the only meal I ate in the dining hall was lunch, and I usually used that time to cram for a class. There were other kids in my cadet class who I talked to, but would I consider any of them friends? Probably not. If I was honest with myself, though, something I tried to be, I knew that wasn't what I wanted. I'd have loved friends, or even just one. Someone I could tell something like this to, someone I knew would have my back no matter what.

My thoughts were cut short by the sound of footsteps coming down the path to our left. Both Elliot and

I snapped our heads in that direction and froze. Then, as though we'd choreographed it, we both lunged for the letter. Our hands collided, both scrabbling for it in our panic to get it hidden, and it fell into the bubbling water of the fountain and vanished. I blinked at the spot where it had disappeared. What had just happened? I'd never seen paper dissolve like smoke before.

Before I could say anything, Elliot had my arm in a vise grip. I looked up at him, still baffled, and he held a finger to his lips and silently slipped over the edge of the fountain and into the water, dragging me behind him. I let out a low hiss as I descended into the thigh-deep water. The sound of the footsteps got louder and Elliot let go of my arm so he could duck behind one of the large statues in the fountain. His hand snaked out a second later, and he pulled me behind the biggest statue and into a small hidden alcove. A metal electrical plate made it obvious that this was some kind of service area for the fountain, and I crouched down in the icy water next to Elliot, barely feeling the cold as adrenaline shot through my system. From our hiding spot, I could see out through the tangle of statue legs to the spot where we'd just been sitting. A moment later a security officer came around the corner. I'd thought the danger of the Cocoon had been real before, but now that I was on the verge of getting caught, it all seemed to hit home just that much harder. Thankfully the guard appeared to be doing a routine check of the grounds. He scanned the fountain without showing much real interest before strolling around the perimeter. A moment later he headed off down the path that led back toward the Academy dorms.

"That was close," Elliot whispered. His hot breath tickled my ear uncomfortably, and I hunched my shoulders up and turned to look at him.

"You couldn't think of a better place to hide than in the fountain?" I asked, a shiver running through me now that the terror of the situation was starting to fade.

"What are you complaining about?" he whispered back. "Your grand plan appeared to be waiting until you got caught with a Cocoon. I'd say my idea was better."

"Fair point," I admitted. "I didn't even know this was back here."

"Neither did I, until a certain princess gave me a solid shove for no good reason."

"Don't call me princess," I said. "And you're welcome. If I hadn't shoved you in, you'd never have found this spot."

"No," he contradicted me. "*You're* welcome. I just saved your neck."

I decided to ignore this and held up my empty

hands. "But what happened to the letter?" I asked. "I've never seen anything like it. It's like it dissolved."

"I noticed," he said, his wrinkled forehead mirroring my own confusion. Then his face brightened, and he looked at me. "It's like it never happened."

"But it did happen," I said. "You saw it. Now we have to figure out what to do."

"We do nothing," Elliot said. "I'm not risking everything I've worked for because of a stupid letter I didn't even write. I'm leveling up tomorrow, so any future Cocoons you get, just keep them to yourself."

"But the letter said you couldn't level up tomorrow, that something bad was going to happen if we didn't start working together," I said.

"That sounds a lot like a you problem," Elliot said. With that he stood up and made his way over to the side of the fountain. Putting both hands on the concrete ledge, he levered himself up and out.

"But," I protested, then stopped myself, because, really, what was I supposed to say? He was right, he had no skin in this game now. I stood in the freezing cold fountain as he stalked off down the dark path, leaving a dripping trail behind himself like the bread crumbs in the story of Hansel and Gretel. A trail I couldn't follow.

CHAPTER SEVEN

ELLIOT

I couldn't think about this. Not now. Not with the test tomorrow. The letter was gone. I'd watched it dissolve like sugar in water, no trace. As long as Fitz hadn't shown anyone, which she claimed she hadn't, I was in the clear. My name scrubbed off the only incriminating piece of evidence.

I slipped silently into the same window I'd left less than an hour before. Standing in my dark room, I waited to feel the relief I'd felt at the fountain when I'd realized that I was off the hook, but it didn't come. Instead I felt a gnawing sense of guilt. But for what? For leaving her standing in the fountain? That would be incredibly stupid since she'd done the exact same thing to me once.

My eyelids felt scratchy but my brain was still going about a thousand miles an hour, and I knew that sleeping wasn't in the cards for the night. I found myself pacing my tiny dorm room. After the cool expanse of the campus at night, the tiny six-by-ten room felt like a cage. I needed something to disengage my brain. Something I could use to forget about the mess of the last few hours.

Like I always did, I turned to books. Opening my backpack, I grabbed the book I'd checked out of the library just that morning. I flipped it open and paged through to the section on the Battle of the Bulge. I'm not sure how long I sat there before my eyes slid shut and I fell asleep.

I woke up still sitting at my desk with my head resting on my book. I sat back, disoriented, and looked around at my sunlight-filled room as I tried to figure out why I was at my desk and not in my bed, and then everything came crashing back to me. I jumped to my feet. It was ten till eight, and my test was supposed to start at eight clear across campus. Dashing to the bathroom, I splashed some cold water on my face before throwing on a fresh uniform and bolting out my door. I practically flew through campus, dodging other students who had the luxury of walking to class instead of sprinting, and the entire time I was seething inside. This was all Fitz's fault. I slipped through the door of the simulation room with less than ten seconds to spare. I stopped, breathing hard, with my hands on my knees as I fought to collect myself for one of the most important tests of my life.

"Cadet Mason," said Professor Brown, "good of you to make it. Cutting it a little close today, aren't you?"

I stood up straight and forced a smile onto my face. "Sorry, ma'am. I just got distracted with some last-minute studying."

Professor Brown nodded and stepped aside, revealing the cadet I'd be competing against today for my advancement. The cold blue eyes of Regan Fitz met mine, and I froze.

"Are you ready to lose, Mason?" she asked. Her voice sounded different, harder somehow.

I whirled as Commander Fitz walked into the room. The sight of her made my already jumpy nerves practically sizzle, and I barely remembered to get my hand up in a formal salute. As soon as the commander had taken her seat with the panel of professors who would decide my fate, I turned and glared at Regan.

"This isn't fair," I said.

Regan looked at me, her blue eyes snapping. "Gosh, Mason. This sounds a lot like a *you* problem."

CHAPTER EIGHT

REGAN

Sometimes it was good to be the commander's daughter. Today was one of those days. I'd run home in the dark, dripping wet and freezing. I'd never felt more alone in my entire life. I don't know why I'd been surprised by Elliot's flat-out refusal to help, but somehow his words had still cut. Slipping back into my dark house, I'd found myself wandering into my mom's office. I probably should have changed first; it would be hard explaining to anyone who found me there why I was soaked. But after seeing that Cocoon, the risk felt far away and unreal, like it belonged to someone else's life and not my own. Everything about the last few hours felt unreal, and instead of blinding panic, I felt oddly numb and detached. Hopeless, I realized. I felt hopeless, and it was a sensation I wasn't sure I'd ever felt before. At least, not at this gut-deep level.

My wet clothes clung to my goose-bumped skin, and I leaned over and flipped the switch to light the gas fireplace. It gave a low grumble and click and then lit, the flames instantly warming my skin a few degrees. Sitting down at my mom's desk, I stared at the flickering flames and let my brain churn over everything that had happened. Now what? Elliot had his final test tomorrow, and then he'd move up and be gone.

More for something to do with my hands than because I was really interested, I started organizing the papers on Mom's desk. Most of the nitty-gritty details that went into running the Academy were just plain boring, payroll and bills, the new outline for the Butterfly detection prototypes, but every now and then there was something interesting, a simulation Recap transcript or a discipline form. My brain was still chewing over Elliot's "sounds like a you problem" comment when I realized that his name wasn't just in my head, it was on the memo in my hand. Jackpot.

The memo showed the list of students who were participating in the sim test tomorrow morning at eight. The only kid with enough points for advancement was Elliot, but I was surprised to see how many points my fellow classmates had managed to accumulate while I avoided the tests like the plague. It looked like there were only five cadets signed up for tomorrow, which meant there was an odd man out. In this case, Elliot. My mom had made a note about asking a fourth-year cadet to participate for extra credit, and I wondered if that was why she'd bugged me about it. All I knew was that whoever she found to compete against him had better be good, because while that Cocoon had been vague about almost everything else, it had been crystal clear about the fact that Elliot Mason couldn't win tomorrow. And then it clicked. There was one way I could guarantee he'd lose.

Suddenly, despite my flat-out refusal to my mom earlier that night, I was all in. The stakes had changed, and feeling dumb in front of my peers was a price I was willing to pay. I bounded out of the chair and headed for the door, a plan already forming in my head. I needed to change and wake up Mom. It was time I started living up to all that potential she was always talking about.

Hours later, I stood in the freezing cold simulation room, waiting as my mom prepped the Lincoln assassination simulation, again. If I passed this, she'd let me take the test at eight. If I didn't, then I could watch from the audience as Elliot leveled up. I hadn't played my cards right when I'd busted into her room to tell her that I'd do the simulation test. I'd been too eager, and she'd eyed me suspiciously as I rambled on about deciding to live to my full potential. I honestly had thought she'd be so excited that I actually wanted to do a sim test that she'd jump on board immediately. Instead she'd decided to take my change of heart as an opportunity to get me past what she called my "Lincoln Block." If I wanted this, I was going to have to prove it and beat the Lincoln assassination once and for all.

I didn't have much time to dwell on my mistake, though, not if I wanted to compete. The first simulation slot opened at seven, and my mom had pulled strings to get me in at the last minute. Professor Treebaun walked in a moment later, looking decidedly grumpier than usual at being called in so early to monitor a test he'd watched me fail less than twenty-four hours ago. But he just nodded to Mom and took another sip of coffee as he sat down behind the monitor.

"Simulation starts in five," Mom told me, moving to sit beside Treebaun. "Good luck." I nodded as everything went black, and I opened my eyes in seat 10B for the sixth time.

Five minutes later I opened my eyes in the icy simulation room again, a wide grin spread across my face as I looked at my mom for confirmation of what I already knew. I'd nailed it. She grinned back, but only for a second as Treebaun cleared his throat and stood up without even glancing at the screen over his head that showed me successfully cuffing the Butterfly I'd discovered hiding behind the curtains of the Lincolns' theater box.

"Nicely done, cadet," he said, tapping the screen on his tablet. "Now if you'll excuse me, this morning is going to require more than one cup of coffee." When the door slid shut behind him, my mom wasted no time in unhooking my simulation probes so she could give me a tight hug.

"I'm not sure what put a fire under you, but I'm proud of you," she said in my ear before releasing me.

"Thanks, Mom," I said, feeling a tug of guilt because I knew exactly what had put that fire under me. I craned my head to get a look at her watch, and she followed my gaze.

"You have ten minutes," she said. "Head over there now. I need to stop by my office to meet with a professor before I go. Besides, it's probably best we arrive separately."

I nodded and hurried out of the room. Mom wouldn't be personally evaluating my test, but I knew she wouldn't miss the opportunity to watch me compete in my first one. I couldn't stop the wide smile from spreading across my face as I hurried down the hall toward the testing room. I'd finally done it. Finally beaten the Lincoln simulation, and I didn't even care that it had been about 90 percent dumb luck that I'd looked up at the Lincoln booth just as the Butterfly peeped their head out from behind the curtain to look at the stage. I stopped cold in the middle of the hall as goose bumps ran up my arms, prickling like needles along my neck, because it hadn't been dumb luck. The letter had practically told me where I was supposed to look for the Butterfly. That first bullet point had said *behind the curtain.*

I stood there in the hallway feeling like a puppet who had performed exactly as the puppeteer wanted, and if the puppeteer had been anyone but my future self, I'd have run screaming in the opposite direction. But I couldn't. Not now. I was too far in. I probably would have stood there forever, trying to wrap my mind around it all, if a very nervous-looking Calvin and Ella, two cadets in my year, hadn't bumped into me in their hurry to get to the simulation test.

"Hey," I called, and they stopped and looked back at me. "Do you have a piece of paper and a pen?" Calvin looked annoyed at the request, but Ella dug around in her bag and thrust a crumpled scrap of paper and the nub of a pencil into my hand. I mumbled a thank-you and quickly sat down against the wall, propping the paper against my knee as I scribbled down the bullet points from the letter as best I could from memory.

Behind the curtain.
Something about under a deck?
Break a window?
Grab a key card. (What am I supposed to
grab it off of?)
Don't forget about a pocket.

I stared down at that list, racking my brain. I was forgetting something. I'd been almost positive that there were more than five. Two more cadets rushed by me on their way to the simulation test, and I hurried after them and into the testing room, my eyes immediately combing the room for Elliot. To my surprise, he wasn't there yet. The other cadets stood by their respective simulation tables, pale and nervous, and I realized that, for the first time, I wasn't nervous for this simulation at all. I wasn't competing for an advancement point; I was here to hijack Elliot's test. I glanced up at the clock. Elliot was always obnoxiously early to everything, so where was he?

When he finally rushed in with mere seconds to

spare, I enjoyed every moment of his eye-popping surprise as he caught sight of me. He looked rough, like he'd slept even less than I had, which would be a real trick since I'd been so hyped up about my new plan that I'd only managed to grab a few hours. Maybe it was the way he stared at me, like I had no business being there, or maybe it was the memory of him walking away last night, but everything inside me solidified in cold determination. I was going to kick his arrogant butt, and not because that letter told me to either. Because I wanted to with every fiber of my being.

"Attention!" said a firm voice behind me, and I turned and saluted with everyone else as my mom entered the room. She'd changed since my Lincoln simulation and looked every inch the commander in chief in her fitted black uniform. The Glitching medals across her left shoulder and chest flashed impressively in the fluorescent lights, and every eye followed her as she walked across the room to take her seat. She didn't even glance in my direction, which didn't surprise me. In here I was just another cadet. Elliot took a half second longer than everyone else to salute, since he was still staring at me like I had four heads.

"Better get it together, Cadet Mason," I said under my breath as Mom took a seat behind the control panel. He scowled at me, and I smiled back my most winning *watch me screw this up for you* smile. Professor Brown began explaining the logistics of the test, and we turned our attention back to her. We would be entering the same simulation, but there would be only one Butterfly. The first cadet to find and remove them would be the winner and receive the advancement point.

Elliot moved to stand next to me, his arms crossed over his chest. "What are you doing here?" he whispered.

"I thought that was obvious," I breathed.

"But why?" he asked.

"You know why," I said, and I saw him stiffen.

"You don't stand a chance," he hissed, and I rolled my eyes.

"Then why do you look like you just swallowed a goldfish?" I asked, fighting the urge to laugh at the sour, pinched look on his face. Even if I did lose, irritating Elliot to this degree would almost make it all worth it. But while I smirked back at Elliot, a small part of me, the part that always shriveled when a teacher realized that the mediocre student sitting in front of them was the commander's daughter, felt a pang of doubt. Why in the world did I think I could beat Elliot?

I squared my shoulders and pushed those thoughts away. Even a blind squirrel finds a nut sometimes, I reminded myself. Especially, I remembered as my insides squirmed uncomfortably, when that squirrel has some help from the future. Future me had ensured that I'd made it this far with the curtain tip, and I could only hope that meant that today was my day to find the nut. I mentally ran through the bullet points that I could remember. If they were in order, then I needed to keep an eye out for something under a deck. Whatever that meant.

"Cadet Fitz?" Professor Brown asked, and I glanced up to see everyone staring at me expectantly. I'd apparently been asked a question.

"I'm sorry," I said, feeling my face flush with embarrassment. "Could you repeat that, please?"

"I asked if you had any questions, seeing as this is your first simulation test," she said.

There was the slightest titter of a laugh to my left, and Brown narrowed her eyes at the guilty cadet. The laughter cut off immediately, and I felt an embarrassed flush creep up my neck and into my ears, turning them beet red.

"No, ma'am," I said, making sure not to look in my mom's direction. If I was embarrassed, I'm sure she was too, although, knowing her, she would be sitting as cool as a cucumber. Why couldn't I have inherited her unflappability instead of her hair color?

"If there aren't any questions, please take your

seats," said Professor Brown. I sat down, swung my legs onto the supports, and put my arms on the armrests as a tech came forward to place the simulation wires with their sticky cold pads over my legs and arms. Elliot hesitated for a second before finally climbing into the chair next to mine, resigned. A moment later, the countdown began, and I hazarded a glance in my mom's direction. She sat, the picture of a professional, but there was a tightness around her eyes that let me know she was a little worried. My vision went black. The simulation had begun.

CHAPTER NINE

ELLIOT

I opened my eyes in the past. When exactly in the past? I had no clue yet. Usually we had this information before a simulation began. We were told what event our simulation would be of, and then we were given the week to study and prepare for it. That was the part I was good at, the studying and preparing. Unfortunately, for a sim test we had no time to prep. It was all about thinking on our feet, about using our instincts and our training.

A quick glance down showed me that I was wearing fitted brown pants with high kneesocks and a white button-up shirt. I was in a room with a tall, soot-stained ceiling. A large furnace and bellows were set up at the far end of the room, complete with stacks of horse-shoes and bits of iron. Okay, I thought as I worked to calm down my racing heart, I was in a blacksmith's shop, and judging from the rudimentary-looking tools hanging on the wall, I was somewhere in the 1700s. My white shirt was smudged and dirty from sitting in the soot, and I brushed myself off and walked over to look out the window. The sun was just beginning to set, and the street outside was primitive, nothing more than packed dirt between poorly built wooden houses.

What historical event was about to take place that I had to keep intact? I looked around, hoping for a clue, but a second later I heard footsteps and a door being unlocked behind me. I barely had time to duck behind a large iron anvil before the door burst open and a tall man tumbled inside, quickly turning to lock the door behind him. That job done, he turned and looked around the dimly lit room, his blue eyes flashing in a pale frightened face. I slouched even lower, pray-ing that the shadows would hide me. Apparently they did, because he sagged in relief before walking over and picking up a large crowbar. He tested the weight in his hands before discarding it for a smaller option. He moved around the space uneasily, and I had the distinct feeling that this wasn't his blacksmith shop. So why was he here? And what was with the crowbar?

The man turned back to the door and stared at it expectantly. The white shirt he was wearing had large dark splotches of sweat under his arms, and he fidgeted from foot to foot. Man, this guy was twitchy. What was he up to? Thankfully he didn't have to wait very long before a knock came at the door. Three short taps, a pause, and then three more taps, like it was some kind of code.

The man quickly opened the door so that more men could enter, bringing a cold gust of air in behind them. The group had a nervous energy that seemed to hum around them, and I scrutinized each of the men carefully, looking to make sure that none of them was just a cleverly disguised Regan. She was *not* going to mess up this test for me.

"He gave the signal," said one of the men, taking off a thick wool coat and throwing it onto a chair. "The time to act is now, while the meeting is still underway."

"You're sure?" asked the first man who'd come in. "There is no doubt?"

The man turned to glare at him. "I was there, wasn't I? I heard him say '*This meeting can do nothing further to save the country,*' and if there is one man we can trust in all of this, it's Samuel Adams."

Then I knew. I was in Boston, Massachusetts, and it was December 16, 1773. The men in front of me had to be part of the secret society called the Sons of Liberty that was formed to protect the rights of the colonists from British taxation. In my time, these men would be some of the most well-respected in history. But tonight, they were nothing more than criminals about to commit a crime so extreme that it would change history forever. All the information about the event was as fresh in my mind as though I'd just read about it in one of my textbooks.

More men were coming into the room and quickly stripping off their own jackets and shirts. The chair near the door now had a stack of discarded clothing wobbling precariously as the men talked in the hushed voices of conspirators. The first man I'd seen had grabbed a large bucket of ash from inside the blacksmith's forge, and the men were picking up the soot in handfuls and rubbing it over their faces, arms, and torsos. Another man had appeared with what looked like roughly woven blankets, while yet another produced a box of hatchets. Seeing my opportunity, I stripped off my own shirt, grabbed a handful of ash, and scrubbed at my face and arms, turning myself the same dingy color as the men in front of me.

Satisfied with my coverage, I waited until the room was so full that I wouldn't be noticed before slipping out and grabbing a blanket that I knew was supposed to represent the Mohawk Indians. The disguise was a lame one and not even culturally accurate, my fact-driven brain was quick to point out. Besides being offensive, the blanket itched as I pulled it over my head. But, I reminded myself, the Sons of Liberty hadn't chosen this disguise to be accurate, or even to be political; they'd chosen this disguise to identify themselves as being American—not British. Knowing how the rest of history would play out, I found this sadly ironic as I grabbed a hatchet from the basket. That done, I made sure to slip to the edges of the group and back into the shadows. As I stood there waiting for the men to finish donning their ragtag disguises, I said a silent thank-you to whatever committee member had conveniently given me a test simulation where disguises made it easy for me to blend in, despite the fact that my skin was a few shades darker than the men surrounding me. I knew that a few black men had participated in the Boston Tea Party, but even so, the last thing I needed right now was to stand out. Although, I frowned as I followed the Sons of Liberty out into the cold December night, the only participants in the Boston Tea Party were men. So how in the world was Regan going to pull this off? I brushed away all thoughts of Regan as I slipped through the dark streets toward the harbor. It was time to commit treason.

CHAPTER TEN

REGAN

For a half second after I opened my eyes, I thought I'd landed back in Ford's Theatre and this was another Abraham Lincoln assassination simulation. The building I was in had the same old ornate feel, with its tall ceiling and arched windows and rows of hard wooden seats. But this was no theater, and surrounding me was not the well-groomed and washed crowd that had attended that infamous production of *Our American Cousin*. No, this was something else entirely.

The room was crowded, bodies pressed in on me from all sides, and the air had an angry hum that reminded me of a beehive I'd accidentally hit with my baseball when I was nine. The smell washed over me a moment later, and I had to swallow hard to get my gag reflex in check. Man, I hated time traveling to years before regular bathing was a thing.

A quick glance down at myself showed that I wasn't in an ornate and cumbersome dress like I usually was when I did a simulation this far back in the past; instead I was dressed like one of the many men surrounding me. My brown fitted pants were heavily patched and the shirt I was wearing probably hadn't been washed, well, ever if the dark yellow stains covering it were any indication. I lifted my hand to my head and discovered a wool hat that was barely containing my hair inside it. I was disguised as a boy. Lovely.

But where was I? This was obviously pre–Civil War, and I stank at pre–Civil War simulations as a general rule. I scowled, which wasn't a big deal since everyone in the room was wearing a similar disgruntled expression, although I was pretty sure it wasn't because their simulation test hijack wasn't going as they'd planned.

Someone was calling the meeting, or whatever this was, to order, and I turned my attention to the front of the room, where a familiar-looking man stood. He wasn't particularly tall or impressive, but there was something about the way he held himself that made it clear that he was in charge. Or maybe it was the way the crowd immediately quieted and turned their eyes on him that did that. Either way, I knew that I *should* know him.

I squinted at him, trying to remember all of America's Founding Fathers. Was that Ben Franklin? I wondered. He wasn't wearing glasses, though, and I was almost positive that Benjamin Franklin wore those. Maybe George Washington? The man smiled grimly at the crowd, and I threw that idea out too. George Washington had lost almost all his teeth by the time he was in his forties, and this guy had a full set. They weren't particularly good-looking teeth, but that was par for the course during this time period. I racked my brain as I stared at the man. Why did so many of them have to look the same? Same no-nonsense faces, same vests, same stupid-looking shirts.

The man started talking about the British East India Company and the taxation problems the colonies had been having, and I finally knew where I was in history. Maybe. For a half second I actually considered turning to the guy next to me and asking if we were in Boston. But, of course, I didn't. I could just imagine the lecture I'd get for that one.

The first rule in a simulation was not to talk to anyone unless it was absolutely necessary. We were to tiptoe through history like soldiers walking through a land-mine-riddled field where one misstep could cost you life and limb. Time was that tricky. If I stopped someone to ask them a question, and that thirty-second delay caused them to accidentally get taken out by a runaway horse or something, I could completely alter history. Or it would be fine. The thirty seconds wouldn't change anything, no one would get run down by a horse, or miss a ride, or not meet someone they were supposed to meet, and time would march on as though a trespasser hadn't snuck in the back door.

The past was this gigantic domino game, with a billion moments all stacked end to end, and if you took just one domino out, or moved it an inch to the right or left, the whole thing came crashing down. It all made my brain throb, so I pushed the thought away. What mattered now was finding the Butterfly in the middle of what I was pretty sure was Boston. I turned back to stare hard at the man speaking. Gosh, he was familiar. Maybe John Hancock? Or Paul Revere? I made a mental note to study more.

"This meeting can do nothing further to save the country," the man in front said, his voice heavy and sad. The reaction of the crowd was immediate. As though it was choreographed, cries of outrage rang out, and I wished I'd paid more attention to what the guy was saying. Like the mob it was turning into, the people around me all started moving angrily toward the too-small exit. I was forced along with the tide, squished and squeezed as someone in the front of the room begged for everyone to come back, informing them again and again that this meeting wasn't over. I hated to break it to him, but this meeting was most definitely over.

After what felt like an eternity of pushing and shoving and enough up-close-and-personal encounters with body odor to last a lifetime, I was finally outside in the mercifully fresh air. Well, fresh-ish air, I conceded. The heavy smell of wood smoke and cooking food was almost as overpowering as the smells had been inside the meetinghouse, but under it all I could smell a saltiness I was pretty certain was the ocean. An icy wind whipped past me, almost taking my hat before I could smash it more securely onto my head.

As the crowd dispersed into the streets of what I was almost positive now was Boston, Massachusetts, in seventeen hundred and something or other, they grew quieter. Some of them grouped together, talking in low voices before disappearing into the doorway of a house or down a side street. Meanwhile, I just stood there in front of the meetinghouse like a goober as the crowd thinned out around me. I was lost. I didn't know who I should follow, or even which way the harbor was, and weren't there a lot of harbors in Boston? Which one had been the one that had the tea party? All of my bravado from hijacking Elliot's simulation test was draining away, and I was left with a familiar feeling of uncertainty. Only this time, that uncertainty was lined with panic. Because if I didn't beat Elliot in this, he would go on to the next level of the Academy, and I'd be left behind, waiting for whatever awful future the letter forecasted to come true.

Squaring my shoulders, I caught sight of one of the last groups of colonists moments before they turned down a side street, and I broke into a jog to follow them. I might not know where the harbor was that held the infamous ships of the British East India Company, but they sure did. It was time to hunt down that Butterfly.

CHAPTER ELEVEN

ELLIOT

As I wove my way through the sleepy streets toward what would soon be the infamous Griffin's Wharf, I started my search for the Butterfly in earnest. Considering the time period, the odds were that the Butterfly would be a white male, probably in his twenties so that he would easily blend in with the event. When people first started trespassing into history, they weren't careful about that kind of thing. They floundered about in the wrong clothes with the incorrect haircut and speech patterns like the proverbial bull in a china shop. Or, to steal the words of one of my favorite professors, like a whale in a bathtub. They stuck out. As time went on, though, and the Academy started sending Glitchers in to capture them, the Butterflies got smarter and a lot sneakier. Especially the Butterflies that joined up with Mayhem.

The first step was to figure out what about this event could be easily derailed. How could someone forever alter the future? Usually that question was clear, but tonight it wasn't. The event was too large; too many people were involved and spread across too wide of an area. Even an incredibly skilled Butterfly wouldn't be able to completely stop this event. So where was I supposed to look?

Before I could figure it out, we were at the harbor, and I was following the stream of men on board the closest of the three boats. There were only a few sailors guarding the cargo, and they quickly decided that tangoing with a pack of angry colonists with hatchets was a bad idea and got out of the way. The Boston Tea Party began. Barrels of tea were dragged across the deck of the ship, laid on their sides and hacked at with the crude hatchets until they cracked open like eggs, revealing the rich dark tea inside. Some of it spilled out onto the deck, filling the air with the pungent odor of distant lands, before the barrels were hurled overboard into the water.

Not wanting to gain any unwanted attention, I got to work and was just levering my first barrel across the deck when I caught sight of the other British East India ship under attack, the *Beaver*. Glancing in the other direction, I could just make out the third ship, the *Dartmouth*, as it was converged on by more angry Sons of Liberty. I must be on the *Eleanor*, then, I thought, and even as I felt the familiar smugness of knowing the details of this historical event inside and out, I felt a tug of fear. What if the Butterfly was on one of those other ships? How would I ever know? And that's when I saw Regan Fitz board the boat.

I almost didn't recognize her without her signature tumble of blond hair, but there was something about the way she held herself, a lofty arrogance even in her dingy men's clothing and frumpy hat, that set her apart. My distraction made me lose focus and my next hatchet hack hit the metal ring that held the barrel together and glanced off. A moment later I felt a searing pain in my right leg and looked down to see a bloom of blood already darkening the calf of my brown trousers.

The hatchet fell from my suddenly numb hands as I bent instinctively to grasp my bleeding calf muscle. Pain momentarily fogged my brain, and I sat down hard on the wooden deck of the boat.

This isn't real, I told myself as I gritted my teeth against the all too real pain. My leg was perfectly intact back in the simulation room. But while my brain might have believed that, my body wasn't buying it. My head felt light and disconnected from my body as I attempted to stop the stream of blood that was running over my hand and onto the deck. I was going to lose major points for this screwup.

"That was really stupid," said a voice in my ear, and I looked up into Regan's annoyed blue eyes.

"What are you doing?" I said through gritted teeth as I blinked at the tears I hadn't even noticed until now.

"Saving your neck," she said. "What does it look like?"

"My neck doesn't need saving," I said.

"Your neck may be fine, but you really jacked up your leg," she said, wrinkling her nose. "How badly are you hurt?"

"I don't know," I said, shaking my head. Why was she doing this? Did she think she was going to get extra points for helping me? I didn't think it worked that way. One of the main rules of this competition was that you weren't to interfere with another Glitcher under any circumstances. It was every man for himself, just like it would be in a real simulation someday.

"Helpful," she said as she shrugged out of the coat she was wearing, inspecting it for a second before grabbing at something, a thread I think, and giving it a yank. She did the same thing two more times, picking at tiny threads and pulling until the entire sleeve dropped neatly from the coat. That done, she bent to wrap the sleeve around my bleeding leg, and as I watched her knot off the makeshift bandage, I became aware again of the clamor around us. Barrel after barrel was being rolled across the deck to be maimed and tossed into the sea. Every now and then one of the disguised men would yell out something about no taxation without representation and everyone would cheer. What had started as a covert and sneaky operation was now a full-blown mob scene.

"Get up," Regan said, already hauling on my arm. "If you keep sitting on the deck like a beached whale, someone is going to notice you." I tried to shake her off and succeeded in freeing my arm only to have my bad leg give out and drop back onto the deck with a tailbone-bruising thump. She raised an eyebrow at me. "Smooth. Really smooth."

"Just stay out of my way," I said, getting awkwardly to my feet, careful not to put too much pressure on my throbbing calf.

"Your gratitude is heartwarming," she said. "A simple thank you would be fine."

"Thank you?" I sputtered. "This is your fault! If you hadn't distracted me I wouldn't have almost chopped my leg off. Now scat. I might still have a chance at this."

"Suit yourself," she said, and stalked away. I turned

my attention back to the chaos of the ship. Zeroing in on every colonist, looking for something, anything that would show them to be a Butterfly. But there was nothing. Everyone seemed to be working with the same resolute focus as they systematically destroyed barrel after barrel of tea. Meanwhile, I was running out of time.

In desperation I turned, just in time to see Regan dart belowdecks with a single-minded purpose I'd recognize anywhere. She'd spotted the Butterfly.

CHAPTER TWELVE

REGAN

Spotting the Butterfly was 100 percent dumb luck. Not that I'd ever in a million years admit that. But it was. Pure. Dumb. Luck. For one thing, he practically took me out as he charged away from the action at the rail of the ship. I barely managed to get out of his way before he shoved past me, making a beeline for one of the hatches that led belowdecks. And it was that word, *deck*, that brought me up short and made me give him a second glance. I was almost positive that the word *deck* had been in the Cocoon. The fact that I noticed any of this at that moment was a minor miracle because I was still fuming over Elliot's rude dismissal.

Going on gut instinct, I turned and followed the

man. There was nothing about his outfit or his haircut to give me the usual clues, but there was something off about him all the same. This was what I was good at. The actual catch. The nitty-gritty details of the historical event itself might slip in and out of my brain like water through a screen, but this, this I could do. I waited a half second for him to disappear down the hatch before slipping in behind him. Right before my head dipped belowdecks, I looked up to see Elliot watching me. And I know it was childish, and I knew my mother would roll her eyes when she saw it live on the simulation, but I pulled a face and stuck my tongue out at him anyway.

Grinning wickedly, I hurried down the last few rungs of the ladder into the darkness of the ship. Above me the thud and scrape of thirty-plus men shoving barrels of tea around was almost deafening and the interior of the ship had an overpowering musty smell that made my stomach roll a little. The joy of sticking it to Elliot faded quickly as goose bumps prickled up my neck. *Remember, Regan,* said the voice in my head that sounded suspiciously like my mother, *people are never more violent than when two powerful entities collide—the soul-deep conviction of being right and the liberating freedom of having nothing to lose.* I squinted in the dark, looking left and right, not sure which way the Butterfly had gone, and that's when I saw it. The flick and click of a lighter being lit. A lighter that wouldn't be invented for another two hundred years. Bingo.

I put my hands out to either side of me, using them to feel my way quickly down the passage in the dark, using the memory of that flash of light as my homing signal even after it went out. A sense of urgency pushed me faster and faster, and I barely registered the pain as my shins hit stray barrels and crates in the dark. The farther down the passage I got, the less it smelled like must and the more it smelled like something else. But what was it? Gasoline? No, that couldn't be right. The smell was definitely chemical, though. It had a sharpness to it that set off alarm bells in my head.

The flash of light came again less than ten feet, but this time it didn't go out immediately. The Butterfly moved it in a quick arc, and with a speed I wouldn't have thought possible, that flickering speck of light leaped from that lighter to the wall of the ship's passageway and ignited. The flame illuminated the face of the Butterfly just as he turned toward me, a look of shock and surprise on his face at being discovered mid-arson. I skidded to a stop, yanking my shirt up above my mouth and nose as the flames licked hungrily up the walls. Smoke burned and blurred my eyes as the Butterfly whirled and raced away down the passageway.

I felt frozen, unsure what to do. Should I turn and run back the way I'd come and hope I could find the ladder to the top deck in the dark? Or should I charge through the flames after the Butterfly? The damage was done, though, I realized. It was too late. Even if I caught the Butterfly now, this entire ship was going to go up in flames. There would be fatalities as the Sons of Liberty leaped into the sea to escape. Not only that, this ship was moored dangerously close to other ships. Ships that were also made completely of wood. On a night like this one, with the cold December wind pushing at the flames, the harbor would ignite. The entire town of Boston could go up in flames, for all I knew. I might be foggy about my history, but I knew what a fire could do in this time period, and it was devastating. What was supposed to be a violence-free protest would turn into one of the most horrendous events in America's history. If America even existed after this, I realized, remembering the vital impor-tance of this very night to the United States gaining its independence.

I'd just made up my mind to turn and run for help when a bucketful of ice-cold water hit me in the back, drenching me and knocking my hat off as it hit the crackling wall of flames. They sputtered for an instant, and some of them even went out, but the old wood of the ship was too flammable, and it quickly regained momentum. I turned to see who'd thrown the water just in time to catch the second bucketful right in the face. Elliot didn't even pause to acknowledge me. He ripped off his coat and began beating hard at the last of the flames that were still valiantly trying to spread. Within moments they were out and the passageway plummeted into a smoke-filled darkness.

"Which way did he go?" Elliot asked.

"How did you—" I started, but my words were choked, and I bent over, hacking hard as the smoke tightened in my lungs. Elliot asked the question again, and I pointed down the passageway. He charged past me, using the sides of the narrow passageway as a makeshift crutch as he hobbled on his bad leg. Still coughing, I followed him, my wet hair hanging in soggy ropes around my face. I made a half-hearted attempt to find my hat in the dark but gave up almost instantly and stuffed my hair haphazardly into the neck of my shirt. It would just have to be enough.

I caught up to Elliot just as he reached the cargo hold. What had once been filled wall to wall with barrels of tea was now almost empty. The few remaining barrels were being rolled to the open hatch to be hefted on deck by a handful of waiting men in their haphazard blanket and coal soot disguises.

"What did he look like?" Elliot said, his face a study of intensity as he searched each of the men's faces in the moonlight.

"I don't know," I said.

"Tall? Short? Dressed like a Mohawk or in a different disguise?" Elliot said, his words fast and efficient as he scanned the remaining men.

I squeezed my eyes shut. "Tall," I said. "With blue eyes and no beard. He definitely didn't have a Mohawk."

Elliot rolled his eyes. "Not the hairstyle. The tribe. Was he wearing something like this?" he asked, grabbing at the rough blanket around his shoulders.

I shook my head, "No. Normal 1800s dress."

"It's 1773," Elliot said, his tone as condescending as it could possibly be.

"Whatever," I said, throwing my soggy hands in the air so a few drops of water sprayed out. Elliot flinched and stepped farther away from me like I was a snake he didn't want to bite him as he continued scanning the crowd. "How in the world did you know to bring two buckets of water down with you?" I asked.

"I didn't," he said, and he turned to look at me for the first time, an amused smirk on his face.

"What?" I asked.

"Nothing," Elliot said. "So, he was tall. I can work with tall." With that he turned and hobbled awkwardly toward the small group of men who were just hefting a barrel up toward the waiting hands of their fellow Sons of Liberty. It was then that I noticed the smell that the smoke-filled tunnel had been masking. A blast of what I could only describe as raw sewage hit me full on, and I gagged as I realized why Elliot had smirked like that.

"You threw a chamber pot on me?!" I screamed. Every man in the ship's hold turned to look at me, but I couldn't have cared less. I had a right to scream. Elliot had essentially thrown the contents of a toilet used by a boatful of sailors over the top of me.

Elliot turned, a huge grin stretching from ear to ear. "Two chamber pots," he said. I stared at him in horror.

"I had to put the fire out somehow," he said. "I probably could have missed you, but"—he paused and shrugged—"where's the fun in that?"

An inarticulate scream ripped from my throat, and I charged, careening past the gaping Sons of Liberty to launch myself at him. I didn't have a plan other than to do some damage. Rip out his hair? Punch him? Smear some of the nastiness on him too? All of the above would be fine, thanks.

I hit him full force, and he fell backward as his bad leg gave out. Our combined momentum sent us right into the small group of men just as they hefted a barrel of tea toward the top deck. The barrel they'd been holding fell sideways, cracking open on impact. For a minute it was just one jumbled mass of arms and legs and yelling men, but I think I landed at least one solid punch to Elliot before everything got too tangled to tell which way was up.

Luckily, I ended up on top of the heap, and unluckily for Elliot, he ended up somewhere on the bottom. I managed to roll myself clear of the fray and stumbled to my feet as the men angrily attempted to untangle themselves. I took a wary step backward. Taking out a group of hyped-up colonial rebels was probably not my best idea. Before I could decide if now was a good time to run for it or not, I spotted the Butterfly. He must have been lurking near the back of the men hoisting barrels, because he was struggling to get out from under a rather large man. I hesitated a moment. This guy was way bigger than any Butterfly I'd ever dealt with before. My hesitation cost me the element of surprise as he spotted me and redoubled his efforts to free himself.

My Chaos Cuffs found their way into my hands without my even realizing I'd grabbed for them, and I lunged and snapped the first one onto the Butterfly's right hand just as his left connected with the side of my head. I lurched backward, black spots blooming in my vision as he attempted to pry the cuff off his arm. Blinking hard, I ducked his next swing and grabbed ahold of his left hand. His elbow popped me hard in the jaw and I bit down on my tongue, my mouth filling with the sharp, metallic taste of blood. Then Elliot was there, grabbing the man's flailing left arm and holding it steady for the half second I needed to get the other cuff on. I hit the activation button on the cuffs and everything around us went instantly dark. The simulation was over.

CHAPTER THIRTEEN

ELLIOT

I sat bolt upright in the freezing simulation room, breathing hard as the very real adrenaline from the very fake simulation raced through my system.

"Disqualify her!" I said, yanking the probes from my arms. The simulation technician rushed forward, all fluttery hands and big worried eyes as he tried untangling me from the costly machinery before my temper could do any real damage. Usually I'd care about something like that, but at the moment I felt like nothing mattered except how unfair this all was.

A wire managed to get tangled around my arm and I flapped at it in frustration, only looking up when I noticed that the small group of test evaluators had come out from behind their panel of computer screens, where they'd watched every nightmarish detail of what had to be the worst simulation test in the history of simulation tests. There were only supposed to be six evaluators at a leveling simulation like this one, but of course Regan's mom had decided to sit in as well, so there were seven. I wasn't quite sure if she was participating in the final panel or not. All the members were wearing similar expressions of disapproval on their faces, although more than one looked like they were trying very hard not to laugh. My blood felt like it was boiling inside my veins. Nothing about this was funny. Nothing. Regan had not only hijacked my entire test, but she'd broken every single rule with the flippancy of someone who'd been getting away with it her entire life. Which, as the commander in chief's daughter, she had. I gritted my teeth to keep from saying something else stupid and stopped moving so the poor technician could attempt to untangle the mess I'd made.

"Me?" Regan said, sitting up and pulling off her own probes in a way that made the technician still busy with me flinch. Poor guy was having a day. "Oh, you have *got* to be kidding me. You threw a chamber pot on me!" she yelled. "A chamber pot! After I saved your life!"

"Don't flatter yourself," I said. "You didn't save my

life. It was a simulation! I would have figured out how to stop the bleeding."

"Well, you were doing a bang-up job of it," she said. "Standing there staring at your bleeding leg like a moron. Brilliant strategy."

"It was two chamber pots!" I shot back.

"Enough!" said Commander Fitz, her voice sharp, and we both stopped yelling and snapped to attention. The commander in chief of the Academy did not ask twice. I glanced over at Regan out of the corner of my eye and saw her grim expression as her mother looked from her to me and back again. "Cadets," she went on, her voice quieter but no less commanding, "you will not scream at one another and make a bigger scene than you already have. Now hold still so you can be unhooked properly." She paused, eyeing us both so we knew just how much she disapproved of our yanking at our expensive simulation probes. To her credit, Regan didn't even flinch. I, however, felt the distinct need to hide underneath my simulation chair. Commander Fitz waited for us both to nod before continuing. "Obviously, this test went off the rails."

Regan snorted, and her mother gave her a sharp look. "As such," she went on, "we will deal with the consequences for both of you and your actions in private." Commander Fitz flicked her eyes upward and

Regan and I both looked up to the observation balcony. A balcony that had been empty when we started this simulation but was now full of students. Students who, unlike the supervising professors, were doing nothing to hide their amusement at our situation as they laughed and pointed.

Commander Fitz looked like she was about to say something else, but a professor I'd never seen before came up to whisper something in her ear. Her face stayed neutral and detached as she listened, but her eyes did flick to Regan for the tiniest half second. I wondered if anyone else had noticed. Finally, she nodded and turned her attention back to us.

"Meet me in my office in ten minutes for your recap," she said, turning to stalk out of the simulation room before either of us could reply. My heart sank. This was bad. Really bad. I'd sat in on enough of these tests to know that protocol dictated that we sit and watch our recap in front of the panel. I'd never heard of a private recap in the commander's office. My mind flicked back to the Cocoon, and I felt my skin prickle. What if the private meeting was because somehow they'd figured it out? I tried to remember what Regan and I had said to each other in the simulation. We were too smart to mention the Cocoon when an entire panel of Academy officers was watching. Right?

A quick glance around showed that Ella, Calvin, Molly, and Sid were very busy pretending that Regan and I were invisible. Which was exactly what I would have done had the situation been reversed. I noted that Calvin and Sid looked enormously pleased with themselves, a look I'd worn on more than one occasion when I won a sim test. But not today. Today the last thing I felt like doing was smiling. Today I was a raw nerve.

"How much trouble are we in?" I asked Professor Brown as she came over to help the technician remove the probes from my left leg with a painstaking slowness that set my teeth on edge.

"It might not be as bad as you think," she said as she gently removed the two from my calf muscle, the calf muscle I'd hacked into in the simulation. If I'd done something that dumb during an actual time-travel mission, I'd have Glitched back to the present missing a chunk of my leg. The thought made my stomach turn a bit, and I felt a familiar rush of relief that real time travel was still a long way off. I was going to be the best of the best someday, commander in chief, but today's simulation showed just how far I still had to go to get there. Especially with Regan's shenanigans. She was deadweight, and the sooner I could distance myself from her, the better.

As though my thoughts had called her, I looked up to discover Regan standing inches from me, her arms crossed as she waited for Professor Brown to remove the last of my probes.

"What are you doing?" I asked when Professor Brown finally finished up and walked over to help one of the other kids.

"Waiting for you," she said. "I thought that was obvious."

"Why? Haven't you done enough?" I asked.

"I hope so," she said, hurrying to keep up with me as I stormed out the simulation door. "Although I only wanted to screw up your test, not get myself in trouble."

"Well, you should have thought of that before you tackled me," I said.

"Solid point," she said.

"We didn't, you know, mention the you-know-what by accident in the simulation. Did we?" I asked, because that question could not sit in my brain one more second.

Regan stopped walking so abruptly I almost ran into her. She turned to me, her face white.

"I don't think so. Did we?"

"I don't think so either," I said. "But if we didn't, then why are we doing this in your mom's office and not in the recap review room with everyone else?"

Regan shrugged. "Your guess is as good as mine. Besides, I thought you were going to pretend that the *thing* never happened."

"I was," I said. "But you seem determined to screw that plan up for me."

Regan sniffed. "I am."

"You're kind of hard to like," I said. "You know that?"

She nodded. "I do. And right back at you."

I gritted my teeth. "Let's just get through this meeting with your mom first, and then we'll worry about that headache."

"You're a headache," she muttered under her breath.

"What was that?" I said, although I knew perfectly well what she'd just said.

She looked me right in the eye. "You. Are. A. Giant. Headache," she said. "A hammer pounding between the eyes, it feels like my head is going to explode headache. We could have avoided this if you weren't such a jerk."

"Well, if I'm a headache, then you're a royal pain and dumb as a rock if you thought I was going to let a letter keep me from being the youngest cadet to level up," I said a tad too loudly, so that we both glanced nervously up and down the empty hallway before continuing.

"You're right," she said with a smug smile. "It took me. You're welcome." With that she turned and strode off down the hall.

I scowled at the back of her stupid blond head the entire rest of the way to the staff offices.

I'd only been in the staff section a handful of times. Once when my schedule had been messed up, and I'd needed the Academy secretary to un-mess it for me; the other times were for office-hours visit with this professor or that. But I'd never, not even once, gone in the commander in chief's office, and had Regan not decided to totally mess up my life, I probably never would have.

Regan looked like she was ready to meet a firing squad when we finally arrived outside her mom's office door. If *she* was this nervous, I was definitely in trouble, I thought grimly. Doing my best to ignore the sinking feeling of dread that was pulling at my heart like a lead weight, I squared my shoulders and held my chin up as the door slid open a second later. We walked inside the cavernous office as the doors slid shut behind us with an ominous click.

CHAPTER FOURTEEN

REGAN

Mom's office was big and impressive, and I hated it. I avoided the place when I could, and barely tolerated it when avoidance didn't work. But it wasn't the office itself that bothered me. It was who my mom became when she sat behind that big desk. Here, she was the commander in chief, not Mom. Here, she accepted nothing less than perfection. Here, I was just another cadet. I knew that was how it had to be, but it didn't mean I had to like it.

To my surprise, though, she wasn't alone behind that desk today. Sitting to her left was the mysterious professor who had whispered in her ear, and to her right was Professor Green looking smug about something.

"Sit," Commander Fitz said, and Elliot and I obeyed immediately, both of us perching on the front edge of our chairs like we were about to take flight.

"Now then," Commander Fitz said, taking her own seat behind her desk. "It is time to discuss your simulation." She leaned over and pushed a button on her desk and the entire wall behind her flickered to life. It was a recap screen, smaller than the one in the recap review room, but still impressive. It showed a split screen; on the left was a frozen image of Elliot crouched in a blacksmith's shop, and on the right was the image of that big meeting I'd Glitched into.

This was going to be ten kinds of terrible, I thought, crossing my arms over my chest. My mother slipped out from behind the facade of Commander Fitz for a second to shoot me a disapproving glance, and I immediately unfolded them and placed them on the chair's armrests. No use making this worse for myself than it already was.

"You will watch your recap, and then we will address some of the issues that came up during this test," Commander Fitz said, and hit play.

The beginning was fine. I had to admit that Elliot's quick thinking was pretty impressive, while I bumbled around, obviously clueless about what was going on or where exactly I was. To my credit, though, I did find my way onto the correct ship just in time to see Elliot hack into his own leg. The previous split screen melded into one as our simulation test collided in a bloody mess.

I glanced at Elliot from the corner of my eye to see his reaction to this, but his face didn't give anything away. I wondered who'd taught him not to fidget, because he was doing a killer impression of a statue. Although his face was looking almost as pale as the version of himself on the screen, so he wasn't a complete robot. I should have found this comforting, but I didn't. I wondered again why, of all the people at the Academy, my future self had thought it was a good idea to lump me with this guy. Why Elliot Mason? Remembering the letter made my insides squirm.

The simulation jumped back to a split screen as I stomped away from Elliot and followed the Butterfly belowdecks. What would my mom say if she knew that her own daughter was a time-traveling criminal? That one of the only reasons I'd spotted the Butterfly on the screen, or the one in the Lincoln simulation for that matter, was because I'd been tipped off by my future self.

I clenched my jaw as I watched the Butterfly slosh lamp oil over the dry wood of the ship. I'd stopped watching Elliot's side of the screen, but I tuned back in in time to see him grab the two chamber pots and heave them at the flames. Professor Green and the mystery professor grimaced as my on-screen self was drenched. Commander Fitz didn't so much as flinch. Elliot smiled. Jerk.

It took everything in me to stay sitting calmly in my seat as the simulation careened from bad to worse. Finally, mercifully, the screen went dark.

"Is there a winner?" Elliot asked, and I glanced over at him in surprise. It wasn't like him to blurt out something like that. He was sitting ramrod straight in his chair, his eyes on the panel of professors. He always sat like he'd attached a steel pole to his spine, but it was even worse now. He wanted that win in the worst possible way, and for a half second I felt bad about ruining his chances. But then I remembered the Cocoon and the "sounds like a you problem" and the chamber pots, and I stopped feeling bad.

"There is not," said Commander Fitz. "I'm sorry, Cadet Mason, but this test did not count as an advancement point."

"But it's not my fault that she tackled me!" he said.

"Cadet Fitz's interference is not why you did not earn your point," she said. "It *is*, however, the reason why you are *both* moving to a different branch of the Academy."

"What?" Elliot and I both yelped at the same time.

Commander Fitz held up a hand to stop us, and we both snapped our mouths shut. She turned to the mysterious professor on her left and motioned him forward. "Professor Callaway will explain, since this is his area of expertise."

I stared at Professor Callaway, trying to place him. Had he ever been to our house for dinner? What could his area of expertise be?

"Today was a test," said Professor Callaway, looking from Elliot to me and back again. I fought the urge to roll my eyes. No kidding it was a test. Who was this guy?

"To be more accurate, it was a test within a test," he went on. "On the surface, today's simulation test was just another opportunity for advancement points, but for the last year or so, there has been another test embedded within each of these simulation tests. It was designed to see if you would let your own triumph and success get in the way of a successful mission, or if you'd work together for a common goal. One of the downsides to the current program is the competition element. We realized a few years ago that while we were turning out excellent Glitchers, those Glitchers often ignored other Glitchers in their need to succeed. That resulted in more than one failed mission and even the loss of some of our best and brightest. So, around five years ago, we started a new program to see if we could develop Glitchers who could work in collaboration with one another for the greater good. To further that end, and as a way to test our theory, we found two young Glitchers who we could train as the first partner team. Those Glitchers lived together, trained together, and worked together until they could finish one another's sentences. It was a test program and as such has been kept under wraps, so to speak."

"Wait a minute," I said, holding up my hand. "You mean that our top secret Academy has another even more top secret layer?"

Professor Callaway chuckled. "That about sums it up, Cadet Fitz, but like I was saying," he went on, "that first partner pair just graduated from our prototype program and entered active duty, and they are surpassing their single counterparts in almost every way. Especially when it comes to identifying and taking down members of Mayhem. As such, we have recently received the go-ahead to make the program permanent. I've been sitting in on all the simulation level tests to watch for compatible matchups."

"So, we failed on an epic level," I said flatly.

"On the contrary," Callaway said. "You two scored off the charts for partner compatibility. Your strengths and weaknesses complement one another nicely, and had it not been for your rather unusual brand of team-work, the entire simulation mission would have been lost."

"What are you saying exactly?" Elliot asked.

"I'm saying that you have both been admitted into the Lewis and Clark partner program." Callaway grinned expectantly at us, obviously waiting for us to cheer or hug him or something. He was about to be sorely disappointed.

Elliot stood up again. "And if we refuse the position?"

Professor Callaway shook his head. "I'm afraid you can't. The Academy has made their decision. This is an honor not given to everyone, Cadet Mason."

"The honor I wanted was to beat the record for youngest cadet to advance," he said. "Are you saying that's just gone?"

"I know you were eager to beat my record," Commander Fitz said, "but you will just have to be content with being the youngest partner pair admitted to the program. The other partner pairs have all been taken from cadet levels above your own."

"Fine," Elliot said. "Then I want a different partner. Anyone but her." He pointed a finger at the side of my head, and I scowled at him.

"I'm not too thrilled about you either," I said as I

gave his finger a shove that I hoped hurt. I turned back to the panel. "What about personality compatibility? You have to take that into account too, right?"

My mom's eyes narrowed slightly at my tone, and I swallowed hard.

"No, Cadet Fitz, ensuring the safety and security of our future is not dependent on whether or not you enjoy your partner's personality. What matters is whether or not you can work together successfully, and everything shows that you two have the capacity to do that. Whether or not you decide to make it easier on yourselves and get along? Well, that's on you."

"But this doesn't make any sense," Elliot went on. "I'm at the top of my class and everyone knows Regan is . . ." He trailed off, and I shot Elliot a dirty look.

"Is what?" I asked. "Go ahead. Say it." But Elliot's eyes flicked up to my mom and then back to me, and he just shook his head.

"Cadet Mason," Callaway said, his tone making it clear that this discussion was over. "You may be at the top of your class, but your evaluators have found you sorely lacking when it comes to gut instinct and intuition. You can only learn so much from studying. A large part of being a successful Glitcher is inherent. What Cadet Fitz lacks in academic retention and self-control," he said, raising an eyebrow at me that earned him a few chuckles from Professor Green, "she makes up for with an uncanny innate ability to spot a Butterfly without any visible signs of a time discrepancy." I scowled even though I knew that tackling another Glitcher showed an extreme lack of self-control. In my defense, I'd been covered in sewage, so my judgment might not have been at its best.

"You begin tomorrow," Callaway went on. "You will both move into a separate barracks just for cadets in the L and C program. You are one of only three sets chosen to work in the program, and I'm sure you will make us all proud." He looked like he was about to sit down, but then he stopped and turned back to smile at us. "Oh, and cadets. While we found your simulation test to be most amusing and the use of chamber pots to be inventive and resourceful, please remember that from now on you are a team. If one of you fails, you both fail. There is no going back to the regular Academy track after this." He sat back down as goose bumps prickled up my neck like spiders. No going back. The very same words that had been in the Cocoon.

CHAPTER FIFTEEN

ELLIOT

I stomped back toward my room to start packing. My future, a future where I rose to glory on the back of my own hard work and devotion to Glitching, had just gone up in smoke. All the extra hours studying, the extra time in the simulation rooms, the extra books and essays I'd read on every obscure historical event known to man didn't matter. Because now I was saddled with a parasite of a partner. My mind jumped to the Cocoon, and I felt a fresh surge of anger. Obviously, those future versions of ourselves had known that we were going to end up in the stupid partner program, so why hadn't they just told us what was coming?

I stopped dead in my tracks as a realization hit me

like an oncoming train. This whole thing wouldn't have happened without that Cocoon. That letter had caused a domino effect of events that pitted Regan against me in a simulation test that just so happened to also be testing for compatibility for the partner program. What had Callaway called it? The Lewis and Clark partner program?

Suddenly I felt light-headed, and I made my way off the main path I'd been walking to take a seat at one of the stone benches that peppered the campus. People called out to me, but I ignored everyone, lost in my own angry bubble as I sat there stewing. Because try as I might, I couldn't find a way to be mad at just Regan and ignore the fact that *I* was the one who picked up that letter in the hall. *I* was the one who just had to show it to her to demand answers she didn't have. Why hadn't I just chucked it directly into the trash?

Now I was going to have to pack up and move into a dorm with Fitz of all people. With a resigned sigh I shoved myself to my feet and headed toward the dorm I'd called home for most of my life.

Still lost in my preoccupation, I was almost surprised when I found myself back at my door. I unlocked it and slammed it shut behind me for good measure. I was just contemplating opening it so I could slam it shut again when a sharp knock behind me about made me jump out of my skin. Whirling, I saw Regan standing outside my window.

I moved over to stand in front of my window without making any move to open it. "What do you want?" I asked.

"Let me in," she said.

"No," I said.

This brought her up short, and she glared at me through the glass. "Why?" she said.

"Because I don't want to," I said.

Regan scowled and then took a step back. "Fine," she said, her voice suddenly louder than before. "We can just discuss the letter out here then!" As I hurried to unlock the window, I had the absurd thought that if we ever played chicken, she'd win by a landslide.

"What are you doing here?" I said.

"I followed you back," she said, coming into my room. "Not that you noticed," she said, peering at my bookshelf as she wandered around. "Although that really isn't saying much. I could have lit a rocket off under you and you wouldn't have noticed. You have impressive tunnel vision, my friend."

"I am *not* your friend," I said, removing the book she'd just picked up from her hands. I didn't like her touching my things.

"You're right," she said, turning to face me, arms crossed. "I'm not your friend. I'm your partner. So you could consider not being such a grade-A jerk."

I raised an eyebrow at her. "As opposed to a grade-B jerk?"

She rolled her eyes and huffed in exasperation, taking the book back out of my hand and chucking it haphazardly onto the bed. "You know what I mean," she said. "I'm willing to put your horrendous behavior at the fountain behind us in the interest of starting off fresh."

"That wasn't horrendous behavior," I said. "That was what you call self-preservation." I glanced around my room nervously, although if this room *was* monitored, the security officers would have arrested me the minute I opened that stupid life-ruining Cocoon last night.

"It's safe," Regan said as though she was reading my mind. When she saw my expression, she shrugged. "For the most part, dorm rooms aren't monitored. Besides, I already checked the database in my mom's office to make sure yours was camera free."

"When did you do that?" I asked.

"Last night after you left me at the fountain with your oh so charismatic *sounds like a you problem* comment."

I shrugged. "Grade-A jerk, remember? Anyways, about the letter," I said, and then paused, biting my lip as I considered the domino of events that were already in motion.

"What about it?" Regan prompted. "You look like

your brain just took a wrong turn and fell off a cliff."

"Do you realize that without that letter, we never would have gotten stuck in this stupid partner program?" I asked.

Regan opened her mouth to say something but then snapped it shut again as the realization hit home.

"Did your brain just fall off the same cliff as mine?" I asked. "Because I'll warn you, the landing really hurts."

"No way," Regan said, sitting down on my bed and flopping backward so she could stare up at the ceiling.

"Way," I said, plopping down in my desk chair so I could face her.

She sat up with a jerk a second later and stared at me. "Do you think the Lewis and Clark program was why we got the Cocoon in the first place?"

I shrugged. "Who knows."

"So maybe we already did what the letter wanted us to do," Regan said, biting her lip. "Maybe whatever bad thing was going to happen won't happen now because I went all out to ruin your test."

"You went all out, all right," I grumbled. "How in the world did you spot that Butterfly so fast?" I asked, because if I was honest with myself, it had been eating at me that she got the jump on me like that. It was uncanny.

To my surprise, I saw a blush spread across her face, turning her ears a bright red.

"Um," she said, biting her lip. "I may have had some help with that one."

"What do you mean?" I asked.

"The bullet points on the Cocoon," she said, pulling a wadded-up piece of paper out of her pocket and flattening it in front of me. I glanced down at her list of bullet points, and froze when I saw the one that mentioned a deck, because there *had* been a list of bullet points on that letter. How in the world had I forgotten about that?

"You cheated," I said, pointing my finger in her face. "You knew the Butterfly was going to be belowdecks. That's not fair."

"Really?" she said, raising an eyebrow. "Because I'm pretty sure you had access to the exact same information." I opened my mouth to protest, but, of course, she was right. I glanced back down at the list and frowned. "This is all you could remember?"

She nodded. "But I know I'm missing one."

"You're missing two," I said, reaching over to snag a pen off my desk. I sat down, pulling her crumbled piece of paper over, and fixed the list, adding the two points she'd forgotten.

Behind the curtain.

~~*Something about under a deck?*~~ *Belowdecks.*

~~Break a window?~~ *When the window breaks,*
grab me.

Trust the door will open when it needs to.

The prototypes are a bust.

Grab a key card when you have the chance.

~~(What am I supposed to grab it off of?)~~

Don't forget about the one in ~~his~~ a pocket.

That done, I put a big check next to the point next to belowdecks.

"Put a check next to the one about the curtain too," she said, and I looked up at her, eyebrow raised.

"The Lincoln assassination simulation," she said, sounding sheepish. "I had to pass it in order to hijack your test. The Butterfly was hiding behind the curtain in Lincoln's theater box."

I thought about calling her out for cheating again, but honestly, what was the point? The damage was done. Together we looked down at the last few bullet points on the list, a list that I'd disregarded in my single-minded focus to level up. I wasn't going to make that mistake again.

"So, what now?" she said.

"What do you mean?" I asked. "You won. Now we have to wait to see how the rest of those bullet points play out."

157

Regan grimaced. "I'm not sure if I'd consider this one a win for me. I mean, you're my new partner."

"So?" I shot back.

"I mean, have you met you?" she asked. "When you thought that Cocoon didn't affect you, you totally ditched me. You're a little self-centered."

"Driven," I said. "The word you are looking for is driven. That Cocoon put everything I'd worked so hard for in jeopardy, so it was pretty easy to shrug off."

"And now?" she asked.

I sighed. "And now I guess we are stuck together. Whether I like it or not." I suddenly felt exhausted. I shut my eyes. Maybe if I didn't look at her, she'd magically disappear.

"Hmm," Regan murmured. "That doesn't sound like the Elliot Mason I know. Did you hit your head a little hard when I tackled you?"

"Don't be dumb. You know any injury in the simulation stays in the simulation," I said, rubbing at a pain in my temples as I willed Regan to leave.

"That's the problem," Regan said.

I opened one eye to peer at her. "What are you talking about?"

"I'm dumb," she said. "You practically said it in my mom's office, and I know you thought it when you saw my pathetic attempt at remembering that list, and if that wasn't bad enough, Professor Callaway practically spelled it out." She twisted her face and puffed out her chest in a pretty spot-on imitation of Callaway. "Elliot has the academic knowledge, but Regan has the intuition." She relaxed back into her normal posture and threw her hands in the air in exasperation. "He might as well have said Elliot has real smarts and Regan has similar talents to a really good German shepherd."

"I'd rather have a German shepherd as a partner," I said. I glanced over at Regan and shrugged. "No offense."

She flipped her hand dismissively. "None taken. I'd trade you for a gerbil."

"You're impossible," I grumbled. "And annoying. I hope you know that."

"I've been told," she said.

"Queen Obnoxious and the Grade-A Jerk," I said. "What a team."

"Either that or a really delightful children's book," she said. With that she turned, clambered back out the window, and disappeared.

CHAPTER SIXTEEN

REGAN

If anyone thought I'd be reluctant to move out of the mansion on the hill and into student housing, they'd be wrong. I'd been begging, literally begging, my mom for most of my life to let me live in one of the dorms. All the other kids at the Academy had a camaraderie with one another that I just hadn't been able to achieve, and I was pretty sure it was because I wasn't a part of their inside jokes about the cold showers or the tiny closets. Or, I reminded myself, it could be that I really was the queen of being obnoxious, like Elliot said. Either way, I was getting my wish and moving into student housing at last. I knew I wouldn't make friends right away, especially since I was saddled with Elliot, but maybe eventually. A girl could hope.

Mom had insisted on helping me with the move, but I'd have given anything to make this walk across the misty early-morning campus by myself. I'd really wanted to begin this fresh start, well, fresh. I shivered despite my warm cadet jacket. A glance out of the corner of my eye showed that my mom was just as preoccupied as I was. She'd gotten called away for an emergency meeting right after I'd gotten home from my visit to Elliot's room, and the dark circles under her eyes were more pronounced than ever.

"So, what happened last night?" I asked in an attempt to break the silence.

"Nothing I can talk about," Mom said with a distracted half smile.

"Oh," I said, and pressed my lips together. Seeing my reaction, she sighed and put an arm around my shoulders and squeezed.

"Besides," she said. "The last thing I want to talk about on the day my daughter moves out is work. I'll miss you, you know."

"Now I'll be just like every other cadet," I said, "only seeing my mom every now and then."

"You, my dear, are not just like every other cadet," she said, but before she could go on, there was a shuffling noise to our right, and Elliot came around the corner, his blue regulation duffel bag slung over shoulders that were hunched against the cold.

"Hello, Cadet Mason," Mom said, her voice too loud in the early-morning stillness. Elliot jumped about a foot and looked up in surprise.

"Right," Elliot said, and glanced at me. "Good morning."

"I know this situation isn't what either of you wanted, but I hope you both make the best of it," Mom said. "The Academy needs every good Glitcher we can get, especially if those Glitchers come as a package deal."

Elliot winced at the words *package deal*, and I knew it was because I was part of that particular package.

"A secret package," I said, turning to my mom as something occurred to me. "Why are we still a secret if the program has been approved?"

Mom smiled a grim smile. "Security reasons," she said. "The board thought that it was best to diversify our program."

"Diversify?" Elliot asked, eyebrow raised.

"Maybe *diversify* is the wrong word," she said. "What I mean is more along the lines of keeping all your eggs in one basket. For security reasons, the board decided we should keep at least a few eggs in a basket no one knows about."

"That doesn't make any sense," I said. "What basket. What eggs?"

"We're the eggs," Elliot said. "And I'm guessing that's the basket," he said, pointing to the large border wall where security officers stood by an open door, the blue of the ocean showing just behind them. I came to such an abrupt stop that Mom almost ran into me, catching herself just in time.

"The Lewis and Clark partner program is off campus?" I said, not believing what I was seeing. I'd spent my entire life within the safety of the Academy walls, and I'd expected to spend the rest of it here as well. I turned to my mom in disbelief.

"The L and C program is on an outlier island about a ten-minute boat ride away," she said. "Don't worry— the security there is a tad unorthodox, but you will be just as safe there as you are here."

"But—" I said, turning to see the same shock on Elliot's face. He hadn't had a clue either.

"But nothing," Mom said. "You were chosen for this program, and you will do your very best to excel at it, regardless of its location. Now let's get moving; the extra security detail for this transfer is needed else-where by nine o'clock."

Still in utter shock, I trailed behind my mom as she walked up to the security transfer.

"Have you ever been off the island?" Elliot asked as he came to stand next to me.

"Never," I whispered. "You?"

"I came over when I was a baby, just like everyone else," Elliot said. "So yeah, I guess I was off the island once upon a time, but I don't remember it." His shoulder pressed against mine and I leaned into it a little in some kind of unspoken solidarity.

"The ocean looks bluer than it did from the wall observation platforms," I said. "Can that be right?"

"I have no idea," Elliot said. His brow furrowed, and he turned to look at me. "The only reason the board would need to put their eggs, or us, or whatever, in separate baskets would be if the Academy was vulnerable. But that's impossible, isn't it?"

I shrugged as I watched my mom talk to the transfer security officer. I thought about mentioning the emergency meeting Mom had been called away to or the way Officer Salzburg had hinted at a threat from Mayhem, but decided against it. "The Academy is one of the safest places on earth," I said. But even as the words left my mouth, I wasn't sure which of us I was trying to convince.

"Liar," he said, and I stiffened and looked over at him.

"What did you call me?" I asked.

"A liar," he said. "That was the phoniest thing I've ever heard."

"Was not," I said.

Elliot rolled his eyes. "If that were true, would we even be standing here right now?"

"I don't follow," I said.

"Shocking," Elliot muttered, ignoring my glare.

"Just spit it out," I said as all the solidarity I'd felt a moment before washed away, and I took a step to the left so our shoulders weren't touching anymore and blinked hard. Grade-A jerk, I reminded myself. What did I expect? For him to warm up to me after years of being at each other's throats just because we'd been forced together?

"Think about it, Fitz," he said. "If everything was peachy, we'd never have gotten the you know what that landed us in this stupid program in the first place."

Not trusting myself to say anything else, I just nodded as I looked back toward the ocean, where a small powerboat was pulling up with more security transfers on board as well as a beaming Professor Callaway. He waved to us excitedly as the boat docked, and despite the tight coil of nerves in my stomach, I smiled back. It was hard not to. He was wearing an orange life jacket across his wide chest, the buckles stretched so tight they reminded me of rubber bands about to bust.

"Here you go," Mom said, walking up to hand us each our own orange life jacket.

"Where's yours?" I asked.

"I'm not going any farther," she said. "Professor Callaway will take you from here."

"Really?" I said, turning away from the ocean to look at her. I was going to get my wish and enter this new program alone? I waited to feel the rush of relief, but it didn't come. Instead, a knot of anxiety tightened in my stomach. Faced with all this brand-new territory, I wanted nothing more than my mom at my side, and if I didn't care so much about Elliot thinking I was a baby, I would have said as much. But as it was, I just nodded and squeezed a little tighter when she wrapped her arms around me for one last hug.

"You'll be fine," she whispered in my ear. "More than fine. You'll be great. You're my girl, after all."

I nodded again and bit my lip.

"Good morning," said Callaway. "How are my newest recruits?"

"Surprised," I said.

He chuckled. "I was too the first time I left the Academy, but you'll love the mountain. So if you've said your goodbyes, it's time for us to be off." We nodded and followed him onto the dock. The wind whipped off the water and almost took my breath away as it brought with it the salty smells of the sea. I looked back at the Academy walls, feeling like a turtle suddenly deprived of its shell. Resigned, I stepped onto a real boat for the first time in my life.

CHAPTER SEVENTEEN

ELLIOT

The Academy was all that I knew. All I'd ever known, and now it wasn't much more than a spot on the horizon.

"Do you see it!" called Callaway over the roaring of the wind. Regan and I turned to see the small speck of brown in the distance that was getting larger by the minute. "It's much smaller than the Academy," Callaway said. "But that makes it easier to secure and hide."

Five minutes later we were coasting up to a small dock on an island that was almost completely taken up by a large craggy mountain. Where the Academy had the polished and manicured look of a college campus, this looked every inch the uninhabited wilderness.

"Where's the wall?" Regan asked, and I turned to her in surprise. Why in the world hadn't that been my first question? Where *was* the wall?

"We don't need a wall," Callaway said, coming to stand next to us.

"I don't understand," Regan said. "Mom said the security here was just as good as at the Academy. How do you not *need* a wall?"

"Because we have a mountain," Callaway said.

"I'd still like a wall," I said under my breath, glancing around at the vast ocean surrounding us on all sides.

Callaway chuckled and motioned with his hand for us to follow him as he climbed out of the boat and onto the rock-covered shore. Regan followed, looking just as leery about all this as I felt.

"What in the world have we gotten ourselves into?" she whispered as the security officers climbed out of the boat to flank us on either side.

"I'd like to point out that I wanted nothing to do with this," I hissed back.

"Hurry up, cadets!" Callaway called over his shoulder as he headed down a thin dirt trail that appeared to lead straight into the woods. One of the security officers handed me my duffel, and I swung it over my shoulder, the weight comfortingly familiar. Regan already had her things and was hurrying to catch up with Callaway.

The path was really nothing more than a thin slice of trodden-down dirt between waist-high underbrush that sloped continually upward. As we followed Callaway over rougher and rougher terrain, I couldn't help but wonder if this was all some kind of joke. Maybe it was a hazing ritual done to cadets who were in too big of a hurry to level up. But as I watched the security officers walk beside us, their heads on a swivel as though someone was lurking behind every tree or bush, I knew this was for real.

Callaway stopped beside a large outcropping of rocks at the base of the mountain and turned to the security patrol. "Is the coast clear?" he asked.

The officer closest to me nodded.

"Very good," Callaway said, and then he turned back, took two large steps forward, and disappeared into the rock.

Regan gasped in surprise, and my jaw dropped as my brain fought to make sense of what I was seeing. The security detail smirked at one another, and then the guard closest to me stepped forward, disappearing just as seamlessly. It reminded me of the way the Cocoon had dissolved in water, like it had never even been there.

Suddenly Callaway's head popped back through the

rock, a wide grin on his face. "I love seeing people's reactions the first time I do that," he said. "Please, step right on through. The rock is an optical illusion, a very well-crafted hologram." To prove his point, he popped his head back inside the rock and then back out again like some kind of deranged jack-in-the-box.

"Step lively now," said the security detail behind me. "We don't like having anyone loitering around the entrance." I nodded and was just reaching my hand out toward the holographic rock when Regan shouldered past me and walked right through.

Not wanting to be outdone, I leaped after her. Part of me still expected to ram face-first into solid rock, and I closed my eyes in anticipation of impact. When no impact came, I opened my eyes to discover that I was standing in front of a large steel door. Turning, I saw the shimmering image of the rock, thrown up by multiple projectors mounted to the surrounding mountain.

"That's brilliant," I said.

"Brilliant is an understatement," Regan said, leaning forward to inspect one of the projectors. She put her hand in front of the lens and suddenly the rock projection had a large hole.

"Stop that," said a security officer, snatching her hand so that the projection returned to normal.

"Sorry," Regan muttered.

"This facility is testing out some new innovations in security," Callaway explained as he walked over to the steel door and pressed his hand against a large black panel to the right of it. "The Academy has its wall and security detail, but it is still too conspicuous. Despite the no-fly zone and the water patrol to make sure no unsuspecting boater stumbles upon it, some still have. This way, a boater could go right past the island and have no idea we were even here." The panel lit up green around his palm and the door slid open, revealing a large, well-lit walkway.

"The L and C program is located inside the mountain," Regan said. "That's amazing."

"It took about ten years to build," Callaway said, leading the way down the hallway. "Luckily this particular mountain had a fairly extensive cave system already in place, so we just expanded on it. The Lewis and Clark program is small; you two will make the fourth partner group admitted into the program. Sam and Serina, our original partner pair, will pop in every now and then to assist with your training as well. We hope to grow the program a bit more each year, but finding compatible partners is proving to be harder than we expected."

It was then that I noticed our security transfer hadn't followed us. Callaway noticed my look and waved a hand flippantly. "Don't worry about security, Elliot. They've headed back to the Academy. We don't need them once we are inside the mountain."

We rounded a corner, and the corridor opened up into a gigantic circular room the size of the auditorium at the Academy. Glancing up, I saw that the domed ceiling was chiseled right out of the rock of the mountain.

The room was completely open without a partition or a dividing wall in sight and set up like a pie, with each slice of the circle housing something different. I guess if there were only six of us training here, walls were kind of pointless. Directly in front of us was what looked like a smaller version of Professor Watt's gym, complete with a training mat. To the right of that was a classroom with only ten desks and a floor-to-ceiling projection screen on the wall. My eyes kept tracking around the room, taking in a small library, a simulation setup, lounge area, and cafeteria. It was like they'd taken the sprawling complex of the Academy and shrunk it. I was so busy looking at everything that I almost didn't notice that there were other people in the room until Regan elbowed me hard in the ribs.

"Stop gaping like an idiot and look alive," she whispered as Callaway excitedly motioned a small group of kids over from where they'd been sitting around a table eating breakfast. Realizing that Regan's gaping like an idiot description was 100 percent accurate, I shut my mouth with an audible click.

"Good morning, cadets!" Callaway said. "It's time to welcome our newest team to the program." I wondered if Callaway was always this cheerful. I hoped not.

"This is Cadet Regan Fitz and Cadet Elliot Mason, our youngest recruits to the program to date," Callaway said, and Regan and I both nodded greetings. Callaway motioned forward two boys who I was pretty sure were the year above us. I'd seen them on occasion in the dining hall, and we'd bumped into one another at the library, I was almost certain. The taller of the two had inky black hair and skin a shade or two darker than my own. The other boy was much shorter, with pale, almost translucent-looking skin and hair so blond it might have been considered white.

"This is Corban and Blake," Callaway said, and the boys nodded to each of us. "These two scored high in compatibility during a sim test, just like the two of you. And," he said, turning to the other pair, "this is Tess and Eliana. These two were tested for compatibility because they were first cousins." The girls stepped forward, smiles on their faces. Both of them had wavy red hair that was pulled back into a ponytail, but their similarities stopped there. Tess was heavier set, with broad shoulders and bright green eyes, where her cousin Eliana was taller by a good three inches, her face a study of angles that accentuated hazel eyes. They had to be sixth years, I thought, trying to place them and feeling a tug of embarrassment when I couldn't. Considering how small the class sizes were at the Academy, I should know everyone. But, to be honest, learning everyone's names seemed like a waste of time when I could be learning about the nitty-gritty details of George Washington's role as our nation's first spymaster.

"You will have an opportunity to meet Sam and Serina a little later," Callaway said with a grin at all of us, as though we'd all just performed some sort of impressive trick. I shifted nervously as I took in the four faces staring back at us with a friendly, expectant look I wasn't quite sure what to do with.

Suddenly I felt Regan's sharp elbow digging into my ribs for a second time, and I glanced over to see her smiling cheerfully back at our new classmates. I forced what I hoped was a friendly smile onto my own face, but it felt stiff and awkward so I stopped.

"And this," Callaway said, motioning to the large room, "is where all of our training takes place." He snapped his fingers and two men wearing the Academy staff uniform came forward to take our bags. They disappeared with them down the far corridor and Callaway clapped his hands. "Now we should begin our first simulation of the day. We are already running a bit behind because of our newest recruits. So, no time to waste!"

I jumped in surprise. I'm not sure what I'd expected, but I hadn't thought we'd start training, let alone a simulation, within the first five minutes of walking into the place. I'd obviously thought wrong.

"But we haven't prepped for a simulation," I said just loud enough so Regan could hear me.

"That doesn't seem to matter," she said as Callaway ushered us over to the part of the room that had ten simulation chairs set up. Unlike the chairs at the Academy, which were always in a room all by themselves, these chairs were set up in pairs with one joint recap screen directly in front of the set. Each partner group quickly sat down, buckled themselves in, and began attaching their probes to their foreheads, arms, and legs. Not wanting to be left behind, I hurried forward and jumped into the open set of chairs on the far right. I was halfway through attaching my probes when I realized that Regan had jumped into one of the chairs in the empty set on the left. The other kids smiled, some even laughing outright when they noticed, and I felt a hot wave of embarrassment wash over me for the second time in five minutes. The giggles alerted Regan, and she looked up in surprise.

Spotting me across the way, she groaned.

"Get over here," she said through gritted teeth.

"I'm practically done getting set up," I said. "You come over here." Instead of arguing back, Regan straight-up ignored me and continued attaching her simulation probes. I sat in my chair for another second, fuming, before deciding that it wasn't worth the battle on our first day here.

"Way to make us look like morons," I muttered under my breath as I took the empty seat next to hers.

"Not my fault you got in the wrong chair," Regan said. Before I could respond, Callaway was standing in front of the simulation chairs.

"Ready?" he asked, and I shot my hand into the air.

"Yes, Elliot?" he said, and I almost jumped at the use of my first name. At the Academy I was always Cadet Mason. Here I was Elliot. It was going to take some getting used to.

Noticing my expression, Callaway flashed what I was beginning to think of as his signature smile. "We do things a little differently here. Our staff and student group in the mountain is so small that the formality of the Academy felt out of place, so we have all relaxed a bit."

"Nice," Regan said, and I fought the urge to roll my eyes. I never rolled my eyes in front of professors. I was respectful and followed the rules and protocols to a fault. It was part of my identity, and I felt an uncomfortable tug at Callaway's words.

"Cadet Fitz and I haven't had time to study for this simulation," I said, shoving the feeling aside. The other kids laughed like I'd told some kind of a joke, and I felt my face burn red.

"No one has prepared for this simulation," Callaway said. "The partner teams never prepare specifically for simulations. This is the difference in our training from the normal Academy. At the Academy you are given weeks and months of study of a particular historical event before being sent into a simulation. Here we do a general study on all of history, and you will never know which one you are being tested on. That is the magic and the importance of this specialized program. We foresee you as the Glitchers who will be sent in, in case of an emergency, to salvage a Glitch gone wrong, or to save a historical event from an unforeseen sabotage by Mayhem. Sam and Serina have excelled at this far beyond our expectations. Our hope is that you will develop the skills to think on your feet."

My face must have shown my utter shock at this pronouncement because Callaway chuckled. "Don't look so alarmed."

"So, it's kind of like a level test?" Regan said.

"Exactly," Callaway said. "You'll get the hang of it soon enough. Ready, everyone?" he called. The other two partner groups held up simultaneous thumbs-up. Regan was faster than me on the draw and her elbow cracked me in the head on the way up.

"This is so cool," she whispered as Callaway turned his back to us to work on the huge bank of simulation equipment. "We don't have to study!"

"He didn't say that. He just said we wouldn't have time before the simulation to do it," I whispered back, noting that the other partner groups were murmuring hurriedly to their partners as well. I strained my ears to see what they were talking about, but the low hum of the surrounding equipment drowned it all out. I glanced back at Regan to discover her grinning like an idiot. "And this is *not* exciting," I said. "This is terrifying."

Regan rolled her eyes. "The king of preparation can't prepare. I bet that is terrifying for you. Loosen up."

I gritted my teeth and looked straight ahead at the ominously black recap screen that would show us what an absolute disaster this was going to be in a few short minutes, because there was no way this was going to go well. Regan and I were not cut out to be a team. I was really picking up steam in this freak-out, imagining all the things that could go wrong if I didn't know every detail about the historical event, when Callaway held up his hand to begin the countdown.

Five.

Four.

Three.

Two.

One.

Everything went black and our first official partner mission had begun.

CHAPTER EIGHTEEN

REGAN

I opened my eyes to a war. At least, I was pretty sure this was a war. The sound of gunfire was deafening, and the air was so thick with a dirty gray smoke that I couldn't see more than a few feet in any direction. The sharp smell of gunpowder immediately made my lungs tighten. What was going on? This was *not* protocol. We should have appeared somewhere off to the side of this battle, not in its very heart.

Suddenly someone grabbed my arm and yanked me to the ground so hard I felt my shoulder pop painfully in protest. Before I could put together what was happening, a hand was on the back of my head, shoving my face directly into the soupy mud just as something exploded behind us. I'd forgotten about Elliot.

I yanked my head out of the mud and wiped furiously at my face as I spat out the mucky mouthful I'd almost inhaled. When I could finally look over at Elliot, I discovered that he was just as mud spattered as me, although his face was a whole lot cleaner.

"Where are we?" I yelled over the thunder of gunfire.

"How in the world would I know that?" he called back. He had a point. Another explosion went off, and I hurriedly surveyed our surroundings for somewhere safe to regroup. A little behind us and to the left was a thick line of trees, and I grabbed Elliot by the back of his shirt and hauled him toward them. They were farther away than they looked, though, and we were both huffing and puffing hard when we finally made it.

I let go of Elliot, who I'd held on to more for my own benefit than for his, and put my hands on my knees so I could hack up a mud-caked lung.

Elliot recovered faster than me and walked back to the edge of the trees to peer out at the chaos. I glanced down at myself and noted that I was wearing the same dark blue-gray jacket and coat as Elliot, although with the amount of mud we were covered in it was kind of hard to tell.

"American Revolution?" I guessed, trying to get a look at the back of the jacket.

"No," Elliot said shortly, and I bent over to look at the boots I had on.

"Obviously not Pearl Harbor," I said.

Elliot snorted and turned back to me. "Does this look like Hawaii to you?"

"I *said* obviously not," I said. "Is it World War One?" He ignored me, his dark eyes taking in the chaos that was swirling out in the open. "World War Two?" I said.

"Civil War," he said, turning back to me. "We're Union soldiers."

I peered over his shoulder at the battle that was spread across fields and hills as far as my eyes could see. Now that I knew what I was looking at, it didn't take long to notice that the gray uniforms seemed to far outnumber the blue. "Then why does it look like we're losing?"

"Because we are," Elliot said, jerking his finger behind him. "I'd bet anything that the town down there is Gettysburg, Pennsylvania. This is the battle that decides who wins the Civil War. If the Confederates take the high ground"—he pointed to the hill and its makeshift stone wall—"then they win the war."

"You're really smart," I said, and it wasn't a question or an insult. It was just a fact.

"Yes," Elliot said simply. "But how in the world are we supposed to spot a Butterfly in this mess?"

I bit my lip as I looked at the makeshift rock wall the Union soldiers had erected at the top of the hill. They huddled behind it, every now and then standing to battle back a rush of Confederates as they charged up the hill at them.

"So a Butterfly," I said, thinking out loud, "might be here to make sure they win?"

"That's my guess," Elliot said. "Someone is going to try to help the Confederates take the hill."

"Well, we aren't going to stop them hiding here," I said. "Come on."

"What do you mean, come on?" Elliot asked, hurrying after me as I wove through the trees, all the time angling so we'd be behind that stone wall when we made it to the top of the hill.

"Keep up," I said, breaking into a run.

"But we don't have a plan," Elliot yelled.

"We do have a plan," I called back. "It's called winging it." I heard Elliot mutter something rude about people who didn't make plans, and I smiled despite the chaos going on around us. We made it to the top of the hill, stopped only momentarily by two Union guards stationed in the trees to prevent anyone sneaking up from behind. Thankfully our mud-covered uniforms were identification enough, and we were waved through just as the cry went out that a third charge was coming up the hill.

"Get down," Elliot said, and we dived behind the nearest wall, bullets zinging overhead. The soldiers around us all stood up to confront the Confederates as they charged up the hill. I glanced to my right and left at the exhausted soldiers, most of whom were wounded and bleeding as they rose to fend off their enemies. These men didn't look like they could hold off a charge of bunnies, let alone a group of rampaging soldiers. I wished that we could help them, that I could stand up and fight shoulder to shoulder with the men who stood for freedom, but, of course, I couldn't.

Elliot must have been thinking the same thing, because I saw his hands ball into fists as he watched men fall around us. Gritting my teeth, I willed myself to focus. I was here for one thing, and one thing only. I began looking from face to face, skipping over the ones that were obviously wounded beyond hope. Those men were not my Butterfly. Grabbing Elliot's hand, I began a painstakingly slow creep down the line of soldiers. We crawled through dirt and blood and who knew what else, each of us taking care not to get in anyone's way. I didn't know a lot about the Battle of Gettysburg, but I did know that accidentally getting a soldier killed who was supposed to survive or saving a soldier who wasn't supposed to be saved could alter the future irreparably. We made our way down the battle line, but it was slow going, and at times the gunfire was so loud and so constant it felt like my brain was going to implode.

"Here comes the fourth charge," someone called, and what was left of the men behind the wall staggered to their feet.

"They won't withstand a fourth charge," I said, and I was almost right. The Union soldiers were outnumbered, and within moments the Confederates were close enough that the men gave up on their guns and clubbed at one another with bloody fists and bayonets. It was impossible to stay out of the fray, and I gasped as someone's foot connected hard with my ribs. Elliot yanked me sideways before I could accidentally trip anyone, and we huddled next to what was left of the stone wall as things went from bad to worse. I screamed as one of the men took a gunshot directly to his stomach and fell backward. He lay in front of us for a moment, and I felt my own stomach roll. But before I could throw up, the man blinked and rolled over; glancing down, he removed a smashed bullet from the front of his metal belt buckle, discarded it, and quickly rejoined the fight.

"That's unbelievable," I said, turning to see Elliot's reaction, but instead of looking amazed, his eyes were narrowed as he watched the man throw a punch. I wanted to ask Elliot why he was so worried about the miracle man, but we had to jump apart a second later to avoid getting trampled.

The fourth charge went on for what felt like for-ever, and it was impossible to tell who was winning. I thought for a second that this was it, that the Con-federates had finally succeeded when they retreated back down the hill. As the Union soldiers attempted to regroup, I ventured up to my knees to peer over the wall and watched as Confederate reinforcements arrived.

I ducked back down, my heart in my throat as I took in the mess that was the remains of the Union army in front of me. "These men can't win," I said as Elliot scrabbled over to join me. "There's no way." To my right, one of the soldiers, the miracle man, was listening intently to another soldier, who was inform-ing him that they were down to one or two rounds per man. I looked over at Elliot, eyebrow raised.

"Rounds?" I asked. "That sounds like a lot. Why does the miracle man look so worried?"

"The miracle man?" Elliot asked, then shrugged. "I guess that's as good a name as any. I should know who that guy is. I remember reading somewhere about a colonel who got shot in the belt buckle. He's impor-tant. I know that much."

"Rounds?" I prompted again.

Elliot shook his head. "He means everyone only has one or two shots left. That's not enough."

"Especially since reinforcements just arrived," I said, jabbing my thumb behind me. The entire situation looked hopeless, which made no sense since I knew the Confederates didn't win this battle. I turned back to watch the miracle man as he surveyed his bedraggled troops, his young face pinched with worry. Because I was looking at him, I saw the Butterfly. A Confederate soldier, who I'd assumed was dead, had just rolled over, a revolver already in his hand as he took aim at the man who'd already cheated death once. I lunged to my feet and ran, even though I knew that I'd never make it to the Butterfly in time. Luckily, I didn't have to. The miracle man was still staring over the wall, lost in thought, when I shoved him hard from behind. We both fell forward as a bullet zinged past our heads, missing us by mere inches. I hit the dirt beside him and rolled, fully expecting a second shot. But a second shot never came. Looking up, I saw Elliot wrestling the Butterfly's arms behind his back, and then everything went black.

CHAPTER NINETEEN

ELLIOT

I opened my eyes and immediately looked over to see the same goofy grin on Regan's face that was on my own. We'd been thrown into a completely unknown simulation, and we'd managed to capture the Butterfly. Granted, it wasn't the cleanest capture. Regan had literally tackled that guy, but still. Not bad, all things considered. That's when I noticed that every other partner group was watching us, and my heart sank. Glancing up, I saw frozen images on all three monitors showing the same Butterfly in various degrees of capture. We'd finished last.

"Not bad," Callaway said, interrupting my thoughts. "Considering this was your first experience working together, I would say it went very well, actually." Turning back to the rest of the students, he spread out his hands in invitation. "Now, who can tell me the significance of this historical event?" Four hands shot in the air, and I heard Regan mutter something about show-offs under her breath. I shifted uncomfortably. I should have had my hand in the air, but uncertainty kept them both balled into fists on my lap.

I frowned as Callaway pointed at one of the red-headed cousins. "Who is that?" I whispered to Regan.

"Tess," she said. "I think."

"The Butterfly's target was Colonel Chamberlain. He was a thirty-four-year-old teacher who changed the outcome of the Civil War by helping win the Battle of Gettysburg," said the girl who was probably Tess.

"Very good," Callaway said. "Anything else to add?"

Her cousin waved her hand in the air and Callaway nodded at her. "Yes, Eliana?"

"Had the Butterfly succeeded and killed Chamberlain, he wouldn't have led the charge down the hill that tricked the Confederates into surrendering," said Eliana.

"That guy led a charge?" Regan whispered in my ear. "Was he crazy? He had no ammunition and almost no men left."

I shrugged and flapped a hand at her to be quiet.

"Correct," Callaway said. "Without Chamberlain's

bold move to charge, an event you all didn't have the opportunity to see since all three groups managed to apprehend the Butterfly, the South would have won the war, and slavery would have continued for years to come."

"So the United States would have been divided into two countries?" Regan asked, and Callaway raised an eyebrow at her until she sighed and raised her hand.

"Yes, Regan?" he said, and Regan repeated her question.

"No," Callaway said. "By our calculations, the United States would have divided up into multiple territories, similar to Europe today. Can anyone tell me why that would have been disastrous?" Again, everyone's hand shot into the air except for Regan's and mine. While she sat there, seemingly oblivious to how embarrassing that was, I hunched down in my seat. First day or no first day, we looked like the partner team of clueless and buffle-brain.

Callaway called on Corban, and I sat forward to listen.

"Because if the United States didn't exist as one united nation, there wouldn't have been a country big enough to stop Hitler during World War Two."

"That is correct," said Callaway. "Now, this is all speculation and educated guesses, but it is safe to say that Colonel Chamberlain, from his one decision to charge instead of retreat, changed the course of history."

"Can you imagine if he'd decided not to wear his belt that morning?" Regan murmured.

"What?" I said.

"Think about it," she said. "He survived a direct hit to the stomach because the bullet hit his belt buckle. What if he hadn't worn his belt? Then everything Professor Callaway just said would have potentially happened. Isn't it crazy to think that one little thing, like deciding to wear a belt, can change the course of history?"

I nodded, but instead of a belt buckle, I was thinking about a very innocent-looking letter that I'd picked up that had altered the trajectory of my own life. Regan must have been thinking something similar because I saw her bite her lip worriedly. Callaway talked for a while longer, and then hit the play button so we could watch our recap and repercussion track. The screen in front of us lit up, but instead of one recap at a time, all three were on the screen. Watching my classmates react to being thrust into the middle of an active battle reminded me of something, and I raised my hand.

Callaway paused all the screens with the press of one button on his tablet and looked up, eyebrows raised expectantly.

"Yes?" he asked.

"Is this something different about the L and C program too?" I asked, pointing at the screen where Regan and I had been paused mid-dive into the mud.

"Elaborate," Callaway said, and I shifted uncomfortably.

"Well," I said, "entering a simulation in danger."

"That's correct," came a low male voice from almost directly behind me, and I about jumped out of my skin as I whirled to see a tall blond boy striding down the aisle between the simulation chairs. He was probably around eighteen, but the most striking thing about him was that he was dripping wet. His white button-up shirt was plastered to his broad shoulders and his boots made a loud squelching noise as he walked. I was so busy gaping at him that I almost didn't notice the equally soaked blond girl directly behind him until she'd walked past us in a soggy ball gown.

"Ah!" Callaway said. "Sam. Serina. So good of you to join us, although you could have changed first."

"I wanted to change, but somebody was in an all fire hurry to look at the new recruits," Serina said, pushing a dripping blond lock of hair out of her eyes to glare at Sam. I looked back and forth between them. Same golden hair. Same blue-green eyes. Same high cheekbones. They were either twins, or just freakishly similar.

"There they are," Callaway said, gesturing toward

Regan and me. "Have your look."

Serina and Sam turned toward us, as did everyone else in the room. This had to be what a fish in a tank felt like, I thought.

"Well, this isn't awkward at all," Regan said, breaking the silence. The tension I'd been feeling eased as everyone chuckled. Sam, however, didn't smile. He was still studying us like we had words written across our foreheads, and I found myself rubbing mine before I even realized I was doing it.

"They look young," Sam finally said, turning his attention back to Callaway.

"They are young," Callaway agreed with a chuckle. "You are young too, Sam. Don't forget that." He turned his attention back to us. "Sam and Serina were our first-ever partner pair and coincidentally the first set of twins to both test positive for the Glitch gene. I discovered them doing simulation training together just for fun and realized that we might have something there. It's where the idea for this program originated."

Serina chose that moment to pick up the hem of her dress and wring it out on the floor. Noticing my gaze, she shrugged apologetically. "*Titanic* mission," she said. "We weren't supposed to end up in the water, but somebody got a little overexcited when he spotted the Butterfly cutting the line to one of the life rafts."

Her brother sidestepped the puddle she'd just made on the floor, giving her a disapproving look before turning his attention back to us.

"So, these two really showed compatibility?" he said in a way that made it clear that he found that highly unlikely. It was then that I realized we were literally leaning away from one another, sitting as far from one another as the simulation chairs would allow.

"This is Cadet Regan Fitz and Cadet Elliot Mason, and since you started answering Elliot's question, maybe you'd like to finish it as well?" Callaway said with a jerk of his head toward the simulation screens.

"Right," Sam said, crossing his arms over his chest as he turned to us. "The Mayhem has gotten more and more unpredictable, sometimes launching attacks with the intention of transforming history in less than a minute or two. That means we've had to adjust our strategy. Unlike a normal Glitcher, we don't have the luxury of time or preparation." My face must have reflected the confusion that I felt, because Serina rolled her eyes at her brother and smiled at us.

"Think of it this way," she said. "If a traditional Glitcher is a doctor, or a surgeon even, going into historical events with ample preparation to operate and remove the Butterfly with perfectly executed precision, then the L and C program is the equivalent of a first responder. We are training you to be thrust into situations where thinking on your feet is not only imperative, but life or death."

"That's awesome," Regan said. I wanted to tell her that there was nothing awesome about this, but Callaway had restarted the recap screens, and we all watched each other's recaps in silence. Sam, I noted, never took his eyes off ours, which was unfortunate since it was by far the sloppiest of the lot. While the other partners worked together like a seamless team, Regan and I bumbled along like we'd never done a simulation before in our lives. The whole experience made my skin crawl, and I flashed back to Regan talking about how uncomfortable watching recaps made her feel. I'd thought she was crazy. I didn't think that anymore.

Finally, the recaps ended, and we were dismissed. I sat back, waiting for the techs to come out to unhook us from the equipment, but after a few seconds, I realized that was different here too. In front of us, Corban and Blake were already unhooked, while Eliana and Tess finished taking off the last of their probes.

"Well, that's different," Regan muttered as she started pulling off her own probes and sticking them back on the sensor plate in front of us.

"I think a lot of things here are going to be different,"

I said as I hurried to follow suit. Callaway appeared at our side as we unhooked the last of the sensors and handed us each a piece of paper with a neatly printed schedule on it.

"This seems kind of pointless since our group is so small that everyone sticks together," he said. "But it's always nice to know where you're going next. You'll find all the details about the order of our day here, and as you probably already figured out, you two will be doing all of your classes together. Studying together, practicing together, training together, eating together, you get the idea."

I glanced down at the schedule. The day was going to go very much like a day at the Academy, with combat training, classes on history, costuming, and disguise, a class that appeared to be similar to the nuance and observation class, and so on. The only difference was that I was going to be doing all of this tethered to Regan.

As I followed her out of the simulation section, I thought again of Colonel Chamberlain. If one man could change history so completely, then the least I could do was try to keep that history intact. To do that, I was going to have to start getting along with Regan Fitz.

CHAPTER TWENTY

REGAN

I loved everything about the Lewis and Clark program. I loved the simulation setup that didn't require months of study. I loved the small classes where I was just Regan, not Cadet Fitz. I loved the fact that I was inside a mountain. I was so giddy about it all that I even felt a burst of affection for Elliot. This change was going to be good. I could just feel it.

I was still riding that wave of positivity when the last class of the day ended and we were dismissed to our new dorms for the night. I sighed as I watched Elliot disappear through the doorway that led to the boys' dormitory, making a mental note to tell him that it was easier to make friends when your face didn't look like you'd been sucking on a lemon.

"He pretty much hates you, doesn't he?" came a voice at my elbow, and I jumped and turned to see Serina standing next to me. She was dry now, her blond hair twisted up into a bun on top of her head. I'd been surprised to learn that she and Sam were permanent residents of the mountain and would continue training alongside us when they weren't being sent on missions.

"*Hate* seems like a strong word," I said. Serina waited for me to go on, and I shrugged. "I'm not saying it's not accurate. It's just strong."

She nodded and cocked her head to the side with a smile. "Welcome to the program. As you saw today, there isn't a lot of time for chitchat or introductions."

"I caught that," I said, thinking of the crammed day I'd just had. As though thinking about it made it real, I suddenly felt the bone-deep exhaustion of the day and yawned. Serina smiled and opened the door to the girls' dorm so I could walk through.

I was expecting something similar to the dorms back at the Academy, small no-nonsense rooms equipped with a bed, dresser, and desk, but these couldn't be more different. The first thing I noticed were the bunks on the wall right across from the door. There were ten total, little cubbies carved out of the very rock of the mountain to make bunk beds of sorts. Each bunk had a curtain to give its occupant some sense of privacy. Only three of the ten available bunks were occupied with actual bedding, though. The rest were just rectangular cutouts in the wall with bare mattresses.

"Do I get to pick?" I asked Serina, walking over to get a better look.

"Nope," she said. "You get the bunk where they chuck your stuff." I took a step back and noticed that my bag had indeed been chucked into one of the top bunks. Using the notches carved into the stone between each bunk, I climbed up and into what was apparently my new bed for the foreseeable future. To be honest, I was a little leery of the whole setup. For one thing, I'd never slept in a twin-sized bed before, and the thought of falling out and dropping the six feet to the stone floor didn't seem all that appealing. Once I actually got in there, though, it was deeper than I'd expected. Carved into the back wall of the bunk was a set of shelves for books or personal items and even an antique-looking brass light that reminded me of something you'd see in a mine or a ship. I gave its knob a twist, and it came to life, bathing the cubby in a warm yellow glow.

"Not bad, right?" came a voice, and I jumped and cracked my head hard on the stone ceiling. I bit my tongue to keep from saying something I shouldn't and turned to see Serina watching me, her arms propped lazily on the mattress as she stood on the bunk below mine.

"Not bad at all," I said, grimacing as I rubbed at my throbbing head. "The low ceilings may take some getting used to, though."

"Tall girl problem," she said. "You'll get used to it."

She grabbed something from the end of the bed and tossed it to me, and I discovered that they were sheets. As she helped me tug them over the corners of the mattress, I shot her a look out of the corner of my eye. "I'm kind of surprised you sleep in here with us," I said.

"It's another quirk about the mountain," she said as she adjusted the blanket on the end of the bed. "The Academy keeps everyone so divided they barely know one another, but we work more like a team here. That's one of the reasons that Sam is a little intense about every new recruit. We've proven that partner Glitching can be successful, but one bad screwup and the entire program could be dissolved."

"He's more than a little intense," I said.

She shrugged. "We have our entire careers invested in the Lewis and Clark program being a success. He'll calm down once he gets used to you guys. He was the same way when Tess and Eliana got here a few months ago."

"Well," I said thinking of Elliot and Sam in the dorm across the hall, "I'm glad you are a tad more chill."

Serina laughed. "I like the company. When it was just me and Sam it got really lonely." She handed me the rest of my books and belongings, and I quickly stacked them on the shelf.

"Now what?" I asked once that was accomplished.

"Now you grab a shower and go to bed so we can do it all over again tomorrow," Serina said. I noticed that Tess and Eliana had already disappeared through the door to the bathroom, and I was thankful for Serina, who patiently showed me where to find towels and shampoo and everything else that had always been provided for me without question or hassle at home. As I crawled into my scratchy sheets later that night, I smiled. Scratchy sheets or no scratchy sheets, this was exactly the fresh start I'd been hoping for, and for a moment I forgot about the Cocoon and the ominous shadow it had cast over everything. I forgot about the seemingly random bullet points that seemed to be marching Elliot and me toward something huge, and I fell asleep excited to see what tomorrow would bring.

What it brought was a grumpy Elliot. Which shouldn't have been a huge surprise, but it was still a bummer to sit down to my first breakfast at the mountain to his scowling face.

"Good morning," I chirped with a wide smile as I

set my tray of eggs and toast down next to his.

"Debatable," he said, stabbing another piece of egg onto his fork. I sighed as I dug into my own breakfast. Different location, same old Elliot. Since my dining partner left a lot to be desired, I glanced around the room. The other kids in the program were still in line to get their breakfasts, and behind us, Callaway was sitting at a small table with some of the other mountain faculty. Compared to the expansive staff of the Academy, the mountain was run and maintained by just a small group of professors, a handful of security officers, a few tech specialists, a cook, and a housekeeper. Apparently, they all ate together. It was a sharp contrast to what I'd grown up watching. Callaway sat side by side with the techs and the cook as their equal and friend. Everyone knew he was in charge, but he was also genuinely liked by everyone at that table. Although, as I listened to his big booming laugh fill the cavernous room, it wasn't hard to see why.

Looking back over at Elliot, I noticed that someone had dropped off the day's schedule, and he was frowning down at it like it had just personally insulted him.

"You know if you're not careful your face is going to freeze like that," I said.

"Like what?" he asked.

"Like you just ate something rotten," I said.

"It's not the same," he said, throwing the schedule down in disgust.

"What do you mean?" I asked.

"What I mean is that apparently our schedule is different every day. How in the world are you supposed to plan for that?"

"Um, like this?" I said, grabbing the schedule so I could read it. It was indeed different from the day before, and I was happy to see that the mountain's version of my favorite Sherlock class, officially called Observation and Nuance, was that afternoon.

"Did you notice it yet?" he asked as I wrinkled my nose at the double study block on Pearl Harbor scheduled first thing that morning.

"Notice what?" I asked. Reaching over, I plucked his toast off his plate and took a bite.

"Stop that," he said, snatching it back. He ripped off the piece I'd bitten and took a bite of the remaining toast. "The paper," he said, so quietly I almost didn't catch it.

"We are the only ones at the table," I pointed out. "You don't really need to whisper."

Elliot grabbed the schedule, crumpled it up, and dropped it into my cup of water. Before I could protest, the entire wad dissolved. My heart gave a startled lurch, and the bite of toast I'd stolen stuck in my throat. I stared at my water for another second before reaching over to take a swig of Elliot's.

"Hey," he protested.

"Sorry," I said, "but you polluted mine. What was I supposed to do?"

"Have some manners," he grumbled. "For someone raised with a silver spoon in her mouth you sure don't act like it."

"Thank you," I said, peering inside the glass even though I knew that paper was long gone. "What do you think that means?" I asked.

Elliot shrugged. "No idea. But the mystery of where our future selves get the weird disappearing paper is solved."

"What's going on?" Tess said, setting her tray down and sliding in next to me. Elliot and I both jumped guiltily, and she paused mid-bite to raise a questioning eyebrow at us.

"Nothing," I said, a hair too quickly.

"We just discovered that the schedule dissolves in water," Elliot said. "It's kind of bizarre."

"Oh, that," Tess said, tossing her red hair behind her shoulder. "Most of the products we use here in the mountain dissolve in water. That way we have very little waste to deal with."

"Smart," Elliot said, turning his attention back to his eggs.

"So, before you dissolved the schedule, what did it say?" she asked. The rest of our new classmates sat down, and Elliot began to recite the schedule with perfect accuracy. As I watched him, I couldn't help but be a little impressed. Not that I'd ever tell him that. Everyone groaned at the mention of the double block of studying, and I smiled, enjoying the camaraderie.

"You didn't do half bad on your first partner sim," Corban said around a mouthful of eggs.

"He's only saying that because he and Blake bombed their first practice sim so badly that Callaway almost sent them back to the Academy," Tess said with an exaggerated wink at her cousin Eliana.

"Don't listen to a word Tess says," Blake said, leaning forward conspiratorially. "Rumor has it that she landed face-first in a cow pie on her first sim test. BLAM! Face full of cow poop."

Tess sniffed and took a bite of her toast. "It was horse poop," she said.

"Right," Blake said. "Because that's so much better."

"The point is," said Corban with a smile, "we all have to start somewhere, and all things considered, you two did great."

"So, do you actually like it here?" Elliot said. "Or are you just making the best of things?"

Corban shrugged. "It's fine," he said. "The food at the Academy was a bit better, but the mountain's cool."

"And you don't hate being stuck with a partner," Elliot said, making it very clear in his tone that he thought Corban was delusional.

"I'm right here," I said, elbowing him in the ribs.

"Like I could forget," Elliot muttered, and Corban laughed.

"You two are going to be fun to watch," he said.

"Fun like a train wreck," Elliot said, and Blake snorted orange juice out of his nose all over Corban's shoulder.

The conversation turned into a debate about crunchy versus soggy bacon, but I was too preoccupied with replaying that paper dissolving right in front of my eyes to contribute. Did that mean that the future Elliot and Regan were still in the mountain? It must. The twinge of fear that always came from thinking about that letter curled up inside my stomach like a snake waiting to strike.

"Come on," Elliot said a few minutes later, jarring me from my own thoughts as he stood up.

"What?" I asked, but a second later I saw that we were the last ones at the table and everyone else was emptying their trays and heading toward the far side of the atrium.

"Move it," Elliot said. "I'm not going to be late." I

raised an eyebrow at him, and he narrowed his eyes. "If you're late, I'm pretty sure that means I'm late too. Right, partner?"

"Quick question," I said as we hurried across the main atrium toward the library section.

"What's that?"

"Are you *always* going to say the word *partner* like it tastes bad?"

Elliot sighed, and to my surprise he turned to me, a grim look of determination on his face. "No," he said. "I'm trying to be better."

I couldn't help myself; I snorted right in his face.

"I am!" he said with a grimace as he wiped the flecks of spit off his cheek. "But you don't make it very easy, you know."

"Right back at you," I said. "Although I didn't mean to spit on you. My bad."

He just rolled his eyes as we entered the library. The library took up one pie slice of the atrium, but it felt bigger than the other parts somehow. As I walked between the shelves, it was easy to imagine I was back in the palatial Academy library with its levels upon levels of books. That comparison stopped short when I discovered a fireplace crackling merrily at the back of the room. Overstuffed chairs were clustered around with a table between each. Tess and Eliana were already settled in one set each with a large volume open on their laps while Corban and Blake were busy scrolling tablets, ignoring the books sitting between them. Remembering what had happened last time, I waited to see which empty set of chairs Elliot would choose. He looked between the few remaining sets, his forehead scrunched in thought, before finally choosing the ones closest to the fire, and the farthest away from everyone else. I followed and grabbed the seat next to him. The chairs were surprisingly comfortable, a far cry from the hard wooden ones back at the Academy.

I'm not sure how long Elliot and I sat there, lost in our own thoughts as we waited for a professor to begin the class, before I realized that we were the only ones waiting. Finally, I leaned over and poked Eliana's arm. She looked up from the book she'd been reading, eyebrow cocked.

"When does the professor get here?" I whispered.

Tess looked up from her book and smiled at us. "There is no professor for a study block," she said. "We study with our partners."

"I was afraid it was something like that," Elliot grumbled, and I felt a heavy book land in my lap. Looking over, I saw that Corban and Blake were quietly talking as they pored over something on Corban's tablet. Tess and Eliana were already back in their own little world of studying. With a resigned sigh, I stared down at the book Elliot had handed me. It was called *All the Gallant Men: An American Sailor's Firsthand Account of Pearl Harbor* by Donald Stratton. A quick glance at Elliot revealed his nose buried in the exact same book.

"Read the first three chapters and then we can quiz each other," he said, his eyes never leaving the page. Feeling resigned, I opened it up. The words in the book were tiny, and they marched across the page like overly industrious ants. Firsthand accounts of history were the bread and butter of the Glitching world, and I was lucky this one wasn't in someone's scrawling handwriting or in a crusty old journal that smelled like mouse poop. Still, I stared at those little ant words uncomprehendingly for a while before shutting the book and grabbing the tablet perched on the table beside me. A quick search in the database pulled up the exact same book, and I tabbed through to the first page, making sure the words were enlarged as much as possible. Elliot, meanwhile, flipped through page after page of the firsthand account, ignoring me completely. I tried to read again and made some progress this time. Slow progress, but progress all the same. The words tried to jumble themselves up and reorder themselves, but I willed them back into place and read on. The firsthand account was a good one, and I was just getting into it when Elliot tapped me on the shoulder.

"Ready?" he asked.

"For what?" I asked, blinking at him as I resurfaced from the sailor's story.

"To quiz," he said, and I saw that the other partner pairs were doing just that. What were they? Reading ninjas?

"I'm not ready yet," I said. My face felt hot, and I knew I was blushing like an idiot.

"Why?" Elliot asked, all impatience and judgmental furrowed eyebrows. He could just put those eyebrows away, I thought grouchily as I looked back down at my screen. I was on page five. That was it. He stared holes into my head while I studiously ignored him, but he finally got the picture and went back to his own book with a sigh. A lifetime later I set the tablet down and tapped him on the shoulder.

"I'm ready," I said.

"Were you reading the book or writing a book?" he grumbled, but before I could say something back, he pulled out a notebook and started asking questions rapid fire.

"What was the exact time the first plane was spotted?" he said, looking up expectantly.

"In the morning," I replied.

"Exact time," he said.

"Early morning," I said.

"Are you serious right now?" he asked, setting down the notebook.

"Serious as the grave," I said. "Fine, Mr. Know-it-All, what time was it?"

"Seven fifty-five a.m.," he said flatly.

"Right." I nodded and glanced back down at the tablet in front of me, my brain scrambling for a question I could ask him. I'd prefer it to be something really hard so he got it wrong, but after firing back what I assumed was a real doozy at him and having him answer it with ease, I realized that maybe that was destined to be my role in this relationship. Which was just peachy.

The entire study session took a header after that, with Elliot getting more and more frustrated until I began to worry that he was going to chuck the book at my head. While normally frustrating Elliot was one of my favorite pastimes, today it just made me feel stupid. Right when I thought that I couldn't stand another minute of this torture, Callaway showed up, his characteristic smile on his face.

"Regan, if you'd come with me, please?" he said. I glanced over at Elliot, but he just threw up his hands in a *please take her away* sort of way that made me feel about two inches tall. Thankful for the escape, I put down my tablet and hurried to follow Callaway out of the library section. He led me quickly across the main atrium and down a hallway and into a tiny room I could only assume was his office. It was either that or a broom closet, I thought as I squeezed inside and into the tiny chair Callaway offered me. Without preamble, he pulled out a tablet, typed a few things in, and handed it to me. Before I could ask what was going on, my mom appeared on the screen.

CHAPTER TWENTY-ONE

ELLIOT

Regan didn't come back for the rest of the study session. Which was best for all involved since throttling your partner with your bare hands was probably frowned upon. I glowered over my book at the other partners as they cheerily talked through what they read and took turns quizzing one another. Tess and Eliana reminded me of bookends with their matching red hair and smiles, and even Corban and Blake seemed to go together somehow despite the fact that their appearances were as polar opposite as humanly possible. Why Regan? I wondered for the millionth time since picking up that letter. Every time I thought I'd put my annoyance with that girl behind me, something like this would happen and it would all come rushing back. Where in the world had Callaway taken her? If anyone needed more study time, it was Regan.

Just when I was good and boiling, the double study period ended. Nuance and Observation was next, but no one actually called it that, at least not back at the Academy, where it was always referred to as the Sherlock class. As I followed the other kids out of the library and across the atrium, I could see that they had tried to re-create the circular theatrical seating of the Academy on a smaller scale. A small platform rotated in the middle of the classroom with desks clustered around it in a circle.

"So what's your favorite century?" Eliana asked, coming to walk on one side of me while Tess commandeered the spot on my other side. I suddenly understood what the ham felt like on a ham sandwich, and I didn't like it.

"What?" I said taken off guard.

"Your favorite century," Eliana repeated. "You know, like mine is the early 1900s, but Tess really likes the 1600s."

"I don't know," I said. "I guess I've never thought about it."

"Really?" Tess said.

"Really," I said, but they didn't go away. They kept

me solidly between themselves as we walked across the atrium, insisting that I swing by the dining tables with them to snag an apple out of one of the bowls of fruit that had appeared there. I did, even though my insides were still too knotted with anger to be very hungry. Finally, they left me alone to go use the restroom before class, and I heaved an audible sigh of relief.

"They want to be your friends," Corban said, coming to stand in the same spot where Tess had been just moments before.

"I don't want them to be my friends," I said.

"You say that like you have a choice," Blake said.

I raised an eyebrow. "I don't?"

"Not if you want to make a go of it here," Corban said. "This place is too small to avoid people. Don't worry about it, though; the girls are cool. Tess is practically a genius, although she'd never tell you that, and Eliana is uncanny when it comes to getting the Chaos Cuffs on a Butterfly. She's so quick it's like watching a snake strike. Blam, snap, click and the Butterfly is standing there wondering what hit them. Of course, she's an absolute disaster at actually identifying Butterflies, but she's working on it. Regardless, she'll give you a lesson any time you want to." He clapped me a hair too hard on the back and together he and Blake walked over to Tess, who was chatting with one of the professors like they were old friends. This place just keeps getting weirder and weirder, I thought, turning back toward the Nuance and Observation classroom.

To my surprise, Serina and Sam were already in two of the seats, and I found my eyes drawn to them. It wasn't that I'd never been around active Glitchers before, it was just that I'd never been around ones so young. Seeing them made my future more tangible somehow, and I felt a shiver of excitement race up my spine. That excitement was doused a moment later when I remembered that my future was no longer just mine—it was forever tangled with Regan's.

Serina and Sam must have come straight from another mission because Sam was dressed head to toe in the gear of a soldier from World War I, and Serina was in a matching nurse's uniform. Both of them were liberally coated in mud and what was probably blood. I wrinkled my nose and chose the seat as far away from them as humanly possible. While I appreciated their commitment to furthering their education, the fact that they hadn't showered before joining the class grossed me out.

Everyone else took their seats and a moment later a man who I could only assume was Professor O'Reilly sauntered into the room. He was dressed in the uniform of a British soldier, his bright red jacket neat and pressed over tight-fitting pants and high black boots. Immediately, all eyes focused in. He walked casually around the perimeter of the circle, allowing everyone a closer look before stopping in the middle of the platform.

"Well?" he said. "Who spotted it?"

Five hands including mine shot into the air. He nodded his approval and pointed to Corban.

"What do you think?" he asked, holding his hands out as the platform carried him in a slow spin for the class.

"Is it your belt buckle, sir?" Corban asked, but from his tone I could tell this was a 100 percent shot in the dark.

Professor O'Reilly shook his head. "This belt buckle is authentic iron from a forge in seventeenth-century London. What about you, Tess, what do you think?" he said, looking to my right.

"Um," said Tess, "is your hat the wrong shape?"

"Wrong again," O'Reilly said, relishing the moment as he whipped off his black triangle hat. "This is authentic too, my dears. Any more guesses?" He was just turning to call on me when a loud bang behind us made everyone turn. Regan stood there, cringing down at the copy of *All the Gallant Men* she'd dropped upon her not-so-sneaky entrance.

"You must be Regan," Professor O'Reilly said. "Glad you could join us."

"Yes, sir," Regan said, stooping down to grab the book. I put my hand back in the air. I knew the answer to this.

But Professor O'Reilly ignored me as he watched Regan. I pushed my hand farther into the air. I *knew* the answer.

"Regan," O'Reilly said as she plunked heavily into the seat next to mine, her backpack giving me a good whack in the side of the head for good measure as she settled in.

"Yes, sir?" she asked, looking at him for the first time.

"Do you see it?" he prompted.

"Your buttons," she said as though the answer was automatic and obvious.

O'Reilly smiled. "What about my buttons?"

She narrowed her eyes at him, and I looked at his buttons for the first time too. I'd thought the discrepancy was something to do with his shoes. I silently crossed my fingers and wished for her to be wrong. Let it be the shoes.

"That one," she said, pointing to the second button down. "It's too perfect. Buttons during that time period wouldn't have looked quite so perfect."

"Well done!" O'Reilly said. "I'd heard you had an uncanny knack for this. You did not disappoint. Now, can you tell me what time period this jacket would have been produced in?"

Regan's face went pale, and I smiled smugly as my hand shot back into the air.

"Well?" O'Reilly prompted.

"I'm sorry, sir," Regan said, "but I don't know. Maybe sometime around the American Revolution?"

"It was the late eighteenth century," I said, the words falling out of my mouth without my permission. O'Reilly turned to me, an eyebrow raised in disapproval at my blurting disruption. But it was like word vomit, and I couldn't stop it now. "1775 was the start of the Revolutionary War, although the uniforms were probably made prior to that in 1774."

"Thank you, Elliot," said O'Reilly. "Next time, please wait your turn."

"Or maybe I'll just arrive late and expect special treatment," I muttered under my breath. Regan shot me a look out of the corner of my eye that let me know she'd heard me.

"Where were you?" I asked as O'Reilly called in another professor dressed head to toe in clothes straight from the 1970s.

"My mom called to check in," she said dismissively,

never taking her eyes off the new professor. I squinted at the garish green-striped bell-bottom pants and yellow knit top. Maybe her earrings were off? I'd forgotten how much I hated this class.

Around us our classmates were guessing, and I thought Serina had it when she pointed out that the professor's shoes were rhinestone-encrusted cowboy boots, but apparently that was on-trend for the seventies. Weird.

Beside me Regan raised her hand again, and I ground my teeth into my lip as she spotted the discrepancy in the professor's hairstyle.

"*That* you can remember?" I muttered as O'Reilly stepped back into the center of the platform to begin his lecture on '70s fashion.

Regan shrugged and turned her attention back to O'Reilly and his description of matching knitwear common to that time period. When the class finally ended, I shoved myself to my feet, my stomach snarling at the possibility of lunch. While everyone else walked toward the lunchroom with their partner, I hurried ahead to grab my lunch tray. I sat down at the same table we'd eaten breakfast at that morning, silently sulking over the fact that avoiding Regan was now physically impossible.

A moment later someone set a tray down next to

mine, and I turned, fully expecting to see Regan looking smug. Instead I saw the too-serious face of Sam.
He was still wearing the bloody uniform, and I tried to
scoot to the right without him noticing.

"Are you a jerk?" he said, and I almost choked on
the forkful of salad I'd just put in my mouth.

"What?" I said once I managed to stop coughing.

"A jerk," he repeated. "Are you a jerk?"

"No?" I said, but it sounded unconvincing even to
my own ears.

"Then stop acting like one," he said. "Because if you
don't learn how to work with your partner, you fail."

"And you think that seems fair?" I shot back, glad
I had an outlet for the anger that had been simmering
under the surface of my skin ever since that morning's
disastrous study session.

"Who in the world told you that life was fair?" he
asked, eyebrow raised. I opened my mouth and then
shut it again.

"Here's the deal," Sam went on. "The way I see it,
you get dealt a hand in life, and it's up to you to choose
how you play it. So, you can keep huffing and puffing
about the partner you got stuck with, or you can make
the best of it and become a phenomenal team. From
what I saw back there"—he jerked his head toward the
Sherlock class's platform—"Regan is pretty dang good."

"Shocking, you're already on Team Regan," I said. "That girl has been skating through life like everyone's favorite puppy. It figures the same thing would happen here."

"No," Sam said. "But I recognize talent when I see it. Is that your problem? Everyone likes her? No one likes you?"

"No one likes me?" I said. "Already?"

Sam shook his head. "I'm not saying that. What I am saying is that the gigantic chip you're carrying around on your shoulder is going to get in the way of you becoming everything you could be. You need to get out of your own way."

Before I could respond, Corban sat down, and Tess joined him a second later. I glanced behind them to see that Regan had apparently decided to forgo lunch to sit over in the simulation section by herself, the gigantic copy of *All the Gallant Men* open on her lap. And for the first time, I felt a stab of guilt for my behavior. She hadn't gotten angry when I wasn't spectacular during the Sherlock class. Meanwhile she'd been knocking it out of the park, a fact that I probably would have noticed if I hadn't been so distracted by my desire to see her fail. Which, I reminded myself, was just plain stupid, since if she went down, I went down too. We were on the *Titanic* together, and I was over here yelling "Aim for that iceberg!" And I'd called *her* dumb. No sooner had the words gone through my head than I wished they hadn't. I'd conveniently forgotten what I'd said to her back on the dock. Time for an apology.

With a sigh I shoved myself to my feet and grabbed my salad off my tray. After a quick pass of the lunch counter to grab a second salad, I made my way across the atrium to where Regan sat, her forehead scrunched in concentration as she read chapter two. My first reaction was to roll my eyes that she was only on chapter two, but remembering Sam's words, I shoved down my knee-jerk instinct and took a seat next to her.

"Here," I said, thrusting the salad into her hands.

She looked up in surprise and blinked at me. "What's this?" she asked.

This time I couldn't stop the eye roll. "What's it look like? It's food. Eat it. I don't want you all fuzzy-headed for simulation training this afternoon." She looked from the salad to me and back again, a wary look on her face.

"What?" I asked, making zero effort to hide my exasperation. "You think I spit on it?"

"Did you?" she asked.

"No!" I said, and it took everything in me not to let the old familiar anger fizz back to the surface. I took a deep breath and tried on a smile, which might have been a mistake because it made her look even more nervous. This was not going the way I'd pictured it. "It's a peace offering. You know, for before," I said, flapping a hand that I hoped encompassed twelve years of general rudeness and animosity. She still looked unconvinced, which, considering my peace offering was a lackluster salad with soggy croutons, was not all that surprising.

She studied me for a second longer and then took a bite of her salad. "I can't stop thinking about our schedule dissolving this morning," she said. "The last few days have been so busy that I almost forgot about that Cocoon."

"Shhhh," I said, glancing around, but no one was looking in our direction. "You can't be serious?" I said. My own brain had been gnawing on that letter like a dog with a bone ever since that afternoon at the Academy.

Regan snorted a laugh. "I know, unbelievable. But then that schedule dissolved, and it all came crashing back to me. As cool as this place is, and as excited as I am for a fresh start, it really isn't one, is it? I mean, if something terrible wasn't going to happen, we would never have found that letter in the first place."

"Right," I said, and for the first time I didn't have the desire to point out that being stuck with her as a partner *felt* like a terrible thing to me. Sam was right; pouting over my lot in life wasn't going to change anything. "Or," I said, "maybe we are here to prevent something terrible from happening. Maybe you and I become an awesome team and in five years we save some important event in history from a pack of Mayhem members."

"Maybe," Regan said, sounding unconvinced. "But the letter seemed more urgent than that. I mean, we've already hit two of the bullet points in the letter. It doesn't make sense that the other ones wouldn't matter for five years."

"The next one is the one about a window," I said, thinking out loud. "When the window breaks, grab me."

Regan wrinkled her forehead, and together we looked around the cavernous atrium of the mountain, where not one window was in sight.

"Well," I finally said, "I guess we just have to wait."

"I hate waiting," Regan said.

"Finally," I said, "something we can agree on."

Regan smirked, glancing back down at the book in her lap. "Do you think our simulation this afternoon is going to be on this?" she asked.

I shrugged. "I have no idea. Nothing is what I think it should be. I decided it's probably better if I keep my expectations low."

"Yeah, probably," she mumbled around a mouthful of salad as she turned her attention back to the open page in front of her. I watched her chew for a second, her eyes focused on the book, when something occurred to me.

"Is reading hard for you? Or do you just not like it?" I asked.

She glanced back up at me, her expression guarded. "Why?" she asked.

"Because," I said, pulling the book away from her. "Our study session was a disaster I don't want to repeat." She hesitated and I held up my hands. "No judgments. Promise. We're on the same team now."

She sighed. "Hard. Always has been hard. Always will be hard."

"Explain," I said.

She shrugged. "There's not much to explain. If my mom and my tutors hadn't been working with me every second of every day since birth, there is no way I'd have made it this far at the Academy. Studying is impossible for me. The words just won't stay in place, and my brain is apparently made of Swiss cheese." She took another bite of her salad as she pulled the book back off my lap.

I watched her try to study, my brain churning. I'd always loved to read, devouring book after book in the library in my free time. What did she mean by saying the words wouldn't stay in place? Words didn't move.

It was one of my favorite things about them. I thought back to all the extra tutoring she'd received over the years, a fact that I'd always been more than a little jealous of. I'd always assumed it was yet another perk of being the commander's kid and that she was just plain lazy and slacking off in classes. Before I could ask her any more, the bell rang, and we had to hurry to throw away our half-eaten salads before our afternoon of simulation training began. I ignored Sam's nod of approval as I sat down next to Regan five minutes later. Partially because that nod was obnoxious, but mostly because I was too busy trying to remind her of every important piece of information we may need about the morning of Pearl Harbor. Which, as it turned out, was completely pointless since the simulation ended up being on the launch of *Apollo 11*. Figures.

CHAPTER TWENTY-TWO

REGAN

The days at the mountain quickly developed their own rhythm, despite the ever-changing schedule that always put Elliot in a foul mood. But I was getting used to the foul moods, even learning to read them a bit. It was like he had his own grumpy language, and if you hung around long enough you could pick up a word here or there. Thankfully he hadn't directed all that grumpy at me recently. A fact I more than appreciated.

Even if my mom did insist on checking in every few days, it hadn't marred my fresh start at the mountain at all. If anything, I found her sporadic phone calls to be comforting. I hadn't realized that I'd miss her like I did, and having that one connection back to the Academy made me feel more grounded in this new space. The mountain definitely wasn't home yet, but it was beginning to feel more and more like one every day. I shifted in my bunk to a more comfortable position and tapped the screen of my tablet to wake it back up. It had gone dark while I sat thinking over things, and I only had a few more minutes before lights-out to study. The screen came to life, and I narrowed my eyes at the words as though if I just glared at them hard enough they'd behave and not jumble themselves up like spaghetti.

"Whatcha doing?" said a voice at my elbow, and I jumped so badly that my head cracked the stone ceiling of my bunk. I winced and rubbed it as I turned to look at Tess. Her red hair was piled haphazardly on top of her head, and she was sporting an impressive black eye from our combat training that day. It had been a particularly interesting lesson, since all of us girls had to learn how to take someone down while wearing a gigantic hoop skirt from the 1800s. Tess had momentarily forgotten about her skirt and attempted a roundhouse kick, which sent one of the steel bars used to support the huge bell-shaped skirt right into her eye. She didn't seem to mind, though, and she smiled at me as she peered over at my tablet.

"We only get an hour of free time a night," she said. "Why in the world would you want to spend it studying? Didn't you get enough of that today?"

"Oh, I did," I agreed, remembering how Elliot had tried over and over again to help me remember the important information about the Gettysburg Address with limited success. My eyes automatically flicked past Tess, looking for her counterpart, Eliana, but she was nowhere to be seen.

Tess noticed my glance and smiled. "She was hungry and decided to sneak out to grab something from the kitchen."

"We're allowed to do that?" I asked.

"No," she said. "But everyone does. The security here at night is, well . . ." She shrugged. "As far as we can tell there really isn't any. The professors all go to bed, and the only one you have to worry about is Callaway, and half the time he's raiding the kitchen for cookies and the worst thing he'll do is share with you."

"Really?" I asked, thinking about the nightly patrols at the Academy.

"Really," she said.

"I'll have to remember that next time I'm hungry," I said, wondering if Elliot knew about this yet. The lights flickered, signaling it was time for lights-out, and I made a mental note to tell Elliot about it at breakfast the next day.

But as it turned out, breakfast wasn't on the agenda for the day.

"Good morning," Elliot said the second I walked out of the dorm the next morning. I jumped in surprise, my brain not fully awake yet despite the shower I'd just taken.

"Geez," I said, putting a hand to the cold stone wall to steady myself. "Don't ever do that again."

"Sorry," he said, bouncing on the balls of his feet as he waited for me to get myself together.

"What's all this?" I asked, gesturing at the bouncing. Was he smiling? He was! And it wasn't one of his awkward smiles that always made him look like he was trying to keep a spider in his mouth by clenching his teeth together. It was a real smile. This was getting weirder and weirder.

"I have an idea," he said. "Come on." Without waiting for me to respond, he turned and jogged down the hall. I watched him go, debating whether I could get away with going back into my dorm and hiding in bed. Perky Elliot was just plain bizarre. I stood there a second longer before deciding that he'd probably find me anyway, so I ran after him.

The hallway quickly opened up to the atrium and I stopped, not sure which way he'd gone. A shrill whistle came from the left, and I looked over to see Elliot already sitting in one of the simulation chairs.

"What's going on?" I asked as I sat down.

"We are studying," he said as he quickly helped me attach the simulation probes to my arms and legs. "I have an idea, and Callaway said I could give it a go. You hate reading, right? The words move?"

"And?" I prompted.

"And I decided we should try out something new," he said. "The definition of insanity is doing the same thing over and over again and expecting different results, right? You've tried studying the normal way your whole life, and it has never worked. What do you have to lose by trying it my way?"

"Nothing," I said as my stomach grumbled. "I just wish you'd waited until after breakfast."

"Stop complaining," Elliot said, reaching over to stick the last probe onto my forehead. Apparently I still didn't look convinced, because he rolled his eyes. "Worst-case scenario, you can always activate your cuffs and leave," he said.

"Worst-case scenario," I repeated, wondering what he had up his sleeve. "You know," I said, "it's too bad we don't have team names, because that would have been a solid choice for us."

Elliot snorted as he hit the activation button and everything went black. A moment later I found myself on the deck of a huge ship.

"Where are we?" I asked, glancing around at

the immensity of the ship's deck. The place seemed deserted, sleepy even, which wasn't the usual environment a Butterfly liked to work in. This whole thing was making me feel off balance, but I felt the familiar Chaos Cuffs on my hip and calmed down. Elliot was right—worst-case scenario, I could just leave.

"Where do *you* think we are?" Elliot asked. "Actually, better yet, what time is it?"

With a sigh I decided to play along with whatever this was and looked around until I spotted a clock. "It's seven fifty-four," I said, and then I felt something in my brain click home like a key in a lock, and I turned to take in my surroundings with wide eyes. "Are we?" I asked, and then the clock I'd spotted mounted to the ship clicked to 7:55, and I turned as the buzz of low-flying airplanes hit my ears.

"This is Pearl Harbor," I breathed.

"Sure is," Elliot said with a grin. We both turned as a bomb hit a ship called the USS *West Virginia.*

"But the Butterfly," I yelled over the noise of the explosion.

Elliot shook his head. "There is no Butterfly. Welcome to our study block!" What a study block it was. I'd never done this before, gone into a simulation just to observe and learn. As we dodged bombs and fled a sinking ship amid a pack of terrified sailors, I had to admit that it made sense. Instead of focusing on finding the anomalies in the situation, I was able to actually pay attention to the history taking place.

"So, Cadet Fitz," Elliot said when the simulation was over, his voice dripping an exaggerated formality. "Can you tell me what time the first bomb hit Pearl Harbor?"

"Seven fifty-five," I said as a smile spread across my face. Elliot fired off question after question, and I answered them correctly. Each and every one.

"I guess your brain isn't Swiss cheese after all," he said as he finally sat up to detach his simulation probes.

"I guess not," I said. "That was amazing. Do you think we could do it again?"

"Definitely," Callaway said as he came up behind us. "It appears your idea worked out, Elliot. The only trick will be finding the time in your schedule. I feel it is important that you continue your traditional study blocks with the rest of the cadets. This new method of study is still untested, and honestly, I'm not sure your mother would approve."

"Why not at night?" I said, thinking about what Tess had said about how roaming the mountain at night wasn't a big deal. "Could we come here and study before lights-out? Or early before breakfast?"

"Sounds good to me," Callaway said, turning to walk across the atrium toward where the breakfast dishes were being cleared.

"You know," Elliot said, standing up and stretching, "if we can get this figured out, we might actually make it as partners." And for the very first time, I believed it.

CHAPTER TWENTY-THREE

ELLIOT

An alarm blared, jarring me from a dream where I was doing a Glitch in a trench during what had to be World War I. I sat bolt upright, my hair barely skimming the top of my bunk, and for maybe the second time in my life I was grateful for being short. It took me a heartbeat or two to remember where I was. Regan and I had been meeting up every night for the last two weeks to do study simulations, and the lack of sleep was really starting to get to me. A fact I'd made sure to hide from Callaway just in case he decided our extra training was too much and changed his mind.

I rubbed my eyes and peered out of my bunk. The dorm was pitch-black except for a red flashing light in the corner of the ceiling that I'd never seen before. The alarm blared again, and I clapped my hands over my ears. What was going on? Was there a fire? That thought sent terror racing down my spine as I remembered that I was in the heart of a very big mountain.

A second later, the door to our dorm burst open and a pajama-clad Callaway stood silhouetted in the doorway.

"Get dressed and meet in the atrium in two minutes," he said, flicking on the lights before rushing away. For a half second we just sat there blinking in the harsh light as the alarm continued to blare overhead, and then we sprang into action. I don't even remember taking my pajamas off, but I was in my uniform and following Sam out the door at a run in less than a minute. We met the girls as they came barreling out of their own door in the same rush to button jackets and stumble into shoes mid-sprint. The partner groups paired up automatically as we rushed down the hall that led to the atrium. Regan looked particularly wild, her blond hair, usually straight, waving out in unruly tangles and twists that made her wide frightened eyes stand out sharply in her pale face. Her shirt was also on backward, but now wasn't the time to point that out. Her shoulder pressed against mine as we ran, and she shot me a knowing look out of the corner of her eye, her mouth set in a grim line.

Something bad had happened, and she knew as well as I did that this could very well be the reason that Cocoon had landed in our laps.

The alarm system stopped blaring as we rushed into the main atrium, but the red flashing lights that had been present down every hallway continued in here as well, casting an eerie red glow on the cavernous ceiling. The faculty was there already, but Callaway was the only one still in his pajamas. He scanned the room, mouthing our names as he counted to make sure that we were all present. That done, he clapped his hands for quiet, and the nervous murmuring stopped instantly as all eyes turned to him.

"What's going on?!" Regan called out, and Callaway motioned at her to be quiet, his normally jovial face tight with worry.

"There has been an attack at the Academy," he said, and there was an audible gasp as everyone took that in. Regan's whole body went rigid next to mine.

"What kind of attack?" she asked.

"We aren't sure yet," he said. "All we know is that the entire Academy island has lost communication, and we are on lockdown until we know more."

"What do you mean *lockdown*?" Regan asked, her voice high and shrill. "Aren't we going to help them? Is anyone hurt?"

"Regan," Callaway said sternly. "I am telling you everything I know. And no, we are not going to help them. At least not until we know more."

"But," she started to protest, and I did everyone a favor and put my hand over her mouth to shut her up.

"Thank you," Callaway said as he turned back to the group. Regan sank her teeth into the fleshy part of my palm, and I jerked my hand away. She wiped her mouth and glared at me, and I got the distinct feeling that she was wishing she'd bit me harder.

"All we know right now is that the Academy suffered a security breach after midnight tonight. We were alerted to it so we could make sure our own security was tightened. However, within five minutes of receiving the notification, there was a series of explosions on the Academy island, and we lost all communication." Regan's already pale face got even paler, reflecting the horror I felt flooding through my system like a tidal wave. This couldn't be real. Not the Academy.

"We are kept up to date with the Academy's Glitching activity, down to the second, in case a crisis like this ever occurs," Callaway went on, and I saw the other kids exchanging questioning looks with their partners. I didn't even bother since my partner was a biter. "For that reason, we know that there are four Glitch agents who were mid-mission when the system went down." I saw the face of almost every person in attendance go white at this new bit of information. If there were four agents mid-mission when the Academy lost power, then those agents had no way of making it back to the present. They were stuck in whatever time they'd been sent to. Worse than that, if left in that time period for too long, they would inevitably become Butterflies themselves, meddling with the ebb and flow of time by their very presence. No one asked why agents were Glitching at this time of night, since we knew that missions happened at all hours.

"So now, despite the fear I know you are all feeling, I must ask you all to rise to the occasion for the sake of the Academy," Callaway went on, talking over the nervous murmuring. "We are going to send each partner team after one of those agents. Your job will be to bring them back to the present. Preferably intact."

"But we've never actually time traveled before," said Blake.

"That doesn't matter at the moment," Callaway said. "Trust me, I'm not happy about this situation either, but all of the staff here at the mountain have been deactivated, which means that you are the only option."

"What about the Butterflies?" I asked. "The ones the agents were sent in to catch in the first place? What about their missions?"

Callaway sighed. "Right now, we just need to retrieve our agents. We will have to send them back in once the Academy is online again." His lips pressed into a thin line as he didn't say what everyone there was thinking, that the Academy might never be back online, that we didn't know what was left of the Academy or the people in it. The thought made me feel as if the bottom had dropped out of my stomach. The Academy had been the only home I'd ever known before coming to the mountain. Everything and everyone I knew was on that island, and now we didn't know what had happened to them.

"Is this a hostile takeover by Mayhem?" Regan asked, and my head snapped over to look at her. But she ignored me, her arms crossing over her chest as she stood a little taller and looked at Callaway.

"Well?" she prompted.

Callaway just shook his head. "Regan," he said, his voice tight with warning, "I've already told you all that I know. The clock is ticking, and we need to get ready for the retrieval. The longer we wait, the longer our agents are without a line back to the present." I nodded, trying not to think about how tricky the timing on this one would have to be. If they sent us too early, the agent might confuse us for the Butterfly, catch us, and haul us back to the Academy just in time for it to explode, but if we showed up too late, the agent could have accidentally become a Butterfly themselves.

"Can't we just connect them to our equipment?" Regan asked.

Callaway shook his head again. "If only it were that simple," he said. "But since we didn't send them, we can't bring them back. They will have to hitchhike home with each of you via your Chaos Cuffs. Now, we don't have any time to waste. Each team will be briefed by a professor and costumed appropriately for the jump. Move!"

We moved. Or rather, everyone moved around us as professors started pulling each partner group in a different direction. Callaway hustled Regan and me over to the corner of the atrium that housed the combat mats, Professor Tramble close behind him. Regan walked with a stiffness that made it obvious that it was taking every ounce of her self-control not to pummel Callaway with more questions.

"Keep it together," I whispered under my breath.

"I am," she replied through gritted teeth. "I went through all the same crisis training as you. I know not to fall apart." I raised an eyebrow at her and her hands balled into fists at her sides. "I'm *not!*" she insisted.

"Okay," I said, holding my arms up in submission. "You're not. But remember this is the real deal, okay?

Someone's life is on the line, and the entire history of the United States and possibly even the entire world could be altered if you screw this up."

"We," she said. "If *we* screw this up, and *we* won't." Callaway turned to face us when we reached the combat mats, and he shuffled through the papers in his hands until he found the one he was searching for and looked up.

"What do you know about the Triangle Shirtwaist Factory fire?" he asked.

"Nothing," Regan said at the exact moment that I said, "Everything."

Regan turned to me. "There is no way you know everything about it," she said accusingly.

"There is no way you know nothing about it," I countered. "It's a really important historical event. It's the reason factories changed their labor laws. It's why we have fire extinguishers everywhere. It's . . . ," I said, pausing as I gestured hopelessly in the air for the right word.

"Important," Regan said. "Got it."

Callaway nodded as one of the technicians rushed over with a rack of clothing. Without a word she began holding drab cotton dresses up to Regan.

"Give me the basics of the event," Callaway commanded.

"It happened on March twenty-fifth in the year 1911 in New York City," I said, slipping happily back into my role of top student with all the answers. "A shirt factory located on the eighth, ninth, and tenth floors of the Asch Building caught fire and one hundred and forty-six people died. Mostly women and almost entirely immigrants, if I remember correctly. It was one of the largest industrial accidents in US history."

"Why did so many people die?" Regan asked.

"They were locked in," Callaway said as he began pulling leather shoes off the rack and holding them out for us to try on.

"Locked?" Regan gasped.

"Locked," I repeated. "The owners of the factory didn't want their employees leaving early or protesting for better working conditions, so they locked them all in."

"But the fire department?" Regan said.

I snorted. "You mean the ones with ladders that only reached to the sixth floor and the faulty equipment? They weren't exactly helpful. Those women had no way out and no one who could save them."

Regan's eyes went wide, and I felt my own stomach roll nervously as something occurred to me. I turned back to Callaway as Professor Tramble handed me a dull blue button-down shirt.

"Are we entering before the fire starts?" I asked.

"Unfortunately, in order to retrieve our agent, you will be entering mid-inferno," Callaway said, still looking at the papers in his hand. I let that sink in for a minute as he finally looked up and handed us a page. Regan took it, and I peered over her shoulder at the picture of a slimly built woman in her forties.

"That is Agent Chris," Callaway said. "She's one of our best agents, and she was sent into the middle of the factory to catch a Butterfly that we suspected of tampering with the event. Your mission is to locate her and bring her back using these," he said, and for the first time in my life I was handed a real set of Chaos Cuffs. Even though they were identical in every way to the sets we used in simulations, these somehow felt heavier.

"Study her face well," Callaway said. "Like you, she will be in full disguise." With that he hurried away to talk to Sam and Serina, who were dressed head to toe in what looked like clothing straight from the eighties. I wondered what event they were traveling to.

Regan and I stared at the picture, committing Agent Chris's sharp nose, wide-set eyes, and broad forehead to memory. I was so focused that I about jumped out of my skin when someone brushed something across my cheek. I turned to see one of the technicians with a makeup palette of blacks, grays, and reds as he turned to Regan and gave her the same treatment. Within minutes, we both looked like survivors of a fire, with soot-covered faces and a few bloody scrapes for good measure.

"Are they ready?" Callaway asked as he hurried over.

"Yes," said the tech as he stood back to take us in. He put one last swipe across my nose, gave my shirt-sleeve a good rip to match the one he'd put in the hem of Regan's dress, and then hurried over to Tess and Eliana, who were still getting dressed in what appeared to be the uniforms of Revolutionary War soldiers.

"No," Regan said, so quietly only I could hear.

"Seriously," I whispered. We'd made huge progress over the last few weeks, ever since I'd come up with our unique way of studying, but nothing could have prepared us for this.

"Remember," Callaway said as he straightened a hem here and a collar there. "The Triangle Shirtwaist factory went up fast. You need to locate Agent Chris and get back as quickly as possible."

"Can we switch with them?" I asked, jerking my head to where Corban and Blake were donning scuba gear. "We've only been training as a team for a few weeks."

"That's why I chose this one for you," Callaway said. "Most of the people you meet inside the building won't survive the fire, which means you have very little chance of accidentally changing history. The other missions require quite a bit more tact, finesse, and time. Besides, Regan is one of the best natural Butterfly spotters I've ever seen, so finding Agent Chris amid the chaos will hopefully be easiest for her. Now, follow me, please."

With that, he turned and headed down a corridor on the far right that I'd never gone down before. The other teams filled in behind us, and I was a little relieved to see the same anxious expression on their faces that I'm sure was on my own. Regan was the only one who didn't look nervous, but I'd been her partner long enough now to know that was a very convincing front and her insides were just as knotted as my own. Feeling resolved, I gritted my teeth and attempted to get in the right frame of mind for what was coming.

Callaway stopped in front of an impressive-looking metal door and held his hand up to a sensor on the wall. After a second, the panel lit up, and he keyed in what had to be a twenty-digit code. As if that wasn't enough protection, he then pulled out a key from around his neck and inserted it into a lock, turning it three times before the door unlocked and he ushered us inside.

As I followed Regan through, I saw that the door

itself was over a foot thick, which I would have thought was overkill, except that in front of me were five sets of Glitch platforms complete with the hub of computers that would be needed to send my classmates and me hurtling through time and into the past. A blast of icy air sent goose bumps rippling down my back, and I swallowed hard as Callaway directed each partner group to a different platform. For the second time that day I felt Regan's shoulder pressed against mine as we stepped up onto the thick metal disk.

"I can't believe this is happening," she said.

"What?" I asked. "That we are actually about to Glitch for real? Or what happened at the Academy?"

"Both," Regan said. "But to be honest, I'm doing my best not to think about the Academy or anyone else right now." I saw her swallow hard, and I averted my eyes as she swiped at hers with the back of her hand.

"Don't," I said, clenching my jaw. "If you start, I'll lose it, and then where will we be?"

"Sorry," she said, sniffing as she pulled her shoulders back.

"Me too," I said, and I wondered if I should give her a hug or something. Everyone felt terrible about the Academy, but Regan especially had more to lose. I wondered if she was going to be able to keep it together for this jump.

"Okay?" I asked. I wasn't a hugger.

"Okay," she said as Callaway and the other professors and techs rushed around, turning on the different machines, their brows furrowed in concentration as they set the program for each group's time travel. I watched their fingers fly across the keys and realized that the programming for an actual Glitch was almost identical to the simulation programming I'd learned back at the Academy. I'd assumed it would be more complicated than that.

"Did you realize programming a Glitch was that easy?" I said quietly to Regan.

She nodded, and I decided not to press her on how she knew that and I didn't. Maybe that fact was kept out of our training so cadets wouldn't get any funny ideas.

"Here," said Professor Tramble, walking up with two large pills and glasses of water.

"What are these?" I asked, picking up the pill warily.

"These will give you five minutes of air," he said, holding up his hand as though we'd forgotten how many five was.

"Air?" Regan asked, eyeing the pill suspiciously.

"You are going to travel to the middle of a factory fire," Tramble said. "These will allow you to breathe without damaging your lungs permanently."

"But only five minutes?" Regan asked.

"Think of it like Cinderella and the stroke of midnight," Tramble said. He waited until we'd both swallowed our pill and chased it with our cups of water before returning to his spot behind the control panels.

"Wait a second," I said. "Does that mean we will only be gone five minutes here too?" I'd never thought to ask about the actual passage of time when you were on a real honest-to-goodness Glitch.

Regan shrugged. "I know there is some complicated mathematical equation that figures that out, but no, I don't think it's a one-to-one ratio thing. We can ask after this is all over." She didn't add that we'd have to survive this to ask the question, a fact I appreciated. Still, my insides squirmed like I'd swallowed a nest of live spiders, and I could feel my hands trembling.

"I really hate fire," I admitted to Regan.

"No one likes fire," Regan said. "Let's just get in and get out fast."

"We have to," I said. "This isn't a simulation. If we die there, we don't just wake up back here."

"I didn't really need that reminder, but thanks," Regan said.

"Is everyone ready?" Callaway called, and I glanced around the room as every partner pair reached out and grasped hands. That was kind of weird. I glanced over at Regan, but her hands were balled into tight fists at her sides, her eyes squeezed shut as though she was waiting for a bus to hit her.

"Good luck," Callaway said, and I shut my own eyes as the countdown began. Regan and I were going to need all the luck we could get.

CHAPTER TWENTY-FOUR

REGAN

I'd heard Glitchers talk about what time traveling felt like for my entire life. They would sit around our big wood table after a fancy dinner and compare sensations in the same way we cadets compared the blisters on our hands after a particularly grueling training session. It was different for everyone, with no two Glitchers ever feeling the same thing. My mom said it felt similar to the tingling feeling you got in your foot after it fell asleep, while another professor would say it was like plunging into an ice-filled bathtub. The most notable one I could remember was an active Glitcher who said it felt exactly like someone had caught his stomach with a fish hook and was reeling it in at full tilt.

So as far back as I could remember, I'd wondered what it would feel like. I'd obsessed over it, really, but I forgot to care as the countdown began, because who could care about something like that when their mom might be dead? The second the traitorous thought crossed my mind, I shoved it away. I couldn't go there, not yet, not ever. I'd been trained my entire life to compartmentalize, to give my entire focus to the situation at hand, and I leaned hard on the habits developed from years and years of study and work. What mattered now was the mission. What mattered now was retrieving Agent Chris, and I could shut everything out and focus on just that. I was almost positive.

The countdown hit one, and the air whooshed from my lungs as a sudden intense pressure encased my body. It was as though I was being sucked through a straw. I felt like my skin was shrinking, and if I'd had any air left I'd have screamed. A second later it was over, and I felt the heat. Heat so blistering that I thought for a second that we'd been Glitched directly into flames. I opened my eyes.

The insides of the 1911 factory were ablaze and the screaming of the workers trapped inside was almost deafening. Adrenaline hit my system like a freight train, and I felt my heart rate double in an instant. I'd heard my mom talk about the Glitch rush, but I'd always thought she was exaggerating. She wasn't. In the next instant, I remembered Elliot and turned, expecting to find him at my side, but he was nowhere in sight. My mouth went dry. Something had gone wrong. I was here alone.

My hand went automatically to my belt, and I felt the tiniest fraction of relief when I found my set of Chaos Cuffs there. I might be here alone, but I wasn't trapped. Forcing myself to refocus, I looked around. In a room where everyone was panicked and running, I felt like I was moving in slow motion as I took in the row upon row of upturned sewing machines that cluttered the already packed space, the piles of scrap fabric that lay everywhere just waiting for their turn to catch fire, and the disordered swirl of panic at the far end of the room where workers were still frantically trying to open a door that I knew would never open. And in that moment, I felt the enormity of it all in a way that I never had before in a simulation. Because these people were real. They weren't generated by a computer. They were someone's mother, or sister, or friend, and almost every face that I saw wasn't going to survive the next ten minutes. Someone bumped into me, and I was jarred from my horror and back to the task at hand. I'd already wasted ten seconds. I didn't have ten seconds to waste.

I tried to look at every panicked face, hoping to see something that would let me know that I'd found Agent Chris. The room was unbearably hot, and I wondered that my skin wasn't boiling. I could breathe just fine thanks to that pill, but my lungs still felt thick and dirty from the smoke. Or maybe it was panic that made my chest feel like it was getting smashed by a hundred-pound weight. It was hard to tell.

I glanced out one of the broken windows; since the floor below me didn't appear to be on fire, I decided that I was probably on the eighth floor. Unfortunately, that glance out the window also showed me that most of the women who'd jumped hadn't survived the fall. Below me, the fire department stood staring in horror at their dry-rotted nets that had been torn to shreds. It was almost as bad as the men working to raise ladders that couldn't reach past the sixth floor to the eighth, ninth, and tenth where the fire was in full force. No wonder this event changed things, I thought grimly. Looking up, I spotted what was supposed to be a fire escape partially detached from the wall and crumbling. Was Agent Chris on one of the two floors above me? If I knew this event better, I'd know what other options I had to get up to the next floor, but I didn't. I made a mental note to do a study simulation on this one with Elliot in the very near future, and where in the world *was*

Elliot? The nitty-gritty factual stuff was his specialty, not mine. A fact that was all too apparent as I stood there considering the fire escape. Compared to fumbling around inside a burning building for an unknown exit, this seemed like my best bet. I bit my lip. My next move was going to make or break the mission.

The sound of frantic screams behind me made me turn as an elevator appeared and was immediately rushed, people cramming themselves into the only escape they could see. I caught a glimpse of the elevator operator who'd been brave enough to risk his own life to save others, and I wondered if history would ever recognize him for the hero he was. Not everyone would risk their own life to bring that elevator back. As the doors closed, I made my decision and headed out the window and onto the barely attached fire escape.

I tested the ladder's weight with one foot. It held, so, taking a deep breath, I stepped into thin air with nothing between me and an eight-story drop but a rusty twisted frame of metal, and I was reminded again that this was the real deal. If I fell here, I would be just one more victim of this tragedy.

The fire escape creaked and groaned alarmingly as I made my way upward, so I moved quickly. I was just reaching for the windowsill on the ninth floor when I felt the last metal supports pull free from the wall. On instinct alone, I jumped. The brick window ledge of the windowsill cut into my hands as the fire escape fell away to career to the ground. In that moment, I understood why I'd been forced to train so brutally and intensely for my entire life. Using muscles I'd honed through hundreds of push-ups and pull-ups, I heaved myself upward toward safety. I would have made it too, if someone hadn't chosen that moment to break the window.

I ducked my head a half second before glass exploded around me, accompanied by an overpowering wave of heat. It was like the building was an oven and someone had just opened the door. I lost all the ground I'd gained, slipping backward so I was hanging by the tips of my fingers. My stomach did a sickening flip as I made the mistake of looking down to the pavement nine stories below. I dug my nails into the brick. I would not die here. Not like this. I felt someone grab my wrist, and even before I looked up, I knew it was Elliot. I felt a rush of gratitude and relief so intense I could have cried as he grabbed my other wrist. With his help I pulled myself up and into the building.

"Where were you!?" he yelled directly in my ear as I scrambled to my feet.

"I could ask you the same thing!" I said. "How did you know I was out there?"

"Bullet point number three," Elliot said. "When the window breaks, grab me." I stared at him as my stomach gave a sickening flop of recognition. The Cocoon was now three for three, but I didn't have time to think about the bullet points that were left—we had a job to do.

"Have you found Agent Chris yet?" I asked. He shook his head and together we turned to take in the nightmare of the ninth floor. The clamor inside this floor was just as loud as the one below us as the workers panicked, and I felt like my brain was going to explode from all the heat and noise. My chest tightened, and I wondered if our five minutes of air was almost up.

"Agent Chris must be on the tenth floor or the roof. Follow me!" Elliot said. I nodded and stayed close behind him as he shouldered his way through the crowd, our progress slowed by the rows of sewing equipment that had been shoved to the floor. I was just clambering over a particularly cumbersome piece of equipment when something brought me up short. I reached out and grabbed Elliot's arm, bringing him to a stop, and for a half second we stood frozen as chaos swirled around us. I wondered briefly if this was what it felt like to stand in the middle of a tornado. Elliot yanked on my arm, but I held up my hand and shook my head. I'd seen something, I just needed my conscious brain to catch up with my subconscious.

One second. Two. I'm not sure how long I stood there, my eyes combing the features of panicked worker after panicked worker until I saw her. At first I thought it was Agent Chris—that was who we were here for, after all—but in the next second I realized that I was looking at a Butterfly. Maybe it was the fact that she stood three inches taller than the other workers, or the fact that her face was perfectly clean while those around her were filthy, sweaty, and soot-covered, but I knew it was her. I leaped off the equipment and charged. The woman turned at the last second, and I saw her surprised expression as I took her to the ground. Elliot was there a second later, and before I could stop him, he'd slapped his Chaos Cuffs on her, and they disappeared in front of my eyes.

CHAPTER TWENTY-FIVE

ELLIOT

I was back inside the mountain. The icy air of the Glitch room hit me first, racing into my smoke-filled lungs, and I coughed, doubling over as my body attempted to adjust to the drastic change. It was a few seconds before my eyes stopped watering and my body stopped heaving long enough for me to stand up straight. As I took in the room through streaming eyes, I noticed two things simultaneously. The first was that we were the first ones back—the other platforms sat empty. The second was that there was no *we*. There was just a me. Regan was nowhere to be seen. I spun to look behind me, as though she was playing hide-and-seek, but the only other person on the platform was Agent Chris. Except, was it Agent Chris? The stranger I'd brought back through time stumbled to her feet and whirled to face me, her cuffed hands reaching for my neck as she let out a scream of rage. I stumbled backward just as two techs and Professor Callaway vaulted onto my platform. All three of them grabbed the woman, and it was then that I saw her face for the first time, and it was not Agent Chris's face. In the craziness of the burning factory, I'd done what I'd been training to do—I'd relied on my partner and cuffed the target before I'd gotten a decent look at her.

I watched in numb disbelief as the woman screamed and scratched, trying to escape despite the Chaos Cuffs still firmly around her wrists. It took the techs a moment, but they eventually had her in hand and led her off the platform.

Callaway turned to me, his blue eyes wide. "Where's Regan?"

I swallowed hard. "March twenty-fifth, 1911."

Callaway's jaw dropped in horror. But before he could launch into a lecture about how partners always Glitch in and out of events together, there was a loud popping sound to our left, and we both turned to see Tess and Eliana reappear on their platform, a bedraggled man clutched between them. A second later the same sound echoed to my right, and I turned to see Blake and Corban reappear, each holding the hand of a middle-aged woman with gray hair. Was I the only one who had screwed this up? I shut my eyes, which was a mistake because I was instantly bombarded with the images of the burning building, with the terrified faces of the workers who would never escape, with the smell of the acidic smoke and the screams of people who knew they were about to die. I stumbled off my platform, barely getting my head in a trash can before I threw up.

When I finally ran out of things to throw up, I stood up, turning to see that Sam and Scrina were back with their own agent. Unlike the other two, though, they'd managed to not only find their agent, but also to catch the Butterfly. I watched with a numb detachment as the Butterfly was wrestled off the platform and through the same door the techs had taken the women I'd captured.

I was still staring at the doorway when there was a loud pop behind me, and I turned to see Regan appear, the arm of a white-faced and bloody Agent Chris thrown over her shoulders.

"Help," Regan called. "We need help over here! She's hurt." I rushed back onto the platform just as Agent Chris's legs buckled, and together Regan and I lowered her onto the platform. The mountain's medics hurried to check her pulse and shine lights into her eyes. We stood there side by side and watched as Agent Chris opened her eyes, coughing hoarsely into the oxygen mask someone had put over her face. I knew how she felt; my own lungs felt like someone had stuffed them full of cotton. I turned to Regan, waiting for her to rip into me about leaving her behind, but to my surprise, she didn't. She just stood there watching them work on Agent Chris.

"Are you okay?" I asked.

She bit her lip, not looking at me, and shook her head.

"Me either," I admitted. "I just hurled." I jerked my head toward the trash can when she looked at me in surprise. "I highly recommend it, actually," I said.

"I almost threw up within the first thirty seconds of being there," she said. "It was awful. More awful than I thought possible."

I nodded.

"I never got it before," she said. "But I do now."

"Got what?" I asked.

"Why someone would become a Butterfly," she said. "Why you'd want to go back in time to change something. All those people," she said, shutting her eyes as though she could unsee it all that way.

I watched her, remembering the time back in my fifth year where I'd done a simulation of the bombing of the Sixteenth Street Baptist Church in 1963. I'd almost asked to be deactivated right then and there. What good was it being a Glitcher if you couldn't save the innocent little girls who died that day for the color of their skin? What good was being a Glitcher if I had to stand by as unspeakable horrors took place? Thankfully one of my favorite professors, Professor Abrams, had been there that day, and he'd sat down with me and talked for hours about it all. Maybe it was because his skin color matched my own, or maybe it was because of the way he explained it, but I hadn't asked for a voluntary deactivation that day. "History isn't supposed to be pretty," he'd said. "It's downright repulsive at times, and you don't have to like it or agree with it to preserve it. But remember that the healthiest forests grow the year after a forest fire, and that without extreme pressure we wouldn't have diamonds. You can't hurry history, and you can't fix an injustice until people recognize that it is one." All this raced through my mind as I watched tears run down Regan's soot-stained cheeks, and I wondered if she'd have realized this all earlier if she'd looked like me, or if her mom hadn't been who she was. Probably. Finally, she opened her eyes and shook her head. "I would have given anything to be able to save them."

"You saved one," I said, motioning with my chin to where Agent Chris was getting helped to her feet. "Where was she anyway?"

"On the ground," she said. "After you disappeared with the Butterfly, I spotted her pinned underneath a fallen beam. I didn't think I'd be able to get her out, especially since that pill ran out about ten seconds before you disappeared, but I did."

"Nice work," I said, and Regan raised a surprised eyebrow at me.

"I'm serious," I said. "I have no clue how you spotted that Butterfly *and* Agent Chris in that mess."

"It didn't help that I Glitched to the wrong floor," she said, brow furrowed. "I wonder why you and I got separated."

I shrugged. "No idea. But it's probably because you and I are the worst partners in the history of ever."

"I don't know," Regan said. "I think we did okay, all things considered." Before I could respond, Callaway was there, herding us off the platform.

"Are you both all right?" he asked as the rest of the partner pairs joined us.

"We are," Regan said. "But something went wrong. We didn't Glitch together like we were supposed to."

Callaway furrowed his brow. "That's extremely odd," he said. "Were you holding hands?"

"Were we supposed to hold hands?" I asked.

"Of course," Callaway said, his eyebrows shooting up in surprise. "Don't tell me that was never covered in your training?!" When we both just stared at him, he waved a hand. "Well, now you know. That was an atrocious oversight on our part, but of course, since it only applies to actual Glitch jumps, your professors may never have mentioned it in the short time you've been here."

"Do we have to watch our recap?" I asked, my still-queasy stomach rolling a little at the thought of reliving any of it.

Callaway shook his head. "There are no recaps in a real Glitch," he said.

"Oh," I said, feeling supremely stupid because of course there wasn't a recap. Nothing about what I'd seen was computer generated, and if I hadn't already thrown up everything I'd ever eaten, I'd have done it again now.

"Any news about the Academy?" Serina asked, hurrying to walk next to us.

Regan's face went white, and the relief I'd felt upon her safe return evaporated instantly. I'd forgotten about the Academy.

Callaway sighed, like he was a tire someone had just punctured, and turned to face us. We all stopped, taking in his expression, and it was like he didn't even have to tell us. That look alone confirmed everyone's worst fear. The Academy was gone.

CHAPTER TWENTY-SIX

REGAN

It didn't make any sense. The world couldn't just go on without the Academy. It was impossible. It was like the earth continuing to revolve after the sun had disappeared. I'd stood there listening to Callaway explain that Mayhem had discovered the location of the Academy and at one o'clock this morning had discharged enough explosives to wipe out the entire campus. No survivors.

The entire mountain was in shock and mourning. Every single person there had grown up within the Academy walls. I was not the only one who had lost something or someone, but I was pretty sure I was the only one who had lost their mom. But even that felt unreal, because I couldn't imagine a life where my mom didn't exist. She was too tough, too strong, too in control to let something like this happen. It couldn't be true. But it was.

As the early hours of the morning turned into the late hours of the afternoon, I sat with everyone else in the atrium as reports trickled in. Even though none of the adults said it, we all knew they were scared. We were all too aware that the only thing protecting the last people with the equipment and training to Glitch for the United States was a hidden door in the side of a mountain.

I remembered again what my mom had said about putting all their eggs in one basket. Had she known? Glitching to the future was impossible, but she must have had some idea that things could go wrong. I sat beside Elliot, wrestling with emotions so big I thought they might suffocate me.

"We need to talk," Elliot said in my ear, jolting me from my own thoughts. I looked up to see that someone had put food on our table, but no one was touching the sad-looking sandwiches. Glancing around the table at my classmates, I noticed that, like us, they were still in full costume and makeup. It made for a very weird table dynamic.

"Why?" I said, quiet enough that only Elliot could hear.

"Because I just figured something out," he said. I stared at him for a moment, trying to read his expression. What could he have possibly figured out? There was nothing left to figure out. The Academy was gone. Game over.

"Good for you," I said, my voice sounding dead and flat in my own ears.

Elliot's elbow dug painfully into my ribs, and I glared at him. If he kept digging his elbow into my ribs like that, I was going to dig mine into his nose. Today was *not* the day to mess with me.

My anger fizzled slightly as I watched Elliot open his eyes wide and jerk his head toward the far exit and then back to me. He was either trying to tell me something or he was having a seizure.

"Just say it," I said. "No one is paying any attention to us."

With an exasperated huff, Elliot leaned in so that his mouth was practically on my ear and whispered, "I wanted to say this somewhere, I don't know, not here, but you are utter garbage at taking a hint."

"Thank you," I said, straight-faced. "Spit it out."

Elliot scowled and then leaned in even closer, his voice so quiet I could barely hear it. "I think this is why you and I got that Cocoon," he said. His words were like lightning to my system, and I sat bolt upright

271

so fast that my shoulder cracked Elliot in the chin. He jerked back, clutching his jaw, but I couldn't have cared less. The Cocoon. The letter that had pulled all the strings to get Elliot and me here in the first place—was this why?

We'd been given strict instructions not to leave the main atrium until further notice, but this couldn't wait. "Follow my lead," I whispered, and shot my hand into the air. Professor Tramble walked over, his eyebrows raised questioningly.

"I need to use the restroom," I said.

"Me too," Elliot said quickly. Too quickly. I groaned inwardly. Smooth, Elliot. Real smooth.

"We aren't supposed to allow more than one student at a time to leave the atrium," Professor Tramble said, thankfully too distracted to notice that Elliot looked like the proverbial kid with his hand in the cookie jar. "Can you wait?"

Elliot shook his head. Professor Tramble turned to me, and I shook my head as well. Tramble sighed and motioned for us to go. "Be quick about it," he said. I leaped out of my chair, and it tipped backward and hit the stone floor with an earsplitting bang. Everyone in the atrium jumped and turned to look at us. My face burned, and I muttered an apology and righted the chair before sheepishly following Elliot toward the bathrooms.

I was barely around the corner when Elliot grabbed me and yanked me the last few steps out of sight.

"So much for a discreet exit," he hissed in my ear.

"You should talk," I shot back. "You were practically twitching when you asked Tramble to use the bathroom; way to play it cool."

"Whatever," Elliot said, waving his hand. "Are you thinking what I'm thinking?"

"Maybe," I said. "But to be honest, I think I'm a few steps behind you. I feel like my brain stopped working the minute Callaway told us about the Academy. I've been sitting in that atrium stuck inside my own head, where nothing makes sense."

"I was too," Elliot said. "At first, but then I started thinking about how lucky we were to be here and not there, and then it all clicked into place."

"Remember?" I said. "I'm a few steps behind. Catch me up."

"The Cocoon," Elliot said, his voice dropping so low I had to lean in to hear him. "*This* was the reason we were sent here. Not to be the worst partner team in the history of forever, but because you and I are supposed to fix this."

"How?" I asked, wanting more than anything for what he was saying to be true. "If we travel to the past, we become criminals. You know what happens to Butterflies who get caught."

Elliot leaned forward. "Haven't you realized it yet? Almost all the US Glitchers who catch Butterflies are dead."

His words brought it all home again, and I sank down to sit with my back against the wall. Elliot joined me, and we sat shoulder to shoulder in silence for a minute.

"Sorry," Elliot finally whispered. "That was really crummy of me to say."

"It's the truth, though," I said.

"Yeah. Doesn't make it any less crummy," Elliot said.

I turned to look at Elliot as I searched for the right words. "You were so dead set against this when we first found that letter. You swore you'd never become a Butterfly, no matter what. You lectured me over and over again about how history cannot be changed."

"Right," Elliot said, but then he paused, biting his lip. "But what if we are *supposed* to change it?"

"Explain," I said.

"In the future," Elliot said, "you and I travel back through time to leave that Cocoon. If we hadn't, you and I would have been at the Academy when the attack happened. Right?"

"Right," I said.

"So," Elliot said, his brow furrowed, "if I'm understanding this right, we already fixed this."

I stared at him a second, my thoughts in tangled knots. "Are you saying that me and you, in the future, made sure that we survived so we could save the Academy?"

Elliot nodded. "Have you thought about what the future looks like without the Academy? I mean, really thought about it?"

"I've been trying not to," I said, grimacing as the tears I'd been holding back swelled in my throat again. I swallowed hard, wiping at my eyes with the backs of my hands.

"I'm sorry about your mom," Elliot said. "But if we can figure this out, maybe we can save her."

"Right," I said, unconsciously squaring my shoulders in the way my mom had taught me. Successful people don't slouch.

"Take a second and think about it," Elliot said. "What happens without the Academy?"

"Butterflies happen," I said automatically. "A lot of them, I'd imagine."

"It will be a free-for-all," Elliot said. "When news gets out, every time-traveling criminal with the ability to Glitch will be jumping into the past and doing who knows how much damage. That's on top of whatever Mayhem is planning to do now that the Academy is gone."

I felt the blood drain from my face to puddle

somewhere by my toes, because what Elliot was saying was absolutely true. I'd been in such a fog over losing my mom that I hadn't thought through what losing the Academy was going to mean for the world.

"That's not even the half of it," I said as my brain raced with horrible possibility after horrible possibility. "We have to do something."

"That," Elliot said, "is the biggest understatement I've ever heard."

CHAPTER TWENTY-SEVEN

ELLIOT

I lay in bed that night with my eyes wide open. The mountain was still in major lockdown since we didn't know who we could trust, and the professors had set up a schedule to patrol the corridors twenty-four hours a day. Every hour or so I could hear one of them open our door to check that four boys were safe and sound in their bunks before continuing on down the hall. It was going to make everything that much harder.

Regan had insisted that we make our move tonight, arguing that the longer we waited, the more we could potentially mess up the future. Because, she argued, the future hadn't really happened yet. As of right now, all the reports were that no one knew the Academy was gone except us, Mayhem, and a few high-ranking government officials. But we knew all too well that any minute it could get out and the whole landscape of the future would shift. The sweet spot—Regan's words, not mine—was now, when things were essentially in limbo, and we could make the jump back in time untethered by a future that was already set in stone. The problem was, how in the world were we going to make this jump?

The longer I lay there, the more my brain churned. If my thoughts were milk, they would have turned into butter a long time ago. Around me I could hear the other boys shifting restlessly in their bunks, and I knew that I wasn't the only one who couldn't sleep. I glanced again at the clock and groaned inwardly when I discovered that while it felt like I'd been lying here for a lifetime, it had really only been two hours. In exasperation, I threw my arms over my face, because if I stared at the stone ceiling of my bunk much longer I was going to punch it. The movement made me grimace. Every inch of me was sore from my Glitch jump today, and I had more than a few bruises and burns to show for my romp through 1911. After years of simulations that felt real but never left a mark, this was something that would definitely take some getting used to.

Finally, just when I thought I couldn't lie there for

one more second, the clock ticked to eleven p.m., and I snuck out of bed and out the door like a shadow.

As I entered the dark corridor, I felt an irrational surge of anger at my future self, and for the first time it wasn't because Regan was my partner. It was because future me had held all the cards, known all the answers, and still chosen to only hand out bits and pieces of information, leaving almost everything up to chance and luck. I knew Regan had been the one to write the actual letter, but it was clear now that I'd known about it. That bullet point about the window had sealed that for me. There was no way Regan would have known to put that on there. But I was a detail person who left nothing to chance if I could help it. What happened to me in the future that threw all that out the window?

I stood there mulling this over outside the girls' dormitory while I waited for Regan. I thought back to the Cocoon, wishing for the first time that it hadn't dissolved in the fountain. I was almost positive I remembered everything it had said, but what if I'd forgotten something? I mentally went down the list of bullet points at the bottom of the list. The last one we'd checked off was about the window. If the list was in order, and it sure seemed to be so far, then the next one on the list was about a door opening. It was on this bullet point that we had hinged our entire plan. If you could call winging it a plan, I thought glumly. A second later, Regan tiptoed out of the girls' dormitory. She paused a second outside the door, scanning the dark hallway before she finally spotted me. With a quick glance left and right, she was across the hall and next to me. Together we stood there, our backs pressed against the cold stone of the mountain.

"It's not too late to go back," I said, not really sure where the words had come from. I sure hadn't meant to say them out loud.

"It is for me," she said, and before I could protest she was heading down the hallway at a jog. I realized that I already knew what had happened to change me in the future. Regan happened.

The fastest way to the Glitch room was straight through the atrium, but even at this time of night, it probably still contained a handful of professors and staff desperately trying to figure out the mountain's next move. So we took the long way around, winding through the hallways and corridors that led us around the atrium and toward the hallway with that thick metal door I had no idea how we'd get through. As we slunk through the shadows, I couldn't shake the feeling that we were being watched. The hairs on my neck were permanently at attention and the goose bumps on my arms and legs were big enough to hatch into actual geese. I thought about mentioning this to Regan, but she was the picture of cool, calm, and collected, and I decided against it. Even though I was learning that this was just a facade she put on and took off like a well-worn coat, it was comforting to pretend she had everything under control. I was probably just paranoid. People about to break about a hundred laws were bound to be a little twitchy. Right?

Finally, after almost getting spotted twice by two different professors, we made it. There in front of us was the thick metal door with its three different locks and safeguards that we had no way of getting through. We both stood there, staring at it as the clock crept toward midnight.

"We are never going to get through that door," I finally said, so softly I wasn't even sure if Regan had heard me.

"We have to," she said. "And we both know that we do, or we wouldn't be standing here. All of the bullet points have been spot on so far, this one will be too."

"Bullet point number four said to trust that the door would open when it needed to. It didn't say what door. What if this isn't the door?" I said.

"Well." Regan shrugged. "Let's hope this is the door."

"Future us are not my favorite people," I said. "In fact, we stink."

Regan covered her mouth to muffle her surprised

snort as she turned to me, the intensity of her face lifting for a brief second. "What?" she said.

"We do," I said, gesturing toward the door. "How hard would it have been to include the door combination and a key in that stupid letter?"

"Not hard," Regan admitted. "Except we'd also need Callaway's hand, and I don't know about you, but I'm pretty thankful I didn't find that."

"Didn't find what?" said a voice behind us, and we both jumped and whirled to see Callaway emerge from the shadows like a ghost. We were busted.

CHAPTER TWENTY-EIGHT

REGAN

"**W**hat are you doing here?" I asked. My voice sounded remarkably calm for someone whose heart was making a very solid attempt to escape her chest.

"Funny," Callaway said, "I was about to ask you the same thing." When neither of us said anything, he sighed. "Except I have a very good guess why you're here. You want to change the past."

"I'm confused," Elliot said. "That's illegal."

"And there's the rub," Callaway said. He ran a hand through his thinning hair. "That simple fact is one that everyone in this mountain has known for their entire lives, but the minute the history we have the power to change is our own, they think rules go up in smoke. Poof."

"But," I said as Callaway held up a hand for silence.

"While I appreciate your unique loss in all this, Regan, I would like to remind you that *everyone* in this mountain has suffered an excruciating loss today, and your mother would be the first one to tell you that protocol can't be thrown out the window." Before I could respond, there was the sound of heavy boot steps behind us, and like the partner team we were, Elliot and I whirled as one to see someone coming out of the shadows.

"Officer Salzburg," Callaway said. "You're a sight for sore eyes."

"Who's Salzburg?" Elliot asked in my ear, and I flapped him away as Salzburg stopped in front of us, a look of surprise on his face. I was instantly transported back to that last formal dinner at my house where he showed off his latest security prototype to my hard-to-impress mother. There was something about that word, *prototype*, that rang a very faint bell somewhere in the back of my mind, but before I could think more about it, Salzburg was there, extending a hand for me to shake.

"Cadet Fitz," he said. "I didn't realize that you were part of the mountain program. Although," he said, "that isn't saying much, since I was unaware there was such a thing as a mountain program until yesterday morning." He shot Callaway a disapproving look that Callaway ignored.

"You should know better than anyone the importance of secrecy to security," Callaway said.

"I know that full well," Salzburg said. "However, I didn't realize that secrets were kept from me."

Callaway cleared his throat, clearly uncomfortable with Salzburg, and turned to us, grateful for the distraction. "Regan and Elliot are some of our newest recruits." He smiled at us reassuringly. "Officer Salzburg arrived yesterday afternoon to discuss increasing security measures here at the mountain, and considering recent events, we are incredibly relieved to have his services."

"I'm so sorry about your mother," Salzburg said, but all I could manage was a quick nod. Any time she was mentioned I suddenly felt like I was trying to swallow a golf ball.

"You two need to go back to your dorm with the rest of the cadets," Callaway said, his voice uncharacteristically stern. "I know you mean well, and trust me, you aren't the only ones desperate to fix the unfixable, but you need to trust us to handle this."

"But the Academy—" I said, my words cut off

sharply by Elliot's elbow in my ribs and Callaway's disapproving look.

"Good night, Cadet Fitz," he said sternly, and the formality of that title after weeks of being just Regan stung.

"Follow me," he said to Salzburg, and together they turned toward the door to the Glitch room. A second later I felt Elliot's hand on my arm yanking me back around the corner and out of sight. I was about to open my mouth to protest when, for the second time in twenty-four hours, his hand clapped itself firmly over my mouth. I narrowed my eyes at him. He obviously had a very bad memory, and I was about to bite down hard enough to leave a mark he'd remember when I heard the sound of footsteps coming down the hallway. Twisting my head away from his sweaty hand, I tugged him back into the shadows as a very distracted-looking Professor Tramble came at a trot down the hall, his face mere inches from the tablet he was holding.

He strode past us, oblivious to our presence, and as though we'd decided it beforehand, we silently crept down the hall after him. We peered around the corner as Tramble quickly entered the passcode and placed his hand on the monitor. The door gave an audible click, and he flung it open and strode through. Before

I even realized I was doing it, I was in a full sprint for that door, and it was as though I was watching it shut in slow motion. At the last possible second, I lunged and threw my arm out, my fingers sliding between the door and the frame with a painful but utterly satisfying pinch.

"Trust the door will open," I said. "It's open." I carefully clambered to my feet, my fingers never leaving the space between the door and its frame.

"What's your plan?" Elliot asked. "Storm in there and ask Callaway to be Glitched back to the past?"

"You keep forgetting we don't *have* a plan," I said as I grabbed his arm and slid through the door.

We slipped into the Glitch room unnoticed thanks to the full-scale argument that had every person in the room on their feet and shouting.

Elliot pulled me to the right and down so we sat with our backs against the cold stone wall next to one of the Glitch platforms. It wasn't a great spot—most of our view was blocked by Glitching equipment and a costume rack—but it wasn't horrible either. Especially since it successfully hid us from everyone else in the room. I noticed that some of the agents who had been retrieved today in our mission were there as well, with the exception of Agent Chris, who I could only assume was still in the medical wing. I caught sight of Salzburg again, and I felt a pang of regret that he was the one who had come to the mountain for security talks and not my mom. Had she been here, all of this would have felt so much more manageable.

"Ladies and gentlemen," Callaway called, walking into the middle of the room and holding up his hands for quiet. "I leave for five minutes, and you resort to shouting? Please remember to keep this conversation civilized."

"But we are running out of time," said the agent who Sam and Serina had rescued. He was young, probably in his early twenties, and his eyes snapped angrily as he glared at Callaway.

"Just because the Academy was destroyed does not give us permission to become the very people who we dedicated our lives to capturing," Callaway said.

"So apparently our idea wasn't very original," Elliot whispered. I nodded, too gripped by the argument taking place in front of me to comment.

"Which is exactly why we can't risk it," said another professor in the back. "We only have a handful of people left who can Glitch, and six of them are students! We saw the disaster that was today. Elliot and Regan didn't even manage to stay together in their Glitch, and Corban and Blake were almost killed. If we are about to be under attack, we can't risk sending any of our people back." I shrank down a little at the mention of our poorly executed mission that morning.

"I agree," Salzburg said. "The past is to be left untampered with. What we need to worry about now is the future."

"You're the security expert," said another professor. "Do you know what happened at the Academy?"

Salzburg lifted his hands in a gesture of helplessness. "I am at a loss."

"So he stinks at his job," Elliot murmured in my ear. I nodded, remembering how he'd practically trembled in my mom's presence as he showed off his new Butterfly detector.

"The Academy exploded at around one in the morning," said one of the techs. "That's all we need to know to get boots on the ground and stop it from happening."

Callaway held up his hands and the crowd quieted. "We can't send the last functioning Glitchers our nation has back to the past to hunt for explosives," he said. "Even if we did know the nature or the location of the attack, it's too risky."

"But it needs to be changed!" said someone, and everyone started talking at once again.

It took Callaway longer to quiet the room this time, and I fidgeted nervously.

"The future may judge us harshly for this decision,"

Callaway said, "but what you are suggesting is the very thing we have been trained to prevent. Even if we disregarded that, we can't send any of our remaining Glitchers on what would certainly be a suicide mission."

This elicited a flurry of protests, and Callaway again began the arduous task of quieting everyone down.

"I have the jump programmed and ready to go," said Professor McMillan, his eyes flashing defiantly. "It may be a suicide mission, but it may also be one that saves the lives of our friends and colleagues. Don't you think we owe it to them to at least try?!"

"This isn't like a normal jump," Callaway said. "Have you even considered—" but his words were cut off by the blare of an alarm. Everyone jumped and turned to look at the flashing red light on the wall. It was as though someone had pressed the pause button in the room and frozen everyone where they stood. Blood rushed in my ears as I processed what that alarm could possibly mean.

"We've been breached," Callaway yelled over the alarm.

"Impossible," Salzburg said as he stared in horror at that flashing alarm. A second later there was an ear-shattering boom that momentarily drowned out the alarms. The floor rumbled underneath me as the very walls around us shuddered and creaked, sending torrents of rock dust down onto millions of dollars' worth of equipment. I threw my hands over my head to protect it as the room erupted in screams. It was as though I was back in the Triangle Shirtwaist Factory fire as equipment got knocked aside, chairs were upended, and everybody made a run for the door. Everyone was shouting at once, shoving one another in their panic to escape. Within seconds, the room was cleared. I stumbled to my feet and realized that Elliot was still beside me, his face and pajamas covered in the fine gray dust of the mountain. Before I could formulate a coherent thought, there was another explosion and the door to the Glitch room slammed shut. We were trapped.

CHAPTER TWENTY-NINE

ELLIOT

I couldn't believe it. I was going to die like those women in 1911. The ground shook again, and I was about to run for the door when Regan grabbed me by the arm and pulled me backward. A second later, a huge chunk of the ceiling came loose and crashed to the ground exactly where I'd been standing.

Regan didn't give me time to scream or vomit, which was probably good since I wasn't sure which was the best option. She yanked me backward again, but this time it was to one of the abandoned computers.

"What are you doing?" I yelled. "We have to get out of here!"

"There isn't a way out," she yelled back. "But I

know how we save ourselves." She jabbed her finger at the screen, and I could see that Professor McMillan hadn't been kidding earlier—he really had already programmed the Glitch back to the Academy on the night it was destroyed.

"Come on," she yelled. "We have to do this. It's the only way."

I nodded, and for once, I actually agreed. The mountain would eventually crumble under whatever onslaught it was under, and we'd die. I had no clue what would happen if the equipment we were going to Glitch on was destroyed, or how we could ever come back to this exact moment without it, but none of that mattered now. The lights flickered and Regan dug her nails into my arm. If we lost power, it was all over.

Lunging forward, I hit the activation button and by some miracle the platform in front of us lit up. The computer screen started counting down from ten, and together we raced for the platform, leaping over fallen equipment and rubble that got in our way. We skidded to a stop dead center, and as though we'd planned it, we reached out at the same time to grab hands. More chunks of rock were falling from the ceiling, and I looked across the room just in time to see the door of the Glitch room open and Officer Salzburg burst through, his eyes wide as he spotted us. There was the sound of another explosion and the platform shook under our feet as everything went black.

For the second time in less than twenty-four hours I had the disturbing sensation that I was melting, and a second later, I opened my eyes at the Academy. I stared at the green lawn, the silence of the night almost deafening after the chaos of the last few seconds. I sagged in relief, my knees buckled, and I sat down hard on the dew-damp grass.

"We aren't dead," Regan said, sinking down to sit beside me.

"We aren't," I confirmed. "At least I don't think so."

"When everything went black, I gave us a fifty-fifty shot of being dead," Regan said, and then she sniffed and turned to me. "Are you okay?" she asked.

"No."

"Me either," she said. "In hindsight, that was a really dumb question. Sorry."

"Forgiven," I said, looking around. We'd landed in the grass on the edge of the Academy's large open green space in the center of campus that everyone called the Mall. It was one of my favorite parts of campus, and I'd thought I'd never see it again. I wondered if it would be too dramatic to bend down to kiss the grass like a sailor kisses the shore after surviving a shipwreck.

"What time is it?" Regan asked, pulling me from my

dazed preoccupation with the beauty of the place I'd called home for most of my life. I glanced over to the end of the Mall where the Edison Building sat with its huge clock tower illuminated on top.

"It's midnight," I said, and then all the warm fuzzy feelings I'd been having evaporated instantaneously. "Wait a minute," I said, vaulting to my feet, my weak knees forgotten as my mind raced ahead. "Didn't Callaway say that the Academy was destroyed at approximately one a.m.?"

"Professor McMillan only gave us an hour?!" Regan said, her face pale in the moonlight. "There is no way we can figure this out in an hour. This place is gigantic."

"We don't have a choice," I said, already pacing back and forth as I willed myself to think fast. "We obviously can't go back. There is probably no back to go to. The electricity was about to go out and the mountain was seconds from folding in on itself." I shoved my hands into my hair and pulled it in frustration as I whirled on Regan. "What were we thinking?" I said.

"Okay, you just lost me," she said.

"The letter," I said. "The stupid stupid STUPID Cocoon. Why in the world didn't we put, 'Oh, and by the way, the mountain is going to fall down on your heads'?"

"If we'd told ourselves that the mountain was going

to get attacked, do you think we would have stayed inside of it?" she asked, and the tirade I was about to go on about how irresponsible our future selves were dried up in my throat.

"No," I said, "we wouldn't have. We would have tried to evacuate everyone."

"And we wouldn't have been in the Glitch room with a preprogrammed computer," Regan said.

"Our future selves wanted to make sure that we'd end up here," I said, looking around the dark campus.

"Right," Regan said.

"Well, couldn't they have at least figured out how to give us a bit more time?" I fumed, not ready to let my anger go just yet.

"One hour must be enough," Regan said. "It has to be."

"There is just no way," I said, unable to help myself. "Are we looking for a person carrying explosives? Or lots of people? Or even people? Maybe robots are going to come zooming over the wall at any moment. We don't know anything about this. There isn't research to work off, nothing to reference. No wonder Salzburg thought this was a bad idea," I said.

"If he thought it was such a bad idea, why did he come back into the Glitch room?" Regan asked, her forehead creased.

"Probably because there was no way out of the mountain," I said. "With the way things were falling down around our ears, I wouldn't be surprised if the tunnels all collapsed." I paced away from Regan and then paced back, unable to stand still. Regan, meanwhile, stood like a statue, her face twisted into an odd expression I'd never seen before. I stopped my pacing to peer at her. "Why do you look like your brain hurts?" I said.

"Nothing," Regan said, waving a hand. "What we need to focus on now is our mission."

"You mean the one Callaway called a suicide mission?" I shook my head as my eyes flicked from building to building, recounting the classes I'd taken in them, the professors I'd met, the staff I'd befriended, and worst of all, the kids sleeping in their dorm rooms at that very moment. I'd be so much better at this if it were in the 1800s. I was seconds away from what was sure to be an impressive panic attack when Regan snapped her head up.

"Did you hear that?" she asked.

"Hear what? My brain screaming? Yeah, that's coming in loud and clear, thanks."

"Shhhh," she said, flapping a hand at me, and then I heard it too. Someone was coming our way.

"We have to hide," she whispered, her eyes wide.

"I forgot it's past curfew," I said, glancing back at the clock, which was ticking down with a speed that didn't seem quite fair.

Regan shook her head, her eyes wide. "That's not all," she said. "Don't you get it? We're Butterflies now." I was still processing this when she grabbed my hand and hauled me backward and into the shrubbery that edged the Academy Mall. There was a shout, and the slash of a flashlight followed us into the bushes. We'd been spotted.

CHAPTER THIRTY

REGAN

I wasn't sure where I was leading us, but my main goal was to get some distance from the security guards. Elliot and I zigged and zagged down the campus paths, ducking through shrubbery and doubling back on ourselves whenever possible. This was so not a good start to things, and even as we ran, I couldn't stop thinking about how much time this was wasting—time we didn't have. We hurtled around a corner and skidded to a stop in front of the Trevi Fountain replica. I blinked at it for a second, confused. I could have sworn that we were on the opposite side of campus from this, but it didn't matter now. Elliot was one step ahead of me, already vaulting over the edge of the fountain and into the water. I followed, and we tucked ourselves into the tiny maintenance bay we'd used the last time we were almost caught by security.

Just like before, we huddled together, waiting to see if we'd get discovered, but unlike last time, I realized I was glad that it was Elliot crouching shoulder to shoulder with me. Somewhere in between the teasing and the bickering, I'd come to think of him as more than a mandatory partner. Somewhere along the line, he'd become a friend. I made a mental note to tell him that if we survived this. We both tensed as the security officers ran past our fountain. As their footsteps retreated, I sagged backward against the cool stone in relief, only to stand back up abruptly as something dug into my back. Turning, I spotted a black security camera looking right at us. My first instinct was to grab Elliot and run, but there was something about that camera that felt weirdly familiar, so I paused. That same gut-deep instinct that helped me to identify Butterflies during a Glitch was on high alert as something tugged at my memory. The same something that had been tugging at me ever since I'd seen Salzburg standing inside the mountain. Because I'd seen this camera before, or at least a prototype of it. The missing puzzle piece I'd mentioned to Elliot slammed into place with a certainty and clarity that literally took my breath away.

"What?" Elliot asked.

I shook my head, holding up my hand to silence him as I stared at the camera. Was this it? I turned to Elliot. "Recite the bullet point list again," I said.

Elliot stared at me for a second, then held up his hand as he started ticking things off. "Behind the curtain," he said. "Belowdecks. When the window breaks, grab me. Trust the door will open when it needs to. The prototypes are a bust. Grab the—"

"There," I said, cutting him off. "The one about the prototypes. Say it again."

He did, looking confused. "I don't get it," he said. "What prototypes?"

"How do you destroy an entire island with one explosion?" I asked.

"You couldn't," Elliot said. "Not unless it was nuclear, which it wasn't."

"Right," I said. "So, if you can't do it with one big explosion, you'd have to do it with a bunch of strategically placed smaller explosions. Right?"

"What are you getting at?" Elliot asked.

"Before we left for the mountain, there were a few security breaches, and my mom had a meeting with Officer Salzburg about a new security device that detected Butterflies. A device they'd replicated after they found it on one of Mayhem's members."

"Replicating anything found on a Mayhem member seems like a bad idea," Elliot said.

"Exactly," I agreed. "But Salzburg was so certain of it, he had my mom convinced to let him install them all over campus. Honestly, I think all the security breaches had put her on edge and made her a bit desperate. But what if that Mayhem member got caught on purpose just to pass on a piece of technology? A piece of technology that they could then detonate remotely?"

"I still don't get it," Elliot said, reaching a hand out to touch the prototype. I smacked his hand down and turned to glare at him.

"Obviously," I said. "Think about the fifth bullet point, *the prototypes are a bust*, as in they are going to explode."

"That thing?" he said. "You really think an explosive is hidden inside a security camera?"

I bit my lip and shook my head. "I'm not sure," I admitted. "But I do know these were getting installed right around the time we left. It fits."

"The prototypes are a bust," he muttered darkly. "Future us was so dumb I could just spit."

"Don't spit," I said. "That's gross." Before I could second-guess myself, I'd grabbed ahold of the camera and given it a hard twist. To my utter surprise, it popped off easily, and I stumbled backward. Elliot yelped and covered his head. When nothing happened, he cautiously lowered his arms and took a step toward me again, his eyes wary.

"Not how I would have handled a potential explosive," he said. "But I always knew you were nuts."

I ignored him as I looked at the back of the device, where a small red light was blinking on and off. I didn't know much about what the guts of a camera looked like, but I was pretty sure this wasn't it. "How good were you at our explosives deactivation class?" I asked. It had been a one-year course we were all required to take pretty early on in our training, since oftentimes Butterflies would trespass into the past with the very unoriginal idea of blowing up something or someone, and knowing how to deactivate a bomb was crucial. It did no good to catch a Butterfly if you left a ticking time bomb behind to finish the job they'd started.

"Top of the class," Elliot said in his matter-of-fact way that used to annoy me but didn't anymore. I'd always thought that he was showing off, but really, he was just stating the facts. The facts were that he *was* the best. Which was fantastic, considering I'd barely scraped by in that class. All those wires and buttons had intimidated me, especially since they were so often strapped to a living person I was trying to cuff. I'd never understood the mentality of the Butterflies who didn't mind blowing themselves up as long as they took George Washington or Martin Luther King out with them. Although, I realized, if you'd told me a year ago that I would become a Butterfly myself, I never would have believed that either. It was funny, I'd always thought that the older I got, the more I'd understand and know. But as time went on, the only thing I was figuring out was how much I didn't know.

"Here," I said, thrusting what I now knew to be a bomb out to Elliot, "disable it."

Elliot took it gingerly, and peered down at the mess of wires. "That may take a while," he said.

"How long is a while?" I asked.

Elliot shrugged. "Maybe ten minutes. How many of them are there?"

"Too many to spend ten minutes on each one," I said. "What we need is the schematics map for the installation of these things. Then we'd know exactly where to look."

"This is like the worst Easter egg hunt in history," Elliot muttered, and I almost laughed. He turned the explosive this way and that and then looked at me, eyebrow raised. "Do you think Salzburg didn't know?" he said, voicing the very thought that kept bouncing around my own head.

"I have no idea," I said. "Maybe."

"Pretty convenient that he left the Academy the morning before it was destroyed," Elliot said.

"Yeah," I said, gritting my teeth. "A little too convenient." We both stared at the camera that wasn't really a camera for another second, and then I shook myself, forcing myself to refocus.

"Come on," I said, already sloshing my way out of the fountain. "We have to go break into my house." If one person had a master plan of where all these cameras were hidden, it would be my mom.

"What about this?" Elliot asked, holding up the camera.

"Bring it with you," I said.

"Great," Elliot muttered, shoving it in his pocket so he could use both hands to climb out of the fountain. "Just what I wanted to do. Break into the commander in chief's house with a bomb in my pocket."

"It could be worse," I said.

"Really?" he asked. "How?"

"I have no idea," I admitted. "Let's go."

CHAPTER THIRTY-ONE

ELLIOT

I'd imagined walking into the house on the hill more times than I could count. Sometimes I was the commander in chief in my daydreams, and sometimes I was just imagining what it would be like to live in a place like this. But I'd never, not once, imagined climbing through the second-story window like a thief. Yet here I was, in a tree, waiting for Regan to finish prying the window open. A second later she had it and slipped inside. I followed, not wanting to be left alone in the tree for a passing security guard to catch. The room was pitch-black, and I crouched, waiting for my eyes to adjust. Before they had a chance, Regan had me by the arm and was pulling me out into a hallway.

I did my best not to gape in openmouthed awe, but it was hard. The house was everything I'd imagined it would be and more. The walls were ornately paneled in dark, glossy wood, and the carpet under my feet was so thick it practically squished. I didn't have a chance to look around, though; Regan was hurrying down the wide staircase, and I hustled to catch up. She turned left, and we were inside an office. The office, I realized, of the commander in chief of the Academy. A fireplace sat in one corner, the wood burned down to embers, and on the opposite side of the room was an elegant wood desk. A desk that Regan was ripping apart. Papers rained down around me like snow as she shifted through the piles on the desk like a hurricane.

"Are those them?" I asked, walking over to stare at a pair of Chaos Cuffs in their glass display case.

"What?" Regan asked, jerking her head up to see what I was looking at.

"Are these the cuffs she used to catch the Hitler Butterfly?" I asked, thinking of the jump that had catapulted Regan's mom to fame. We'd studied it in class on countless occasions, recapping how she'd managed to catch the Butterfly who would have reversed the outcome of World War II.

"Are you serious right now?" Regan asked, and I ducked as she threw something, I think a book, at my head. It sailed past me to thump against the wall. "Focus, will you?" she said.

"Right. Sorry," I said, and hurried to help her, grabbing the closest stack of papers and digging in. I wasn't sure exactly what I was looking for. I doubted there was a paper with the heading "Here are the locations of the security cameras that are actually explosives. Have a nice day." But I was really hoping that I'd know it when I saw it.

"Got it!" Regan cried a second later, and I jumped, the papers I'd been holding flying in every direction.

"Sorry," she whispered. "But look, I got it!" She thrust a piece of paper under my nose, and I glanced down to see a detailed map of the campus. On it were tiny red Xs. On the top of the page were the words "BUTTERFLY DETECTION PROTOTYPE INSTALL-MENT" in large block letters. I ran my finger from one X to the next, mentally picturing where each of these deadly explosives was sitting.

"Regan?!" came a surprised cry, and we both jumped, looking up to see Regan's mom standing silhouetted in the doorway of the office.

"Mom!" Regan said, and practically flew across the room and into her mother's surprised arms. Commander Fitz hugged Regan back, looking from her to me and back again. Her eyes widened a moment later when she noticed the mess of papers strewn across the floor.

"Regan?" she said. "What are you doing here? Is everything okay?" Regan stepped back as tears ran down her face. But of course; she'd been told her mother was dead just hours ago. Now here she was talking to her again. "You weren't outside, were you?" her mom asked. "There was a Butterfly alert not five minutes ago, I just got the alert . . ." Her words trailed off as she looked at us, taking in our dripping-wet pajamas and dirt-smudged faces. "No," she said, shaking her head. "You two aren't . . . You can't be . . ."

"I'm really sorry about this, Mom. You know how training drills are. I'll explain later," Regan said, and at first I thought she was apologizing for being a Butterfly, but then Regan whirled and grabbed the glass shadow box holding her mother's famous Chaos Cuffs and smashed it on the floor. The box shattered with a resounding crack, and I threw my hands up as needle-sharp splinters of glass sprayed in all directions. By the time I put my hands down, Regan had already snatched the cuffs out of the box and had one around her mom's wrist and the other around the leg of the desk.

"What are you doing?!" Commander Fitz cried, her voice high and panicked as she yanked at the cuffs. Regan raced back to the desk to grab the map she'd left behind and then ran to the office window. I, however, was still standing there frozen at the sight of Commander Fitz cuffed to her own chair.

"Elliot!" Regan said, and I shook my head and raced for the window. Regan was already halfway out of it, but then she paused and looked back at her mom.

"I love you," she said, and I felt my face burn red. I shouldn't be here for this. If only the office window was big enough to squeeze past Regan and out into night. But since it wasn't, I just stood there as Regan's mom stopped struggling to get loose and stared back at her daughter.

"I love you too," she said. Regan locked eyes with her mom for another second and then slipped the rest of the way out of the window.

Commander Fitz turned her attention to me, and I wished I could sink through the floor. "Sorry," I said lamely, and hurried after Regan.

Regan waited for me to land beside her before taking off back toward the campus buildings.

"How many are there?" I asked, jerking my head toward the paper she still clutched in her hand.

"I don't know," she said, and her voice, so calm and steady mere seconds ago with her mom, now sounded strangled and choked. "Here, you look," she said, thrusting it toward me. I took it from her, deciding not to comment on the tears that were streaming down her face. I glanced down at the map, but it was too dark to see anything, so I skidded to a stop at the next lantern we passed, grabbing Regan so she wouldn't go charging off into the night without me. Considering we were out past curfew and every guard on campus was probably looking for us, the worst place we could possibly be was under a spotlight, but we didn't have time for caution now, not when every second counted. I held the map up to the light and finished the job I'd started in the office before we'd been interrupted by Commander Fitz.

"There's twenty-five," I said. Somehow that number seemed simultaneously small and overwhelmingly large. When Regan first told me about her security-cameras-turned-explosives revelation, I'd pictured hundreds of cameras, a number so big even a fleet of people couldn't retrieve them in time. Twenty-five was definitely better, but it was still terrifying to think about that many explosives sprinkled around campus.

"Twenty-five," Regan repeated. "Salzburg wasn't taking any chances, was he."

"Should we have told your mom about him?" I asked, glancing back toward the house on the hill.

"And said what?" Regan asked. "All we have is a hunch, a hunch that would have taken entirely too long to explain. Besides, last I checked, nobody listened to criminals and their hunches." I winced at the word *criminal* and Regan gave me a sympathetic smile and clapped me hard on the shoulder.

"If it makes you feel any better, there's no one else I'd rather have as a partner in crime," she said.

"In a weird way, that actually does make me feel better," I said. Regan glanced behind her to where the Edison clock tower was illuminated.

"We have exactly forty minutes left to find them all," she said. "We need to get moving."

"It's impossible," I said. "Even if we split up, there isn't any way we can make it all over campus. We don't have enough time." I looked at Regan, waiting for her to join me in my meltdown, but to my surprise she had a familiar smile on her face.

"Now that, I can fix," she said. "I present to you bullet point number six," she said, sounding more than a little smug. Before I could respond, she pulled something out of her pocket and held it up to the light. It was the black metal key card of the commander in chief, a card that hung around the commander's neck until it was time to hand it off to the next commander.

"Grab the key card when you have a chance," I said. "You stole that from your mom?" I asked, remembering how she'd hugged her mom moments before things went south.

"I prefer the term *borrowed*," she said. "Let's go." With that she turned and raced across campus, and I knew without asking where she was headed. What I didn't know was what exactly she was planning on doing once we got there. But as I dashed after her, I realized that it no longer mattered who was in charge or that I had no idea what the plan was. I had to trust Regan in the same desperate way that a skydiver trusts his parachute, and that feeling was uncomfortable for someone like me.

Luckily the Hub, the main building where all the Glitch equipment was housed, wasn't far, and we were hurling ourselves up its wide stone steps within minutes. Thanks to Regan's card, we made it inside without a problem. At this time of night, the building was dark and deserted, and our footsteps sounded too loud in the silent hallways. Three quick swipes of the card later, and we were in the official Glitch room. Regan flicked the lights on, illuminating the gigantic space that was three times as big as the miniature version back at the mountain. Twenty platforms encircled the room, each with their own set of equipment and computers. I'd been here twice before, both times on field trips, and the room had been all hustle and bustle with agents Glitching to the past and back to the present in full costume, Butterflies being taken into custody, and the general clamor and chaos that went with protecting the history of the United States. It had been overwhelming then, but it was even more overwhelming now with its eerie silence.

"Grab six sets of Chaos Cuffs and two belts," Regan said, already booting up the closest computer.

I dashed over to the far wall and collected the cuffs and belts. They clanked together in a way that set my teeth on edge as I deposited the whole lot on the floor at Regan's feet. She typed in one last thing on the computer and then turned and quickly looped a belt around her waist.

"The problem is that these are only designed to carry two sets of cuffs at the most," she muttered under her breath as she attached one set to each hip. She held the remaining set in her hand, her forehead furrowed.

"Here," I said, tossing her the belt I hadn't managed to get on yet. "Throw that over a shoulder and attach the extra cuff." I raced back to grab two more belts. "You know," I said as I attached my own cuffs, "this has only ever been done once before."

"What's that?" Regan said, sounding distracted as she squinted at the computer screen.

"Glitching within a Glitch," I said. "I read about it once. One of our own agents went rogue, and in order to confuse his trail he started leapfrogging through time."

"Did it work?" Regan asked.

"He was never caught, if that's what you mean," I said. "But what we are about to do is really dangerous. You know that, right?"

"Yeah, well, last I checked so was getting blown up, so . . ." Regan muttered, and I snorted. She had a solid point. "Get on the platform," she said as she hit the activation button. Above our platform a countdown started from ten, and Regan sprinted over to join me. Without saying a word, we grasped hands. There was a time that I'd do just about anything to get some distance from Regan Fitz, but right now, at this moment, there wasn't anyone else I'd rather be hurtling through time beside.

"At what point are you going to tell me the plan?" I asked as the numbers ticked down toward zero.

"There is no plan," Regan said as everything went black.

CHAPTER THIRTY-TWO

REGAN

I opened my eyes back inside the mountain. To my relief, Elliot was still right beside me, his hand clutching mine with a death grip that made my bones ache.

"What?" he asked, looking around. "Are you serious? We were *just* here!"

"Come on," I said, bolting down the hallway toward the dorms. We were almost there when I heard something and threw an arm out to catch Elliot as I skidded to a stop. He let out a muffled grunt as my arm caught him in the stomach. Before he could say anything, I slapped my hand over his mouth and dragged him into the shadows. My heart was hammering hard inside my chest, but I could just make out the sound of two hushed but all too familiar voices. Elliot tensed; he'd heard us too. I carefully took my hand off his mouth as a second later a different Elliot and Regan emerged from the darkness, creeping down the hallway in their pajamas. Not a different Regan and Elliot, I reminded myself as we watched the figures disappear around the corner—a past version of ourselves. That was us earlier that night, heading toward the Glitch room with no idea how we were going to get the door open. Present Elliot's jaw had dropped open, and I reached over and put my hand under his chin, closing his mouth with a faint click of teeth. Roused from his shock, he turned to look at me.

"Come on," I said, darting out of the shadows and toward the dorm rooms the past versions of ourselves had just left. Elliot caught up to me right outside the door. "Get Sam, Corban, and Blake and get back to the Academy," I said. "I'll be right behind you." To his credit, Elliot didn't try to ask me a million questions; instead he just turned and disappeared through the dark doorway of the boys' dormitory. I realized that it was because he trusted me. I let that sink in for a second before entering the dorm that I'd left only an hour ago. Well, I amended, the Regan I'd just seen in the hall had only left it a minute ago. I shook my head, choosing not to think about how muddled and confusing

317

time traveling was if you really thought about it long enough, and slipped into the dark dorm room.

My first instinct was to turn on the lights, but as my eyes adjusted to the dark, I decided against it. I was outnumbered, and the element of surprise was going to be key. I moved quickly over to Tess's and Eliana's beds, clicking the Chaos Cuffs onto their wrists before they were even awake. I was just turning to Serina's bunk when I felt an arm snake out around my neck and squeeze.

"Drop it," Serina hissed in my ear as something sharp pressed against the small of my back.

"Serina, it's me, Regan," I said.

"Regan?" she said, removing whatever had been stuck in my back and letting go of my neck. Before she could ask anything else, I had the cuff on her right arm. A second later I was pressing the activation button on her cuffs. Leaning over, I quickly activated Eliana and Tess. Everything went dark, and to my utter relief I found myself back on the platform in the Academy's Hub, but this time instead of Elliot, I was standing next to Tess, Eliana, and Serina. To my surprise Tess was somehow still asleep. Eliana was blinking groggily at the room while Serina stood frozen, her eyes flicking from platform to platform so fast I wondered if she was making herself dizzy. A moment later Elliot appeared mid-struggle with a very angry Sam and an equally confused Corban and Blake.

Appearing on the platform distracted Sam for a moment, and Elliot managed to pull himself free from the headlock Sam had him in to come stand by me.

"Are we—" Serina said, and Sam whipped around to face his sister, his expression relaxing just a hair at the sight of her, and for the first time I understood, because I'd felt a tangible weight lift off my shoulders the second Elliot reappeared.

"Listen up," I said, and everyone jumped as my voice bounced back at us in the cavernous hub. Tess sat up with a start, looking around herself with such a baffled expression on her face that I almost laughed. "Sorry," I said. "But we don't have much time."

"Are we at the Academy?" Sam asked.

"We are," I confirmed. "And in less than an hour this entire island is going to explode, unless we do something about it."

Sam was the first one to catch on, and he walked over to stand next to Serina. "What do we need to do to save the Academy?" he asked.

"Wait a second," Corban said, his head still on a swivel as he looked around. "Is this the past? And if it is, then that makes us . . ."

"Criminals? Butterflies? Time-traveling trespassers?"

Elliot said. "All of the above, welcome to the club."

I held up a hand before anyone could say anything. "Listen," I said. "We'll explain, and then if you want to go back to the mountain, that's your call. We can't force you to be a criminal."

"But, spoiler alert," Elliot said, "the mountain is about forty-five minutes from collapsing in on itself from an attack. So, there's that."

"So, no matter what, in less than an hour, we could all be dead?" Tess said with a nervous glance at her cousin.

"Right." I nodded, hoping my face wasn't giving away how nauseous her words had just made me feel. "But if you stay here, we have a chance to save the Academy and ourselves."

"A very small chance," Elliot added.

"So, what's the plan?" Serina asked, and I thought I heard Elliot snort, but I ignored it and pulled the schematics page for Salzburg's prototypes from my pocket. All too aware of the time we were currently wasting, I jumped into a condensed version of what had happened so far, from the mountain getting attacked, to our initial jump back to the Academy, my deduction about the cameras, and borrowing my mom's key.

"And this guy, Salzburg or whatever," said Blake when I was done. "You really think he's the one responsible for all this? I mean, he's an officer, right?"

"Ten to one says he's a Mayhem member," Corban said. "They are the only ones big enough and awful enough to plan something like this." His eyes went wide as he turned to us. "Whoa, what if there are lots of professors acting as secret double agents? Professor Treebaun was a real jerk back at the Academy, I could totally see him as a double agent. Couldn't you, Blake?"

"Treebaun?" Blake said. "Dream on. That guy's never broken a rule in his entire life. Besides, I'm not convinced this Salzburg guy has anything to do with Mayhem. I mean, isn't it totally possible that he was just stupid and manufactured bombs on accident?"

"He's not stupid," I said, feeling my jaw clench as I remembered his oh so timely transfer to the mountain.

"He might be," Elliot said, and we all turned to look at him.

"Why?" I asked.

"Well, he transferred himself right out of the frying pan and into a fire, didn't he? Why go to the mountain if he was just going to attack it next? It makes no sense."

"Maybe it was an unrelated attack," said Serina.

"One attack at a time," I said. "We fix this one, and then we figure out how to deal with the mess at the mountain."

"So just to clarify, we have less than an hour to find twenty-five bombs," Sam said.

"Twenty-four," Elliot said, removing the small black explosive from his pocket.

"Gah!" I yelped, jumping backward, my hand to my heart. "I forgot about that one."

"I didn't," he said, turning it over in his hands.

"So that's a bomb?" Tess said, leaning in to get a better look at it.

Sam took it out of Elliot's hand and peered at it for a few seconds like it was a bug under a microscope before handing it back to him.

"It's a bomb," he said.

"We can't disarm it?" Eliana asked.

Elliot shook his head. "It would take too long, and I've never seen anything quite like this before."

"So, we don't disarm them," I said. "We find them, all of them, and we get them off the island. We can meet at the West Gate," I said, thinking about the boat we'd used to get to the mountain.

"Wait a second," Elliot said, turning to me. "We can't just send everyone out in their pajamas."

"We can't?" I asked, because honestly, that had been my plan. Elliot and I had been running around in our pajamas.

"That's a good point," Sam said. "If we manage to pull this off, we don't want to be recognized."

I shared a glance with Elliot, because we'd already

been recognized by my mom. It was too late for us. Even if we survived this, we were looking at a life behind bars. For a second that thought made my insides go cold, but then I gritted my teeth. It was better than the alternative, and it would be worth it if we could save lives.

"Right," Serina said, nodding at her brother. "Otherwise we'll Glitch back to the present and find ourselves under arrest."

"Speaking of arrest," I said, jerking my head toward the Chaos Cuffs we'd used to bring them here, "keep those on you. After we get rid of the bombs, we are going to need a quick exit out of here."

"Good thinking," Sam said.

"Well, if we need disguises, we're in the right place," Serina said, already jogging over to the far wall, where rack upon rack of costumes sat, waiting to outfit Glitchers as they traveled to the past. She turned to see everyone else hesitating on the platform and rolled her eyes.

"You said the Butterfly alerts went off on campus, right?" she asked. "So, if they want Butterflies, let's give them Butterflies." She ripped a bloodred ball gown off a hanger along with the matching red feather masquerade mask that went with it. "Try to cover at least part of your face, folks," she said, holding it up so only her blue eyes showed through. "The less of us they can see, the less they can identify."

"Good call," Sam said, vaulting off the platform to join his sister. "I think there are some World War One gas masks in here somewhere." With that everyone sprang into action, grabbing costumes off the rack and yanking them on over their crumpled pajamas. Elliot tossed me an Alcatraz prison uniform, and I glanced up at him, eyebrow raised.

"Trying to be funny?" I said, yanking the shirt on and buttoning it up.

He stared at me in confusion for a second before realization dawned on him and his face went pale.

"Sorry," I said. "I forgot you're not really funny. Probably too soon to joke about life in jail anyway. My bad." Before he could respond I caught sight of the clock on one of the computers, though, and the smile fell off my face. I quickly yanked on the rest of the disguise.

"Everyone ready?" I asked, tying the red bandanna Elliot had handed me into a knot so it covered the lower half of my face. Looking up, I saw the weirdest mismatched group I'd ever seen. There was Alcatraz Elliot and Serina in her full ball gown and mask. Sam had found two World War I gas masks, and he and Corban both were wearing the ratty uniform of a soldier fresh from the trenches. Tess and Eliana had taken a different route, disguising themselves in the raggedy washed-out clothing of Dust Bowl victims, complete with large circular goggles and cloth-wrapped faces. Blake was dressed like Elvis complete with oversized sunglasses and sideburns that took up half his face. It would have to work.

Beside me Elliot snorted, and I turned to look at him, eyebrow raised. For a guy who spent the majority of his life with a scowl permanently embedded on his face, how in the world was he possibly finding this funny?

"Sorry," he said, flapping a hand. "It's just that this went from the worst Easter egg hunt ever to the weirdest Halloween group I've ever seen."

"No trick-or-treater has ever been this historically accurate," Corban said, stepping forward to peer over my shoulder at the map.

"Or good-looking," Blake said as he gave his black Elvis wig a twist so it curled down his forehead in a perfect spiral.

"You two are impossible," Sam muttered as he jerked his head at the map. "Let's get a move on."

I nodded and ripped the piece of paper three times so I was left with four equally sized pieces. "Time to divide and conquer," I said, handing one piece to each of the partner groups. As they studied their section of the map, Elliot leaned in and together we stared at our own section.

"The Revere and Roosevelt Building and my old dorm," Elliot murmured. "Those are big buildings. We need to hustle."

"See you at the gate," Serina said as she and Sam dashed out the door in a swish of bloodred skirts. To my surprise, Tess and Eliana both stopped to give Elliot and me a quick, fierce hug before flying out the door after Serina and Sam.

"What was that for?" Elliot asked, looking after them in confusion.

"It's a friendship thing," Corban said, clapping Elliot so hard on the back he stumbled forward a step. "Don't let it freak you out." With that, Corban and Blake disappeared out the door too.

Elliot watched them go. "Are they our friends?" he asked.

"I think so," I said.

He nodded and turned his attention back to me. "Do you think this will work?"

"Only one way to find out," I said as I jumped off the platform and together we ran for the door. We were outside in the cold night air within seconds, and I pushed myself to run faster. Even with our new reinforcements, we were going to be cutting it close to find our explosives in time.

The first one was located in the Roosevelt Building, and we took a sharp right and raced down the short path, through the dark playground and up the stairs to the wide glass double doors. I'd attended all my elementary-level classes in this building, and I knew the halls well. I gave the doors a firm yank, but nothing happened. I groaned in exasperation. Of course, the building was locked. I was just fumbling for my mom's key when Elliot threw out a hand to stop me. I turned to see him pointing above the door, where a familiar black camera was mounted to the red brick. Bingo.

The next four explosives proved to be easier to find than I'd ever hoped. Instead of being hidden in the heart of the buildings, they were located outside. "Hidden in plain sight," I muttered as I yanked the fifth and final one off the concrete wall of the Revere Building and carefully tucked it inside the backpack I'd found abandoned on the playground. The cloth over my mouth was making it hard to breathe, and I yanked it down around my neck so the cold night air could fill my lungs.

"We might actually pull this off," Elliot said, just as we rounded a corner and ran full force into a group of security officers.

My face collided with the first officer's chest plate, and my nose gave a sickening crunch. Black spots erupted momentarily in my vision as I was knocked flat on my back. A second later, I was blinking up into the faces of four very concerned security officers.

"Cadet Fitz," said one, holding out a hand to help me up. "What are you doing out past curfew? Dressed like that? We had a Butterfly alert. It isn't safe." I let him help me up, my brain going a mile a minute as I worked to think my way out of this. A quick glance at Elliot revealed him clutching his right eye as another officer helped him to his feet. They obviously had no idea that we were supposed to be miles away inside a mountain. That was good. I could use that. I held my hand up to my nose to stem the stream of blood that I could feel running hot and wet down my chin.

"Oh geez," said another officer. "She's bleeding. We just made Commander Fitz's kid bleed."

"Can we get fired for that?" whispered another one.

"Not you," said another one. "Jones, maybe. She ran into him." And then it clicked.

"Quick," I said. "My mom. The Butterfly. He attacked us. I've been trying to find help." I gestured frantically back in the direction of my house, and that was all it took. All four guards snapped to attention at my words and took off at a full sprint toward my house, yelling

328

commands into their communicators as they took my story hook, line, and sinker. Elliot came to stand beside me as they disappeared around a corner.

"I'm impressed," he said. "You didn't even really have to lie."

"I know," I said, swallowing hard. I'd just left out that the Butterfly was me. Before I could think any more about what my mom would say when those officers showed up, I spotted the clock tower. We had five minutes left.

CHAPTER THIRTY-THREE

ELLIOT

There was only one main path that led to the West Gate, and as we raced down it we were joined by Tess and Eliana. Tess held up a lumpy pillowcase, and I felt myself relax the tiniest fraction of an inch. One more section of campus safe. A minute later we almost ran right into Corban and Blake as they burst through the shrubbery and onto the path in front of us. They hadn't managed to grab a bag, and their hands were full of the small black explosives. The sight was unnerving. But where were Serina and Sam? I wondered as the rest of us hurled around the last bend in the path and saw the West Gate.

It felt like a lifetime ago that Regan's mom had

walked us out of those doors and onto the boat that would take us to the mountain. Tonight, though, those thick steel doors were shut tight, and I could only hope that Regan was right and her mom's card would open them. As we hurtled closer, I saw that security officers were standing to either side of the gate, and I felt what little hope I'd managed to muster fizzle.

"Security officers dead ahead," I called to Regan, and I noticed again the ragtag appearance of our group. We weren't exactly inconspicuous.

"Yup," Regan said, and then to my utter surprise she sprinted straight up to them.

"Help!" she screamed, and they rushed toward her, their hands poised above the weapons.

"There's been an attack!" she cried. "A Butterfly, at my house. You have to go help my mom!" It took the guards a second to recognize who was screaming at them, but I could tell the moment that they did, as they stood up just a hair straighter.

I watched this performance feeling more than a little impressed. Thanks to the help of the blood covering her chin and shirt from her busted nose, she was pulling off a pretty exceptional damsel in distress.

"We'll radio for help," said the first guard, reaching for his communicator.

"No, you won't," said a voice behind us, and we all

turned to see Officer Salzburg striding down the path, looking furious.

"No way," I said. "You followed us?" I flashed back to the last image I'd seen before Regan and I had Glitched out of the collapsing mountain. He hadn't come back into the Glitch room because there was no other way out—he'd come back in so he could stop us.

"What's going on?" said one of the guards, looking in confusion from us to Salzburg and back.

"What's going on is that these children have been caught red-handed committing crimes against our nation. They are Butterflies," Salzburg said, his voice ringing out with an icy authority that made the hairs on the back of my neck stand on end.

"He's the Butterfly!" Regan said, jabbing a finger at Salzburg. "He installed explosives all over campus."

"Lies," Salzburg said. "Arrest them. Confiscate the bags they are holding. They've stolen expensive security equipment in an attempt to weaken the Academy's defenses." Regan took a step back and involuntarily the rest of our group huddled together, as though somehow we were going to be able to stop what was about to happen.

I turned to look back at the clock. We had less than three minutes left. Just then, there was the sound of running feet behind us, and everyone turned to see Serina and Sam sprinting down the path with a pack of security officers in hot pursuit. Maybe it was Serina's gigantic ball gown that she had hitched up around her waist, or Sam's gas mask, but I knew in that moment that we were sunk. No one would believe us over an officer like Salzburg.

It was like I was seeing everything in slow motion. The clock ticking down, Regan still trying desperately to convince the guards that Salzburg was the real criminal here, the wide panicked eyes of the rest of the kids, and the small black explosives that were about to detonate and blast apart the Academy. Regan turned to me then, and I could tell from the desperation on her face that she was out of ideas. My mind scrambled for something, anything, and I found myself flipping through every historical event and Glitch mission I could think of like an old-fashioned Rolodex, searching for something that could save us. Nothing had prepared me for this. Not my studying. Not the classes. Not even the practice simulations I'd done with Regan where the worst-case scenario was that one of us would get annoyed and use our Chaos Cuffs to exit the situation, and then it hit me. This *was* a mission. I was in the past, and all I needed to get out of here was a set of Chaos Cuffs.

"Regan!" I called. "Worst-case scenario!" She stopped yelling at the officers to turn to me, and I saw understanding flash across her face as her hand went automatically to her hip, where her own Chaos Cuffs were still clipped. Turning, I rushed for Corban and Blake, hitting the activation button on their cuffs just as Regan hit the activation button on Tess's and Eliana's. The officers yelled as they all disappeared.

"Activate your cuffs!" I yelled to Serina and Sam. I waited a half second to make sure they disappeared before grabbing Regan's hand just as Salzburg lunged for us. I felt his fingernails scrape skin as everything went black.

When I opened my eyes, I had no idea where we were going to be. Back inside the mountain? At the Academy Hub? Our jumps had crossed over themselves so much that it all felt like a confusing spiderweb of time travel at this point. But to my relief, I opened my eyes inside the mountain Glitching room with Regan still holding my hand. That relief vanished a moment later when I spotted Salzburg clutching Regan's arm in a vise grip.

He stood frozen as he took in the empty Glitch platform and the inside of the mountain.

"What did you do?" he asked. I looked over at Regan, who had the same wide-eyed look of horror as Salzburg.

"Where is everyone?" Regan asked, whirling away from Salzburg's grip to look behind herself at the eerily empty Glitch platform.

My heart did a funny hiccup in my chest as I realized that the rest of our friends and the bombs they'd been carrying were nowhere to be seen. What had happened?

I didn't have time to think about it, though, because Salzburg chose that moment to launch himself off the platform and race for the bank of computers. Before I could stop her, Regan threw herself after him. She landed on his back like a monkey and wrapped her arms around his neck. I stood frozen as he dug his fingernails mercilessly into her arm.

"Elliot!" Regan yelled. "Do something!" But I had no idea what to do. I was holding a bag of bombs that were set to detonate at any moment, and my partner had the guy responsible for them in a headlock. What should I do first? Bombs. I decided. The bombs were the priority here. Leaving my bag of explosives on the platform, I jumped off it and rushed past Regan and Salzburg, heading for the computers.

"Thanks for the help!" Regan yelled after me, but I ignored her as I quickly typed a few key words into the computer's state-of-the-art history search engine. I needed somewhere I could ditch a bag of explosives without it causing major damage to the past. The first thing that came to mind was Chernobyl, but I almost immediately dismissed the idea. It was nuclear, which always involved a lot of equipment and prep work, and besides that, we really couldn't mess with Ukraine's history without a sanction from their Glitch department.

What I needed was a big explosion that didn't kill anyone, and that was tricky. I looked up to ask Regan, but she had her hands more than full with the flailing Salzburg. I shut my eyes, thinking hard. There was a test in New Mexico in 1985. If I remembered correctly, and I almost always remembered correctly, it was called Minor Scale, and it was the largest non-nuclear explosion ever detonated.

It would have to work. We were out of time. I quickly punched in the correct coordinates and raced for the platform as the clock above it started counting down. I skidded to a stop on the platform to collect the odd bundle of explosives like some kind of terrible Santa Claus and turned to see Regan leap off Salzburg's back and roll clear as he came up swinging. I'd forgotten just how good she was at hand-to-hand combat when she didn't have a hoop skirt in her way.

Regan looked up then, and I saw the horror register on her face as she realized why I was still standing there. Someone was going to have to take the bombs to their final resting place, and that someone was going to be me. I tried to smile what I hoped was a reassuring smile, but the tears I felt streaming down my cheeks ruined the effect as I prepared for my final Glitch in this lifetime.

Regan stood frozen, watching me for another heartbeat before sprinting for the platform.

"Stay back," I yelled, but when had Regan ever listened to me? With one second left to go on the countdown clock, she grabbed my hand as everything went black.

CHAPTER THIRTY-FOUR

REGAN

We opened up our eyes in the desert. I looked around, expecting there to be a big pile of explosives sitting somewhere, but all I saw was what looked like an aboveground pool about ten feet in front of us. Whatever, it didn't matter now, we were down to seconds before these things exploded, and I had no intention of exploding with them. Elliot was still holding the bag of explosives, and I ripped it off his shoulder and dropped it on the ground.

"Let's go," he said just as we heard a plane overhead. We turned to see that it was carrying something large and rocket shaped.

"It's heading toward that pool," I said.

"That's no pool," Elliot said. I grabbed his hand, and together we activated our cuffs just as the plane dropped its rocket onto the thing that wasn't a pool and everything went black.

I was pretty sure that we weren't dead, that we'd activated our cuffs in the nick of time, but it was still a relief to open up my eyes in the mountain again.

"Where's Salzburg?" Elliot asked.

"There," I said as I spotted him on the Glitch platform directly across from us. Above his head, the Glitch timer was counting down quickly from ten. There was no way I was going to let that slimeball escape. I was mid-leap off the platform when I felt Elliot grab my arm and yank me backward.

"What are you doing?" I said, whirling to face him.

"We'll never get him off that platform in time," Elliot said. "Look." I turned to see that there was less than five second left on Salzburg's clock, and I knew Elliot was right. I felt white-hot anger bubble up inside me at the future version of myself who had let this happen. I'd somehow ensured that I'd beat the Lincoln simulation, but I'd failed to catch the guy responsible for all of this. Suddenly I remembered something. My Swiss cheese brain, the one I'd so often compared to a hole-filled colander, actually remembered something.

"Elliot," I shrieked, "your pocket!" He stared at

me for a half second in confusion, and then all blood drained from his face as he reached into his pocket and pulled out the very first bomb we'd found hidden in the fountain. I didn't even stop to think; there wasn't time for that. I snatched it from his hand and launched it.

"Salzburg!" I yelled. "Catch!"

Salzburg looked up in surprise as the bomb arced through the air and his hands reached up automatically to catch the object zooming at his head. He caught it a half second before his countdown clock hit zero, and he and the bomb disappeared.

"Don't forget the one in his pocket," Elliot said numbly as he sat down hard on the platform beside me. My own legs suddenly felt like wet noodles, and I sank down next to him. Together we stared in disbelief at the empty platform as our raspy breath reverberated around the empty room.

"I can't believe we forgot about the one in your pocket," I said, shaking my head.

"Almost forgot," Elliot said.

"Where do you think Salzburg went?" I said.

"I have no idea, but since he's holding a bomb that could explode any second, let's hope it wasn't the signing of the Declaration of Independence. We can probably pull up the Glitch history on that computer and figure it out. But I need a second for my heart to climb out of my throat."

"But what happened to Sam and Serina and every-one else?" I said. "Why aren't they here? Did they not make it out of the Academy?" I asked, the very thought sending a ripple of fear down my spine as I pictured them holding their explosives in their ridiculous cos-tumes.

Elliot shook his head. "Every one of them disap-peared before we did. We saw it. They made it out of the Academy. I'm positive."

"Then why aren't they here?" I asked again, looking around the room as though they might be playing a very misguided game of hide-and-seek.

"Give me a second," Elliot said, his face furrowed in concentration. "I can figure this out."

"Maybe their cuffs malfunctioned?" I said, looking down at the set I still had attached to my belt.

Elliot snapped his head up and looked at me, his eyes wide. "They didn't malfunction," he said. "Their cuffs took them back to where they came from."

"You're going to have to give me more than that," I said. "We've been a lot of places recently."

"It's confusing," Elliot said, "but you and I Glitched twice, right? Once from the collapsing mountain to the Academy, and then when we found out how many explosives there were, we Glitched back to the moun-tain to get everyone, and then back to the Academy."

"The collapsing mountain," I said, glancing around

the room that was still mercifully intact. "We never warned anyone about Mayhem attacking here!"

"It wasn't an attack by Mayhem," Elliot said, and there was something about the way he said it, a tightness in his voice, that made it clear that I wasn't going to like what came next.

"Just spit it out," I said. "I can handle it."

"It's why Salzburg looked so shocked that night. The attack wasn't one he planned. He had no idea the mountain was going to collapse around our ears."

"Well, if it wasn't him and Mayhem, then who attacked the mountain?"

"No one," Elliot said, looking sick. "There was no attack. There was an accident."

"That's not spitting it out," I said. "What happened?"

"I think our friends Glitched back to where we took them from. The dorm room inside the mountain the night after we found out the Academy was destroyed." My mind raced back to that night, and everything clicked into place. "They brought the bombs back to the mountain," I said. "So, when we were standing in the Glitch room that night, listening to all the professors debate about what to do . . ."

"They Glitched back to a dorm room with no way to dispose of the bombs. So, what we thought was an attack on the mountain by Mayhem, was really just our friends . . ."

"Exploding," I finished, and it was like I couldn't breathe. All the blood rushed from my head, and I put my head between my knees as dark spots swam in front of my eyes. I stayed like that for a full minute before raising my head to look at Elliot. "So they're dead?" I asked.

"That's what I don't know," Elliot said. "If so, they died in an alternate time, a time that won't ever happen now since the Academy was never destroyed. What I don't know is if that act changed the timeline at the mountain enough to save them. So, they might be fine. Or," he said, and he didn't need to finish his sentence for me to know what that *or* meant. I swallowed hard as tears pressed against the backs of my eyes. Had we saved the Academy at the cost of our friends' lives?

"Okay," Elliot said, breaking the sober silence a few seconds later. "We can't sit here and freak out about something we aren't even sure has happened. The odds are that they are fine. What we need to focus on now is us. We aren't out of the woods yet." It was like his very words had jinxed us, because at that exact moment there was a loud bang on the entrance to the Glitch room. We both turned wide eyes to stare as the sound came again.

"Cadet Fitz!" came a voice I knew all too well, and I felt Elliot grab my arm and haul me to my feet as my

343

mother's voice rang out again despite the thick steel door between us.

"Cadet Fitz!" she called again. "I know you and Cadet Mason are in there. Come out with your hands up and no one will get hurt." I turned horrified eyes on Elliot. And then, to my utter shock, Elliot Mason shrugged. Shrugged! Like life as we knew it wasn't over.

"What was that?" I asked, snapped momentarily out of my panic.

"It's fine," he said. "We saved the Academy, but more importantly, we saved a lot of lives tonight. And"— he shrugged again—"that's what we became Glitchers for—to protect the future. So it's okay if they arrest us. It's worth it."

"You're not mad?" I asked.

"Not even a little bit. Now come on," he said. "We are in this together. It's time to face the music."

"Man," I said, shaking my head. "Who are you and what happened to the Elliot who ripped that letter out of my hand that day in the simulation hall?"

"Cadet Fitz!" my mom called again, but I barely heard her as Elliot and I turned to look at one another in horror.

"The letter!" we said at the exact same time.

"Come out, cadets, or we will be forced to come in and take you and your coconspirators down by force," came my mother's voice.

"Coconspirators?" I said, and then shook my head as I realized that she was talking about Tess and Eliana and the rest of the kids we'd brought to the Academy in our attempt to save it. But of course, they weren't here, and their fate was still unknown.

"Get the Glitch programmed," I said to Elliot, glancing around frantically until my eyes landed on a stack of white paper. I grabbed one and turned around to find Elliot holding up an eerily familiar white envelope.

"Do you remember exactly what the letter said?" he asked.

"I think so," I said as I started writing out the letter that would change everything.

"Please, don't forget to put the bullet point about the bomb in my pocket," Elliot said, never taking his eyes off the computer screen in front of him.

"Cadets! We are giving you to the count of ten, and we are coming in," yelled Callaway, and I scribbled off the last of the note. There was something about seeing that rushed bullet point list, and finally understanding why it looked that way, that sent a shiver down my spine. I was already turning to the platform when I remembered something, and whirled to write my name in big bold script across the front.

"Hurry up," Elliot called, and I glanced up to see him tuck his own envelope in his pocket. But before

I could ask him what it was, he'd hit the countdown, and I sprinted for the platform. There was a loud bang from the direction of the door, but I didn't dare look back. I leaped the final steps and grabbed Elliot's hand and together we Glitched back to the moment before it all began.

CHAPTER THIRTY-FIVE

ELLIOT

I'd watched hundreds of recaps of myself, and it had never really fazed me. I'd loved analyzing my every move as I darted through history. But this? This was different.

I crouched with Regan outside the window of the simulation building and waited for the Regan and Elliot who hated one another to come around the corner and discover the letter we'd carefully placed just moments before. As it turned out, it was the second letter I'd drop in the past. The first one I'd already slipped into the campus mail slot. When Regan had asked me what I was up to, I'd been purposefully vague. Calling it the longest of long shots. To my surprise, Regan hadn't pressed the issue. She trusted me.

I was distracted from my thoughts by the other Elliot and Regan. The past version of us came barreling around the corner, bickering and insulting one another like it was our professional career. Even through the smudged window, I could see the look of pure revulsion Regan had on her face as I followed her down the hall, harassing her for all I was worth. Why had I done that? I wondered. Did I really think it made me look better to put her down?

"Man, you were a jerk," Regan muttered, and I turned to smile at her.

"Were?" I said. "As in, I'm not anymore?"

Regan rolled her eyes, but smiled. "Well," she said. "You aren't a grade-A jerk anymore. Maybe a grade B or C."

"First time I've been glad not to get an A," I mused as we watched past Elliot spot the letter that would change everything.

"Just for the record," I said, "you're better now too."

"What do you mean?" she said.

"I mean you used to walk around the Academy like some kind of princess surveying her kingdom. Like you couldn't be bothered to learn anyone's name or care about anyone but yourself."

"Really?" Regan said, wrinkling her nose in a way

I used to think made her look like a bulldog. I decided not to mention that.

"Really," I said.

"That must have been obnoxious," she said, and I snorted quietly. Together we turned our attention back to the versions of us I barely recognized anymore.

"This is so weird," Regan said.

"Unbelievably weird," I agreed. "But that seems to be the theme of our lives ever since we became partners."

"Do you regret it?" she asked, jerking her chin toward the building where the past version of me was just now bending down to pick up the letter.

I shook my head. "Not even for a second." I reached out to grab her hand and was about to hit the button on the cuffs that would return us to the present when she grabbed my arm to stop me.

"What is it now?" I asked, but instead of saying anything, she just raised an eyebrow and held out her arms as she did a slow spin. When I just stared at her uncomprehendingly, she sighed and rolled her eyes.

"Seriously?" she said. "Did you forget that we are wearing Alcatraz prison uniforms?"

"Oh," I said, because, stupidly, I had. "We should probably take those off."

"Ya think?" Regan said, already pulling hers over

her head to reveal her rather sweaty pajamas underneath. I did the same thing, wadding the dirty uniform up into a ball. Regan took it and shoved it unceremoniously into the perfectly trimmed shrubbery next to us.

"What are you doing?" I said. "We can't leave them here."

"Why not?" Regan said as she shoved her uniform in after mine. "Who's going to look in the past for evidence?"

"Good point," I said. Regan paused mid-shove and got a strange look on her face as she looked at me.

"What?" I asked.

"Nothing," she said, shaking her head again. "It's just that I know exactly who finds these. I spotted them on my walk home that afternoon, but I just assumed someone was being careless with costumes and dropped them off at the campus laundry."

"Weird," I said again, and she nodded. We both stared at the uniforms for another second and then I turned to Regan. "If you are going to head this way any second, we better get going. I don't remember how long Professor Green kept us in there."

"Good point," she said just as we saw a very grumpy Elliot stomp away toward Professor Green's room. We both watched as this past version of myself jammed my hand in my pocket, probably double-checking that the letter I'd just swiped was there.

"Let's go," I said. I didn't want to watch that guy I used to be anymore. There was something about the way my face had pinched in anger that turned my stomach a little.

Regan took a deep breath and squared her shoulders in a way I'd come to recognize over the last few weeks. "Right," she said, and then tried to force a smile that came off all wrong. "At least we don't look like criminals anymore."

"No," I said shaking my head. "We are only criminals if we get caught."

"But we're as good as caught," she said. "Didn't you hear that door bust open right as we disappeared? We are going to Glitch back smack dab in the middle of a pack of angry security officers. And my mom," she said, swallowing hard. When she noticed me watching, she gave a sheepish shrug. "Call me a chicken, but I'm not really looking forward to getting arrested."

"We'll see about that," I said as I grabbed her hand and activated my cuffs. The bright sunlight of the Academy faded to black as we traveled back to the present one last time.

We opened our eyes in the mountain in an empty Glitch room.

"What?" Regan said as she turned to take in the empty echoing space. "Didn't my mom and the security officers bust in here right before we left?" She turned to me, finger held up accusingly. "What did you do?" she asked.

"I'm not really sure," I admitted. "I took a chance based on something you said to your mom back in her office. It's the longest of long shots, but since no one is here trying to arrest us, I don't know." I shrugged. "It might have worked."

"So, you mean we might not end up in jail for the rest of our lives?" Regan said.

"There's only one way to find out," I said, and jumped down off the platform. Together we walked across the echoing room, and I glanced up at the perfectly intact ceiling. I would never forget the image of those hunks of rock falling around our heads as we ran for the platform. I remembered again why those hunks of rock had fallen and felt sick. Because of us, our friends had Glitched back to their dorm rooms holding explosives. Please let them be okay, I thought, please.

With a sigh, I turned back to see Regan clambering down off the platform. I walked over to join her, and together we walked across the room and both stopped in front of the thick metal door. We stood there, shoulder to shoulder, and stared at it, and I knew that Regan's mind was churning just like mine was with all the possibilities that could lie on the other side. As long as we stayed in the Glitch room, we could pretend like everything was fine. Like all our meddling in the past hadn't changed the future, but, of course, it had.

"We have to leave sometime," Regan finally said, breaking the silence. "If we get caught in here, whatever you did to prevent our arrest will be a waste."

"Right," I said, swallowing hard. Regan stepped forward and opened the door, and we slipped out into the darkened hallway.

CHAPTER THIRTY-SIX

REGAN

As the steel door of the Glitch room locked behind us, I reminded myself that whatever happened, it would all be worth it. We'd saved the Academy, and in doing so we'd done what we'd been trained to do—we'd protected the future of the United States.

We crept quietly down the darkened halls, but they were just as empty as any other night that we'd snuck out to practice. I was just beginning to think that we were going to pull this off when we came around the corner and ran into Callaway.

"Elliot! Regan!" he said in surprise. "What are you two doing out at this hour?" Elliot and I froze, and my mind scrambled for a reasonable explanation.

"We just finished a practice simulation," Elliot said at the exact same time that I blurted out that we were hungry. I cringed a little as Callaway looked from one of us to the other and back again.

"The simulation training made us hungry," Elliot said, and Callaway nodded knowingly.

"I have to commend you two on all your extra practice. It will come in handy one day, I'm sure."

Elliot and I shot one another a look out of the corners of our eyes, because, of course, it had already come in handy.

"Team Worst-Case Scenario," Elliot said with a smirk, and I grinned back like an idiot.

"Well, you know the way to the kitchen," Callaway said with a conspiratorial wink. "If anyone asks, that chocolate cake was half gone when you found it."

"Yes, sir," Elliot said as we changed direction and headed toward the kitchen. We were about to round the corner when Callaway called out.

"One moment, Regan," he said, and we turned as he made his way back down the hallway toward us, his forehead scrunched in concentration. My pulse was suddenly hammering in my ears, and I felt a cold sweat prickle down my back. Callaway had figured it out.

"Regan," Callaway said. "I meant to ask you about this earlier today, but I received a very strange message from your mother last night."

"Last night?" I repeated, confused as my mind scrambled. "She contacted you before the emergency Glitch jump?" Suddenly I felt Elliot's elbow digging into my ribs, and I realized my mistake. There had never been an emergency Glitch jump last night because the Academy had never been destroyed.

"Emergency Glitch jump?" Callaway said, looking from Elliot to me and back again. "What emergency Glitch jump?"

"She means the simulation we just practiced," Elliot said. "We tried out the Triangle Shirtwaist Factory simulation, and it really threw us for a loop."

Callaway shook his head at us. "You know that's not a simulation we allow cadets to practice. We save events like those until you are in your final training year."

"I can see why," Elliot said with a shudder. I'm not sure what my own face did as I momentarily relived the gruesome fire, but Callaway put comforting hands on our shoulders.

"I don't mind you two training at night, but stay away from the upper-level simulations. Okay?"

We nodded, and I felt a rush of relief that Elliot had successfully saved us from my slipup.

"But back to your mother," Callaway said. "She sent me a message informing me that she didn't want you participating in any more training missions on Academy grounds. Especially after Officer Salzburg mysteriously disappeared en route to the mountain this morning. She said that while she appreciated the formal notice I gave her of the event, that I should send such correspondence electronically in the future," he said, his face a study of confusion. "Do you know what she's talking about?"

I just stared at him, my mouth open in surprise as I tried to make sense of what he was saying. Training mission? What training mission? And what notice had he given her?

"Regan's mom is just super overprotective," Elliot cut in. I turned to him, and he opened his eyes wide and gave me a look that made it clear I was supposed to go along with whatever this was.

"Oh, right," I said. "That. It's just something we talked about the last time she checked in." I glanced at Elliot out of the corner of my eye to see how I'd done and he gave the tiniest of nods of approval.

"Officer Salzburg disappeared?" Elliot said.

"Nothing for you to worry about," Callaway said. "I'm sure it was just a miscommunication and he'll be found in no time."

"You might look into Salzburg's history," I said. "The last time he came for dinner at the house, something about him seemed off."

"Hm," Callaway said. "I'll take it into consideration, Regan. Your intuition is usually pretty spot on."

"Thank you, sir," I said. "And don't worry about my mom. I'll make sure I clear everything up with her the next time we talk."

"Okay, then," Callaway said, and then he leaned in conspiratorially. "Just between us, your mother scares me half to death."

Elliot laughed, and I smiled a smile that I hoped was convincingly nonchalant.

"All right, you two," Callaway said. "Be quick in the kitchen; I don't want you falling asleep during training tomorrow."

"Yes, sir," Elliot said again.

Callaway was just turning away when I stepped forward and grabbed his arm. "Sir?" I said.

"Yes, Regan?" he asked.

"In the training tomorrow, um, will everyone be there?" I asked. "Eliana and Tess and everyone?"

"Why wouldn't they be?" he said, his eyebrows creased in concern. His words were like ice water on the fire that had been burning my heart ever since Elliot's revelation was suddenly doused, and I felt myself relax for the first time in what felt like forever. They were okay. Everyone was okay. Callaway was still looking at me funny, and I realized that it was because tears were making their way out of the corners of my eyes. I swiped at them with the back of my hand and looked away.

"No reason," Elliot said, saving me from trying to explain the unexplainable. "We just wanted to ask Sam and Serina a question before breakfast, that's all."

"Oh," Callaway said. "I believe they are scheduled for a mission involving the Watergate scandal tomorrow, but I'm sure they will be able to spare a minute. You know," he said, giving us a wide smile, "Sam was just telling me how impressed he's been with you two lately. That he thinks you might turn out to be a good partner matchup yet."

"That's great," I said. "That's really great." With that, he headed down the hall toward the kitchen. My stomach gave an angry growl, and I realized it had been a long time since we'd eaten anything. Maybe a kitchen detour was just what we needed to unwind after the insane adventures we'd just been on. The only sound was the echo of our feet on the stone floor as we made our way across the deserted atrium.

"So," I said a minute later as I pulled what was left of the chocolate cake out of the fridge and handed Elliot a fork. "What exactly was in that letter you put in the Academy mailbox? I saw you swipe a form from the Glitch room. What could you possibly have had time to conjure up that fast?"

Elliot shrugged as he popped a bite of cake in his

mouth. "You said something to your mom about us being on a training mission, so I decided that I would create one that explained us being in her office as well as the mess on campus that night. I forged Callaway's signature," he said. "I mentioned a top secret training activity the mountain was doing at the Academy this week, and that for the sake of security she shouldn't mention if she saw any of the mountain students."

"Meaning me," I said around a mouthful of cake.

"Exactly," Elliot said. "I had no idea if it would work, and honestly I just pulled the idea out of thin air as you were scribbling out your letter. I just thought that if that letter could save the Academy, then why couldn't a letter save us too?"

I gaped at him, more than a little impressed. "That's kind of amazing," I said.

"It was the longest of long shots," he said.

"Not that," I said. "That you were okay winging it. That's not you at all."

"Nope," Elliot said, stabbing another forkful of cake. "It's you. You're a bad influence."

I laughed, and it felt so good. Like that laughter had helped loosen the last bit inside of me that was wound too tight. Everything was okay. Our friends were okay. My mom was alive. The Academy was intact. Salzburg was out of the picture, and as far as I could tell, we'd avoided a lifetime in prison. Life was good.

Elliot watched me laugh and a rare smile tugged at his mouth.

"You know what's a shame?" he said after a few minutes of companionable silence had gone by. "The most amazing mission we will probably ever do, and we can't even tell anyone about it."

"You're right," I said. "We can't tell a soul."

"We can't even tell the other kids thank you for helping save the Academy," Elliot said. "Do you realize that? They have no idea."

"Well," I said. "That means we also don't have to tell them that they accidentally exploded in an alternate timeline."

"Good point," Elliot said. "That was really smart of you to think of getting them to help. We never could have done it on our own."

"Thanks," I said, cocking my head to the side. "You know, I think that's the first time you've ever called me smart."

Elliot looked up in surprise. "You are," he said. "Not the same kind of smart as me, but you *are* smart." When I just raised an eyebrow at him, he huffed and put his fork down. "It's true," he said. "It just took me a while to figure it out."

"You're forgiven," I said, popping a bite of the cake into my own mouth. "It took me a while to figure it out too."

"It reminds me of a famous quote by Albert Einstein," Elliot said, his forehead wrinkled in concentration.

"Elliot Mason can't remember something?" I said in mock horror, and smiled when he elbowed me.

"Obviously," he said. "I almost forgot I had a bomb in my pocket." He shook his head ruefully and held up a hand. "Just give me a second, I'll think of it. I'm pretty sure it was Albert Einstein that said it, although it might just be something someone attributed to him. Everyone likes to claim Einstein said this, that, or the other thing, but I like to think Einstein said this one. I'm pretty sure it's about a fish. Got it," he said, snapping his fingers. "Albert Einstein once said that everyone is a genius. But if you judge a fish by its ability to climb a tree, it would spend its whole life believing it's stupid."

"Huh," I said. "I've never heard that before. I like it." I turned to him and raised an expectant eyebrow. "So, if I'm a fish? What does that make you?"

"A jerk, remember?" he said, sliding what was left of the cake back into the fridge.

I shook my head. "You really aren't anymore."

"Thanks," he said.

I stifled a yawn that felt like it was going to split my face in two and hopped down from the counter. "Let's head to bed," I said. "Even though Callaway said everyone was fine, I'll feel better after I see everyone sleeping safely." Elliot nodded, and we left the kitchen and made our way back across the atrium. I ran a hand over one of the simulation chairs as we passed and glanced over at Elliot.

"Want to get an early start tomorrow and do a quick study simulation?"

"Sure," Elliot said. "Why not. Who needs sleep anyways?"

"It's been quite a night," I said, turning to Elliot when we reached our dorm rooms. "I'd say that I couldn't have done it without you. But you know that already."

He smiled back. "I couldn't have done it without you either. Just do me a favor," he said, stretching as he yawned. "If you find another Cocoon, just wait until tomorrow to show me. Okay?"

I laughed. "No problem. Good night, Elliot."

"Good night, Regan," Elliot said with a grin, and he turned and disappeared into his dorm. I stood there a moment longer before turning back to my own door and creeping into the dorm. The other girls were all there, snoring softly in their bunks, and I had to stifle the urge to give them all hugs. That could wait until tomorrow.

I was still smiling at Elliot's joke as I climbed into my bunk. I lay down, tucking myself into the covers as a bone-tired weariness washed over me. Saving the Academy, and possibly history as we knew it, was exhausting. Rolling to the side, I tucked my arm under my head and was just nodding off to sleep when my fingertips brushed against a thick piece of paper someone had tucked under my pillow. I froze, not really believing it. No way. This couldn't be what I thought it was. It just couldn't. I lay there for a few seconds, wrestling with my exhaustion and my need to know if my suspicions were correct. Although, after everything that had happened, there was really only one choice. Whatever it is, I told myself, Elliot and I can handle it. With that I gave in and reached under my pillow. The envelope was thick, the paper eerily familiar as I took in Elliot's name hastily written across the front in his own handwriting. Well, I thought as I opened the Cocoon, at least this time Elliot couldn't be mad about how the letter was written.

AUTHOR'S NOTE

Dear Reader,

The more I write, the more I realize that the majority of my stories came from my time teaching seventh-grade language arts. It was a very different time in my life. I had free time, for one thing, but I was also testing out my wings as a teacher while simultaneously chasing this crazy publishing dream. One of the research projects I taught involved a book put out by *LIFE* magazine entitled *100 Photographs that Changed the World*. It was beautiful, stuffed with full-page glossy pictures, and I promptly took a box cutter to it for my bulletin board. Teachers are allowed to commit book sins like this . . . at least that's the story I'm sticking to.

These pictures, pictures that represented pivotal moments in US history, stayed up in my classroom for a good chunk of the year as we researched and debated the importance of those events. And one day, just to shake my students up a bit, I asked them what they thought would have happened if Hitler had won World War II. What if that church in Birmingham had never been bombed? What if the Triangle Shirtwaist fire had never happened? What would our world look like today? Would it be better? Or would it be worse?

I went home that day with the idea for *Glitch* brewing in my imagination. What if time traveling was possible, and what if some of those time travelers went rogue and started meddling in the past in order to alter the future? I started to picture what the school would look like that would train time travelers to catch those criminals, criminals I would later call Butterflies. Throw that idea in with a deep love of Ray Bradbury's short story "A Sound of Thunder" where a bumbling time traveler accidentally steps off the designated path and kills a butterfly on an ill-fated T. rex hunt, and you have the start of what would eventually become *Glitch*. (If you're shocked that one of my favorite short stories involves dinosaurs . . . you are probably new here. Go check out my Edge of Extinction series and then come back. It's fine. I'll wait.)

As much fun as writing about rogue time travelers was, though, I quickly discovered that this book presented a unique problem that was completely absent when my books contained nothing but dinosaurs, floating boys, and Bigfoot. *Glitch* wasn't just my story, you see; it was also America's story, and America's story wasn't always pretty. It's because of this that I made sure the first time you met Regan she was on a mission to preserve the assassination of Abraham Lincoln, not prevent it. Which, let's be honest, is weird. Shouldn't we want to right the wrongs of history? Wouldn't it make sense to correct the injustices of the past and prevent pain? The answer, in my humble opinion, is no. Elliot struggles with this concept, and one of his professors explained it to him like this:

"History isn't supposed to be pretty. It's downright repulsive at times, and you don't have to like it or agree with it to preserve it. But remember that the healthiest forests grow the year after a forest fire, and that without extreme pressure we wouldn't have diamonds. You can't hurry history, and you can't fix an injustice until people recognize that it is one."

Even Lewis and Clark, the famous explorers I named the partner team program after, have some unsavory details in their story if you look closely enough, but if we don't learn from our ancestors' mistakes, how can we ever hope to create a better tomorrow? So, when Regan and Elliot go into the past, they aren't trying to fix history, just preserve it. History is touchy and the human race has had to learn lessons the hard way as far back as we can remember. But if you remove those hard-earned lessons . . . does anything change? Does anything improve? So, my question to you, dear reader, is this: If you had the chance to change history . . . would you do it?

Until next time,

Laura Martin

GLITCH GLOSSARY

The Chaos Theory: The idea in mathematics that certain systems are very sensitive and a tiny change in a system may cause it to turn out completely differently.

The Butterfly Effect: A term in chaos theory that originated with the findings of theoretical meteorologist Edward Lorenz, who stated that "a butterfly flapping its wings in Brazil can produce a tornado in Texas." Essentially the butterfly effect states that a tiny change in the present can have huge consequences in the future.

Butterfly: A time traveler who travels into the past with the intention of changing a key historical event in order to affect the future in a negative way.

Glitcher: A time traveler trained specifically to journey to the past in order to capture a Butterfly.

Glitch: A trip through time done for the sole purpose of stopping a Butterfly from changing a historical event.

Cadet: A Glitcher in training, usually at their nation's Academy.

Recap: The playback of a cadet's failed simulation that is watched in order for the cadet to learn from their mistakes.

Repercussion Track: A hypothetical analysis a cadet watches after a failed simulation in order to better understand their failure's potential impact on history.

The Academy: A training facility for Glitchers. The location of each nation's Academy is so top secret even the Academy residents are unaware of its exact coordinates.

Commander in Chief: The head of an Academy. Each nation's Academy has its own commander in chief.

The Mayhem: A group of time-traveling criminals willing to alter history for the right price.

The Lewis and Clark Partner Program: A new top secret partner program located inside a mountain where Glitchers are trained to work as a team.

Chaos Cuffs: The high-tech handcuffs used by Glitchers to secure a Butterfly in the past in order to bring them back to the present with them. Named for the chaos theory, Chaos Cuffs always return the Glitcher to the exact location they originally came from. No exceptions.

Class list for the Mountain and the Academy:
Nuance and Observation Class, or "Sherlock Class": Cadets practice identifying the historically incorrect anomaly that identifies a Butterfly as a trespasser in time.

Time Period Combat Training: Cadets train in a variety of hand-to-hand combat training so that they can use period-appropriate techniques when apprehending a Butterfly. Often this training is done in full period-appropriate costume.

Language and Accents: Cadets are trained to speak and understand multiple languages. They are also taught a variety of accents in order to better blend in with whatever historical time period they are sent to.

Costuming: Cadets are taught specific fashions and clothing trends throughout history. They also learn the proper way to correctly wear tricky items such as corsets and waistcoats.

Simulation Training: A way for cadets to practice their Glitching skills in the safety of the Academy using computer-simulated missions.

Physical Fitness: Since being in good physical condition is essential to a Glitcher's survival, cadets are put through vigorous physical fitness training to ensure their health is at its best. This includes strength training and extensive cardio work.

ACKNOWLEDGMENTS

Raising kids takes a village, or at least a grandparent willing to step up and babysit so you can keep your sanity, and I believe that books are no different. And I have the best possible village. From a husband who routinely sends me off to Starbucks or the library on weekends so I can work while he wrangles our three kids, to a mom and mother-in-law who swoop in to babysit so I can do the author visits to schools, I am beyond blessed.

I'm also blessed to have people in my life who love me enough to tell me when my stories don't make sense, my characters are unlikable, or my time-traveling rules are giving them a headache! It's amazing how God brings the exact people into your life that you need to help make your dreams a reality. So I owe a big thank-you to my amazing writing group and my ever-patient editor, Tara Weikum, and her assistant editor, Sarah Homer, for all their amazing input on *Glitch*.

A huge thank-you is also owed to my agent, Jodi Reamer, whose faith in my work opened up the door to publishing that I'd been pounding on fruitlessly for years.

And finally, a big shout-out to coffee and the French vanilla creamer that makes it taste like heaven in a cup. Without you, this book never would have been completed. You're the real MVP here.

Ephesians 3:20

Now to him who is able to do immeasurably more than all we ask or imagine, according to his power that is at work within us, to him be the glory.

DON'T MISS THE NEXT ADVENTURE
FROM LAURA MARTIN!

The morning before I left the *Atlas* forever started the same as every other. I always woke up early, but thanks to Wallace's snoring, this morning was earlier than most. I winced and peered over the edge of my bunk at him. He lay in the middle of the narrow bunk, his arms splayed wide. For a skinny sixteen-year-old, he had the snore of a man twice his age and size. I debated shoving him off his bunk to teach him a lesson but almost immediately discarded the idea. It was the mean part of my brain that wanted to do that. The nice part of my brain, which would probably wake up any moment now, knew that he was exhausted from working with Dad in the engine room the day before.

It wasn't fair to rob him of sleep, even if he'd robbed me of mine—besides, a quick glance at my watch showed that I was supposed to be up in ten minutes anyway. I lay in bed a second longer, wondering why beds were always the most comfortable right when you had to get out of them, before slipping silently from my bunk and pulling on a threadbare sweatshirt to ward off the ever-present chill of our tiny cabin. I was just easing my way toward the door when my dad sat up.

"Heading out already?" he asked, barely stifling a yawn as he slipped out of bed and past the snoring Wallace to see me off.

"I wasn't planning on it," I whispered, "but somebody sounds like he swallowed part of the ship's engine." I jerked my head toward Wallace, eyebrow raised. Dad glanced over at my sleeping brother and stifled a yawn.

"If you're tired enough, you can sleep through just about anything," he said. "Maybe Gizmo isn't working you guys hard enough." He finished this statement off with a wink, and I grimaced.

"That'll be the day," I said. "He has us starting early today, since we're only going to be able to scavenge for a couple of hours."

Wallace grunted in his sleep and rolled over. Dad held up a finger to his lips.

Sorry, I mouthed silently as I slipped the straps of my backpack over my shoulders.

Dad nodded, wiping the sleep from his eyes with the palms of his hands. He still had a smudge of grease above his right eyebrow, evidence of his hard work in the guts of our ship. It wasn't easy to keep a ship like ours in good working condition, but Dad and Wallace and their crew of fellow mechanics and engineers managed it year after year. They had to—our survival depended on it.

"Be careful down there," he said. "No unnecessary risks."

I nodded, knowing full well that unnecessary risks were some of the only ways you found anything useful these days. All the easy stuff had been picked over fifty years ago when everything first went under. Now we were lucky to find scraps. Today might be different, though, I reminded myself. This particular site hadn't been scavenged yet—at least that's what our boss, Gizmo, had told us.

"No unnecessary risks," I repeated with what I hoped was a reassuring smile. My dad smiled back, and I pretended not to notice the worried crease in his forehead as he gave my shoulders a quick one-armed squeeze. I slipped out the door. I knew my choice of occupation on the *Atlas* was a hard one for him to swallow, especially since we'd lost my mom a few years ago, but we both knew full well that there was no such thing as an easy job these days.

If I'd thought our cabin was cold, the narrow hall-way was downright frigid, and I hunched my shoulders inside my sweatshirt as I tried not to think about what the water temp must be today. I'd find out soon enough. Around me the metal of the ship creaked and groaned familiarly as I made my way toward the stairs at the front of the ship. The walls on either side of me showed the jagged marks of years of repairs and reconfigurations, and I ran my finger over one of the many thick welts of metal as I walked. Exactly like scars, I thought. Scars that showed battle after battle that the *Atlas* had fought and won, scars that showed the evidence of its transformations over the years from luxury to lean efficiency. I liked scars. Scars proved you'd survived.

I finally reached the stairs and started making my way up, flight by flight, toward the deck. The chilly damp of the lower level seemed to stay with me, though, and I hurried my pace, hoping that the exercise would warm me up a bit. My legs were burning by the time I finally reached the top deck and walked out into the early morning air of the Mediterranean. I'd asked my dad once why we still labeled sections of the ocean by their original names. It didn't seem to make much sense now that the world was covered by one massive body of water, but he'd told me not to ask such silly questions. That was where he and I disagreed, though:

I didn't think any questions were silly, not when it came to the ocean. I took a deep breath, letting the salty freshness scrub away the musty staleness of the inside of the ship, and headed toward the stern.

The ship was practically deserted this early, but I still kept my head down as I made my way across the worn deck, passing the large chicken coop where the ship's fleet of hens snoozed safely in their nests. They were some of the only domestic animals that had survived the Tide Rising. Animals like cows and sheep required grass to survive, and we didn't have any of that anymore. However, it turned out that chickens could thrive on fish guts and the occasional cockroach, and because of that, we had eggs and the rare piece of chicken in our soup. It was a luxury we didn't take for granted. During the day the hens would peck around, roosting on top of the large storage crates that peppered the deck.

Although, unless you really looked, the crates themselves were almost unrecognizable since every square inch of available surface had a gardening box attached to it. It wasn't much, not like on a grower ship, but the herbs and vegetables we were able to cultivate on deck did help supplement our diet of fish, fish, and more fish. The layout was a far cry from the original deck design, but it worked.

Once upon a time the *Atlas* had been a small cruise ship used for vacations, and if you looked closely, you could still see where there used to be frivolous luxuries like a swimming pool and a running track. The very idea of wasting so much space was laughable now, but I liked to imagine what life was like before, when people sailed on the ocean for fun and not because it was the only way to survive.

We were on the move after having been anchored for two days, and above me on the huge masts the sails were filled with a breeze that moved the massive ship. They seemed disproportionate and out of step with the rest of the ship, for good reason: they had been an afterthought. When the tide had started rising, cruise ships were uniquely suited to take on large groups of people, but they weren't designed to run without fossil fuels—fuels that would be hard if not impossible to come by once the water level rose. So the ship's architects had scrambled to put together a system of sails and rigging that would allow the *Atlas* to maneuver itself using the wind instead of the engines, which would eventually be scrapped and melted down.

A lot of things had needed to be altered or reverted to earlier, less-wasteful forms of technology in order to navigate this new, water-filled world. It had been a bit painful for the human race to take a giant step backward. They'd had to give up so many of the resources, technologies, and conveniences that they'd fought for and rediscover methods of survival carved out by their ancestors, but when your choices are life and death, the decision becomes a lot easier.

I made it to the rail of the ship and glanced around for Garth. He was nowhere to be seen, so I leaned against the rail and watched the horizon, where the faintest line of pink and orange was just beginning to glow. I loved sunrise. I loved sunset, too, but I was usually working or eating when that happened. Sunrise, though, that was mine. She and I had a thing—a standing appointment, you could say—and I mentally forgave Wallace for waking me up early. The few extra minutes of quiet, especially on board a ship that was usually anything but, were a treat. The blaze on the horizon brightened into a warm burnt orange that reminded me of the heart of a fire. I ran my hand over the familiar chips and dents of the railing and sighed. Sometimes it felt like I'd memorized every nook and cranny of this ship. Who knew, by the end of my lifetime I probably would have.

Despite the fact that I had always been fully aware that I would probably live my entire life aboard the ship I'd been born on, the idea still chafed me a bit. It wasn't that I disliked life aboard the *Atlas*—you couldn't exactly dislike the only existence you'd ever known—but that I hadn't chosen it. It had been chosen for me. Just like what I would eat for breakfast was chosen by the ship's cook, how much survival credit I'd receive for the salvage I found was chosen by my boss, Gizmo, and how much electricity our cabin would receive was chosen by the *Atlas*'s captain. That was probably the reason I'd decided to go rogue and become a scavenger: it was literally one of the only ways to get off the ship.

I shook my head and forced myself to focus on the day ahead. A life of choice was a luxury we couldn't afford after the Tide Rising, and that was all there was to it.

"Sorry," Garth said as he skidded to a stop beside the rail twenty minutes later. It wasn't unusual for Garth to be late, but this morning he was an exceptional mess. Half-dressed, with his shirt on backward and only one shoe on, the other held in his hand, he looked like he'd rolled directly out of bed and taken off at a dead sprint. Which he probably had. I raised an eyebrow at him and glanced up and down, not doing a thing to hide my judgment.

"Overslept," he said as he hopped up and down to put on his other shoe.

"Well, if we don't hurry, we're going to have to dive hungry."

"I'm not doing that again," Garth said, already turning to head toward the *Atlas*'s mess hall. "The last time that happened, Gizmo the grump decided to keep us down there for an extra hour on a hunch."

I snorted. "I forgot about that. Didn't you threaten to eat your own wet suit?"

"Let's just say that if Gizmo asks what happened to the chunk by my wrist, I'm blaming it on mice," Garth said dryly, and I rolled my eyes.

Sometimes I wondered if I'd have had the guts to sign up to be a scavenger if Garth hadn't signed up with me. Everyone started to work on the *Atlas* at age eleven. It used to be nine, right after the Tide Rising, so eleven really did feel like a luxury. As far as jobs went, scavenging wasn't one of the most desirable, that was for sure. You weren't even supposed to work as a scavenger until you were fifteen. It was too dangerous to send someone younger than that into water that seemed to get more and more hostile with each passing year. The pressure of diving that deep could kill you if you weren't careful, and the water temperatures could get so cold you risked hypothermia even with a wet suit.

Despite all that, it was the only job on the *Atlas* that seemed tolerable to me. Which, considering I was routinely shoved headfirst down small underwater holes, was really saying something. Scavenging was one of the jobs no one really wanted, which is why bending the age requirement was something Gizmo hadn't even blinked at.

I could smell breakfast long before I saw it. You'd think that, having grown up on a diet primarily made up of fish, seaweed, and more fish, I would have become immune to the overpowering smell, but I hadn't. My stomach rumbled regardless as I made my way up to the counter to collect my halibut wrapped in its seaweed wrapper. Garth grabbed a second one when the worker wasn't looking and tucked it into his pocket. That move should have probably grossed me out, but you couldn't be friends with Garth and let that kind of stuff bother you. He'd definitely stored worse things in that pocket. I gulped my breakfast down quickly, barely tasting what everyone on board called a briny burrito as I made my way after Garth down the stairs and toward the back of the ship to the scavengers' dive room. It was time to go to work.

The dive room was already full of the rest of the *Atlas*'s scavenging crew when we came in. Once, the clatter of gear and the overpowering smell of mildew would have overwhelmed me, but not anymore. This tiny room, with its mismatched jumble of wet suits and half-broken dive equipment, was my smelly second home. I mumbled what was supposed to be a hello around my last mouthful of burrito and went straight to my locker.

"You two better hustle if you don't want Gizmo on our case," said Ralph, a scavenger a few years older than me, as he finished zipping up his thick black wet suit. "We'll only have about two hours to scavenge this new town before we have to move on."

"Do we know the name of the town?" I asked, yanking my own wet suit out of my locker.

Garth groaned and rolled his eyes toward the ceiling. "You always ask that, and we never know. Unless it's something big like Chicago or London or something, no one ever cares about the name of the town."

"I care," I said.

"You're weird," Garth said.

"There's that, too," I said, pausing just long enough in my gear check to grin at him. He chose that moment to burp loudly. When I shot him a disgusted look, he threw his hands up defensively.

"What?" he said, his green eyes crinkling up at the corners as he grinned at me. "If I did that in my mask, I'd be smelling it for the next two hours."

"So instead you made us smell it," Ralph muttered as he shouldered past us and toward the back of the dive room, where I could just make out Gizmo with his customary clipboard and scowl.

"What's that?" Garth said, peering at the small metal box I'd just fished out of my bag.

"I'd have shown you this morning if you hadn't decided to sleep in, Sleeping Beauty," I said.

"Beauty sleep," Garth scoffed. "I'd need a beauty coma, and I'd still look like a walrus sat on my face."

I rolled my eyes. Garth was overly self-conscious of his appearance these days. He'd shot up about three inches overnight, and he'd broken his nose a few months ago and it hadn't set right, giving him a crooked and slightly flattened appearance that I barely noticed but he obsessed about. I decided to let the walrus comment slide and held up the tiny rusted box.

"I'm tired of going into a building with nothing but a headlamp," I said, showing him the square with its flashlights embedded in each side. "I used some broken headlamps and patched them together. Now I can just turn this on and toss it in a window or a chimney or whatever, and I'll know if there is anything unpleasant waiting to greet me."

"Makes sense," Garth said. "But I think you're going to get in trouble if Gizmo sees that," he said. "You remember what he said after he caught you with that . . . what was that thing again?"

"A sand sucker," I said, and I felt my face flush the bright, embarrassed red it always got when I was reminded of a failure.

12

"I believe Gizmo called it a giant waste of time," Garth said.

"That's because it didn't work," I said. "If it had worked, he would have probably liked it."

"Not Gizmo," Garth said. "If it isn't his idea, he'll hate it. Didn't he say if he caught you messing around with junk like that you'd get fired?"

"Something like that," I said as I quickly shrugged my gear on. I tucked my flippers and my face mask under my arm before shutting my locker and turning back to Garth. He wasn't quite finished getting ready, and I tapped a foot to show my impatience.

"Relax," Garth said.

"You know how Gizmo feels about us being late," I said. "It makes him all twitchy.'

Garth grinned. "I like making Gizmo twitchy."

"You would," I said as I followed him out of the dive room and down the hall to where I could hear the other scavengers already queuing up. We got in line at the back of the pack just as Gizmo showed up dressed in his flashy blue wet suit. Unlike the tattered and patched black ones we wore, his was pristine, and I couldn't help but be a little jealous of how well it fit his stocky frame. The worse your wet suit fit, the colder you were. I was always cold.

"Good morning," Gizmo said, and everyone grumbled a half-hearted good morning in return. "Today we have some luck on our side. The town we're scavenging was buried under the sand until the recent storm stirred things up enough to uncover it. I don't have to tell you that it means we have some prime scavenging on our hands today. Captain Brown could only grant us two hours, though, as we have a trade meeting scheduled with the *Blue Oyster* and the *Sundial* the day after next and our schedule is tight, which means no screwups." He paused to look each of us in the eye. "Stick to the methods you've been taught," he said with a special glare in my direction. I avoided his eyes, pretending to be preoccupied with cleaning out my face mask.

"Should be a good haul," Garth said in my ear as Gizmo started in on his usual lecture about the price per pound of iron versus copper. I nodded. "Do you ever wonder how many other towns are out there, just waiting underneath the sand for some big storm to stir things up enough for us to find them?" Garth said, looking dreamy-eyed. It was no secret that he loved scavenging more than the rest of us. For me it was a job, one I'd taken to gain access to the ocean that existed beneath the waves.

"But don't you feel like we owe it to the towns somehow to know their names?" I said. "I mean, if we forget their names, isn't it like they were never even there? It seems wrong somehow."

14

"What seems wrong is only getting two hours," Garth said. "We'll barely be into anything good and it will be time to head back in."

"You'll find something good," I said. "Besides, do you really want just Gizmo in your ear for *more* than two hours?"

"Solid point," he agreed with a smirk. "With all your tinkering, you should figure out a way to turn his mic off somehow."

Gizmo cleared his throat loudly in front of us, and we snapped our mouths shut.

"Better," he said with a scowl that pulled his dark eyebrows so far down they practically connected in the middle. What hair our boss was lacking on the top of his head, his eyebrows more than made up for. "Now, if there aren't any questions, let's do this."